DO OVER

DO OVER

Above the Rain
2021

Above the Rain
abovetherain.editor@gmail.com
North Georgia, USA

Contributing Editors:

J.A. Sexton   Morgan Bowser

Publisher's note:

This is a work of fiction. All characters and incidents are the product of the author's imagination, places are used fictitiously and any resemblance to an actual person, living or dead, is entirely coincidental.

ISBN: 978-1-7377970-0-5

julietrose.author@gmail.com
authorjulietrose.com

Cover graphics and interior formatting by J.A. Sexton
Original cover background photos by Brooke Cantrall
Above the Rain logo artwork by Bee Freitag, text by Jack Freitag

To my children~
You have taught me to see inside myself to recognize my own human vulnerability and purpose of being.

Prologue

The sharp rapping of knuckles on her car window glass jolted Sam awake. She'd no idea where she was, or who the young dude standing outside her car door was. Or, for fuck's sake, why he was banging on her window so loudly. He was motioning to roll the window down. She put it down a few inches and squinted up at him. Her head was killing her, and the sun was cutting through like a knife.

"You can't sleep here," the guy said, pointing at a *no overnight parking* sign in front of her car.

She made out the lifeguard emblem on his shorts and shook her head blankly. He peered in at her, trying to get her to understand.

"It's not safe. And with your windows all rolled up like that, you could overheat."

She nodded and mumbled a half-hearted apology, sti trying to get her bearings. She looked out the front window, an the ocean glittered back at her like the curtain at a Las Vegas loung act. Oh, yeah, she'd driven all night and pulled in just before dawr She'd only meant to close her eyes for about fifteen minutes, but glance at her phone let her know it was pushing eleven in th morning.

He was right though. It was getting hot and sweat wa beading up on her brow, threatening to drip into her eyes. She wa wearing jeans and a long-sleeved, button-down shirt, which wer now damp with sweat. Between those and her head pounding, sh felt like she might vomit.

"Oh, man, I'm sorry. Didn't mean to fall asleep. I was ju resting my eyes. Won't happen again."

He nodded as his eyes flitted to the back of the car, whic obviously contained pretty much everything she owned. She cou tell he was trying to figure out if she was going to be a bea sleeper, which wasn't allowed, made very clear by the sign he pointed at. She wanted him to move on, and fast, before she spill the contents of whatever was in her stomach. She really wished wouldn't take his job so seriously and would just leave her alon She waved her hand dismissively.

"No worries, I was driving all night and pulled in stretch and get my bearings." She motioned towards a small bea shack restaurant. "They open? Just need some coffee and a paper.

His demeanor relaxed, and his smile became friendli "Sure thing. Coffee tastes like ass, but the owner is nice. The take care of you. I'm Smith. I'm one of the lifeguards on duty n if you need any help."

He jerked his head slightly towards a lifeguard stand, appearing picturesque against the sky with a long pier to the left. He was Smith? What did that even mean?

"I'm Samantha. Smith? Like, that's your name?"

He laughed and bobbed his head, apparently used to being questioned about his name. She guessed him to be about mid-twenties. A little too thin and a little too tall but with a friendly face and shaggy light brown hair, bleached out from the sun. A whistle sounded in the distance. Smith turned slightly towards the lifeguard stand where it was coming from. Another lifeguard was gesturing to him from the rail, and he waved back. He turned back to her and set his shoulders, meeting her eyes.

"Duty calls. Nice to meet you. Just remember, they are really strict about overnight parking here. Cops usually patrol into the night after the restaurant closes."

"Noted."

Her irritation with the conversation was apparent. She noticed the parking lot had filled up quite a bit, families spilling out onto the beach over the boardwalk with their chairs, toys, coolers, and other paraphernalia. The sounds of children's pitchy voices grated on her nerves. She needed coffee to try and knock down the crushing headache. She watched him walk away and took a deep breath.

How the hell did she end up here?

Yesterday morning, she woke up in her own bed, cursing a mistake she knew was about to come and haunt her. Yesterday, she was planning what to do for dinner, and how to get out of a work meeting she didn't want to have to sit through. Yesterday, she'd never have guessed she'd wake up at a beach, over seven hundred miles away from where she started. In a town she'd never stepped foot in, with a baseball-sized knot on the side of her head, and everything she owned in the back of her car.

She thrust open the car door and leaned out just in time to heave acidic bile onto the sandy parking lot.

Chapter One

In general, nothing had ever been wrong in Sam's life. Everything was pretty much laid out as expected. She'd grown up in a suburban home, outside a decent-sized, but conservative, city in Indiana. She went to prom, she snuck out and drank with her friends. She smoked a little weed and shoplifted now and then. She made decent grades and played a few sports. She wasn't popular but pretty well-liked. School came easy, but she certainly wasn't a star student. Teachers often said if she just "applied herself" a little more, she could get scholarships. Mostly, she just didn't feel like giving more than she already was. It was enough to keep moving through.

Her parents were busy and distant at times but never mean or unfair, despite what her fifteen-year-old self thought. They ate most dinners together around the table. Their marriage seemed solid, and they were supportive of their children. Her older brother, Brad, was protective and funny but had his own group of friends and interests. Their paths didn't really cross outside of passing in the hallway once they were teens. She never went without but wasn't spoiled either. Life was what it was supposed to be.

After high school, she knocked out a couple of years at community college, trying to decide what her path in life was. Her brother had made it look easy. Went to school for engineering, got a job in engineering. He married his college sweetheart, and they had a couple of kids within the first five years of marriage. They came for holidays and sent a family Christmas card with everyone in matching sweaters every year. Sam just didn't feel the drive. She was successful enough at anything she put her mind to but was disinterested in everything. During college, she met a boy and they decided to move in together, which lasted a few months before she decided she liked her own space. After that, she made sure it never really went past the occasional sleepover stage. The idea of living with someone day in and day out just seemed intrusive.

Having done a plethora of starter jobs and moving to a few towns, she found herself at a steady desk job in an office park with weekends off and enough pay to have her own apartment and used car. Even though most times when she'd look at herself in the mirror, she couldn't connect the person standing there to the person she seemed like inside, life was pretty good. It was flat but not stressful. Sam didn't think about the future much because she saw it being pretty much the same as the day she was on. So, she kept her head down, did her work, and went home at the end of the day. She never felt a need to form friendships and found the social interactions at work to be more than enough.

That was until she met Miriam. Maybe it was a Wednesday. Seemed like a Wednesday anyway. Sam was working at her desk when the manager led a small group of new employees around. A skinny young guy with acne, a middle-aged woman looking like she was trying it out on her own for the first time, per her loud makeup and tight clothing, and a young woman about Sam's age who was trailing behind. As they came by her desk the manager paused and cleared her throat, tapping her finger on the corner of Sam's desk.

"This is Samantha Rutliff. She's been here, what, a couple of years or so and can show you the ropes. Miriam, why don't you take this desk over by Samantha and get yourself situated? Samantha, please show Miriam accounts payable to start."

It ruffled Sam that the manager had spoken about her as if she were a statue. Never made eye contact. Never asked if she wanted to show anyone the ropes, which she didn't. She waited until they'd moved on and glanced over at Miriam who was awkwardly putting her belongings on the desk. Miriam looked like she'd bought the dress she was wearing for the job. Greenish-gray, no real shape, didn't match the shoes she was wearing. She stood there with her hand on the desk, her fingers seeming like they were braced to hold her up. Her dark brown hair against her pale, freckled face made her look like a lost little girl.

"Hey, you can call me Sam. You know you can sit down, right?" Sam waved her hand towards the chair.

Miriam blushed and sat down a little too quickly, hitting her thigh on the arm of the chair and laughed nervously. "I hate the first day at a new job. I feel so stupid. I'm Miriam. Miriam Bryson, but you can call me Miri."

Miri. She said it like it was a cross between Mary and Merry. Sam smiled genuinely and looked back at her paperwork. Miri had kind hazel eyes, which made Sam think she'd never spoken a cross word to anyone in her life. Small talk didn't come naturally to Sam, so she figured she'd let Miri reach out as needed. By the end of the day, they were comfortably talking about work issues. By the end of the week, they were talking about world issues. By the end of the month, they talked about just about everything. The way they comfortably fell into their friendship made Sam wish all people were like Miri.

Over the next few years, they spent much of their free time together. Movies, some holidays, evening drinks, talks on the phone. They weren't the clutching hands, tell your deepest, darkest secrets kind of friends, but Miri was the closest friend Sam had ever had. Miri had a way about her that never made Sam feel like she needed to be something she wasn't. If she was quiet, Miri was fine with it. If she was frustrated, Miri listened. If she was tired, Miri didn't push it. For Sam, it was the perfect friendship.

It wasn't work and they didn't fight. It wasn't a challenge to be together. Miri was just there for Sam and didn't ask for much in return. Sam thought she'd found a way to connect to another person, despite not being able to connect with herself. Miri accepted Sam for who she was and didn't question or push Sam to change. It was all the benefits of a relationship with none of the expectations or responsibilities.

Until that one stupid mistake. One that didn't even mean anything to Sam. But one that would drive them apart forever. One she wished she could go back and change, to let her simple life with Miri go on until they were both old and gray. One which set her on a course that ended life as she knew it. One that would break the heart of the one person she felt mattered the most in the world to her, and prove to both of them that Sam had never really invested herself into the friendship like Miri had.

About three years into their friendship, Miri met a guy named Ty. He was soft-spoken, hard-working and she was head over heels in love with him. He made her eyes twinkle, and she blushed when she talked about him. He never came in between Sam and Miri's friendship. Sam was glad Miri had seemed to find something she couldn't. He respected their time together like she respected his time with Miri. Sam had a feeling Ty was the one for Miri, that their lives together would eventually become permanent. That's why she couldn't understand what drove her to make such a terrible mistake.

It wasn't planned. Nothing led up to it. It just happened. One night she went out with a group of co-workers to have a few drinks. They were coming to the month-end closeout for the accounting books, and everyone was stressed out. Sam asked Miri to join them, but Miri wasn't a drinker and wanted to turn in early. The rest of them loaded up in one car, picking Sam up from her house after work, and headed to the bar for a drink. Or so Sam thought. It was loud and crowded, and Sam immediately regretted her decision. She started to feel anxious and trapped. Her co-workers were pounding them hard and fast. Before long, she wished she'd driven instead, so she could leave. It was apparent they weren't leaving any time soon. It was too far to walk, and she hated calling for a ride.

Across the bar, she spied a familiar face and made a beeline towards it. He was leaning against the bar, bobbing his head to the music. He always dressed about the same. Jeans, work boots, and a solid color, button-down shirt. He was fairly easy to spot.

"Ty? Do you remember me? I'm Sam, Miri's friend?"

He peered at her for a second and nodded slightly, a little confused as to why she was standing there. "Yeah, I know you. How are you?"

She could tell he didn't know what to do with her. They'd only exchanged pleasantries in passing if he was coming and she was going, or vice versa, from Miri's place. It looked like he was there with a few buddies and maybe a few drinks in. He was one of those who always wore a cowboy hat pulled low over his brow, and he peered out from under it, waiting for her to speak.

"Good, good. I came with some co-workers, and they're getting pretty hammered over there. Should've stayed home like Miri, I guess."

She laughed and hoped he would too. He didn't. She pressed on. "So, I was wondering if you were leaving anytime soon if you'd be willing to swing me by my house? I don't think they are leaving in the next few hours, and I'm getting a headache."

He appeared uncomfortable and looked at his beer. Sam looked at it too. Before long, they were both just staring at his half-drunk beer. Sam began to regret even asking. Finally, he picked it up, drained it, and stood straight up.

"Sure, I'm ready to go."

He threw a couple of dollars on the bar and headed for the door. Sam went back to her table and grabbed her purse, waving to a co-worker who appeared like they were seeing things that weren't there. They raised their hand and let it drop. She didn't know who was supposed to be the designated driver but didn't want to get sucked into babysitting all night. She hustled through the crowd and got out of the bar, the cool air immediately making her head feel clearer. She saw Ty waiting by his truck. Climbing up into the passenger side, she whispered a quick thank you.

Most of the ride home was quiet, and she tried to make conversation. He started to loosen up, talked about work and his dog. They chatted about music and the sorts. But they never talked about Miri. Looking back, Sam thought that would've stopped things. Kept their minds right. Miri never came up. Sam kept glancing over at Ty. She'd never really noticed that he was nice looking. Strong jawline, soft brown eyes. When he laughed she could see why Miri talked about how it made her warm inside, his eyes crinkled at the edges. He'd seemed so standoffish and almost rude in the bar, but as they talked he turned into a different person. Younger, more easygoing.

They pulled up in front of her apartment, and he let the truck idle while the conversation wore down. As it fizzled out, she found herself just staring at him, her anxiety starting to bubble back up. To fill the silence she leaned in and kissed him. She didn't know why. Later, as she played it over and over, she couldn't understand it. She wasn't attracted to him in that way. She wasn't drunk. She didn't think he was either. At first, he pulled slightly back but just for a second. Then it took on a life of its own. Before she knew it, she was fumbling for her keys, and they were falling into her bed. It had a form of madness to it. Not like passionate lovers, but like two drowning people, clinging to each other in the hopes they'd hold each other up.

After they finished, they laid staring at the ceiling. The afterglow was quickly replaced with the hot feeling of horror. What had they done? She rolled over and sat up on the edge of the bed. She grabbed a cigarette and lit it with shaking hands. The room seemed to be almost spinning. Her mind raced, trying to find a way to backtrack, to undo what they had done, landing on the reality there was no way to fix this. This was going to end badly.

"That was fucking stupid. Fucking, fucking stupid," she hissed, tears pricking her eyes.

He sighed behind her. Dejected. Broken. He softly whispered the word *fuck* and sat up. She could hear him gathering his things and getting dressed. She couldn't bear to look at him, to face what she'd done. What they'd done. She heard him pause at the door. She thought maybe he'd left until she heard him speak. His voice was low and sad.

"We can never tell Miri about this; it would destroy her. Please. I'm sorry, Sam. We should never have done this."

Sam nodded, never looking over, taking drag after drag from her cigarette. She heard the front door close and his truck start up. As it pulled off, fading in the distance, she set her brain to what she needed to do. She swore she'd never tell Miri. It would kill her. She and Ty had made that promise. A promise she'd keep no matter what.

Except Ty didn't keep his end of the bargain.

Chapter Two

The rising sun brought the renewed horror of the night before. Sam turned over in bed and put her head under her pillow. Nothing changed. She had to face the day. She pushed the pillow back and sat up, catching her reflection in the dated full-length closet door mirrors. She appeared haggard. Her long dirty-blond hair was tangled and frizzy. She rubbed her nose and tried to accept that the person staring back at her *was* her. She touched her forehead and pressed her finger in as hard as she could.

It was like when twins would play "mirror" in front of an empty frame, mimicking each other's every move, to make it look like a mirror image. It seemed like the same person doing it, but it was really two different entities. She lived this existence. She could see it was her but it wasn't. It was the costume she wore, and she couldn't tell anyone. She waved at herself in the mirror, half expecting not to be waved back to. Her twin waved back, her eyes criticizing and cold.

She made her way to the kitchen and started coffee, chewing the skin around her thumbnail. She replayed the events of the previous evening in her head and wondered what had come over her. Why would she do something she knew would destroy her best friend? She pictured Miri's face and shook it away. She'd just have to put it behind her. Ty didn't want Miri to know, he wouldn't risk messing up his relationship with her. He loved her. They were probably going to get married, have a few kids, grow old, and die together. Sam was just a forgettable mistake. A blip on the radar. Things would go back to normal. She could fake it to Miri, she did this with almost everyone else anyway. It was going to be okay.

Sam jumped in the shower to wash the night away, letting the hot water relax her muscles and remove any trace of Ty from her skin. She threw on jeans, a tank top, and a long-sleeved, button-down shirt. It was almost Memorial Day, but this far north was still cool in the mornings. She needed to dress warmly when she first got up, but by the time the workday ended it was hot and the long sleeve shirt was stifling. She couldn't wait until the weather picked a set direction

As she came out of the bedroom, drying her hair with a towel, she heard a light knock at the door. She checked her watch and had another thirty minutes before she had to leave for work. She frowned and hesitated, wondering who would be at the door this early. No one ever came to her door unexpectedly. Did Ty leave something?

When she opened the door to see Miri standing there, in a floral print dress and matching pink sweater, her heart fell. They didn't carpool, so there was only one reason for Miri to be at her door at this time. Her brain raced to cover her tracks, but she knew Miri knew everything. Sam could tell Miri had been crying, her round cheeks were splotchy and her eyes puffy. Sam just nodded, opening the door wider for her to come in. Miri didn't move at first, and they stood in a time freeze for a few seconds, both not wanting what would come next. Finally, Miri put her head down and walked past Sam, making sure not to touch her as she passed.

Miri walked to the kitchen and sat at the table, folding her hands neatly on the surface, her mouth in a tight line. How many times had they sat there drinking wine and chatting? How many times had they laughed so hard they cried? They had eaten, played cards, and shared about guys at that table. Whenever they'd get together, they always ended up in Sam's bright little kitchen. It was their space.

Miri started fiddling with a paper napkin at the table, twisting the corners into tight spirals. She refused to make eye contact. Sam didn't know if she should say something first. Apologize? Beg forgiveness? Blame Ty, the booze, the timing?

"How fucking dare you?" Miri's soft voice cut the silence.

Sam blushed with shame.

"Look, Miri, I don't know what Ty told you-"

"He told me you two fucked. That's what he told me. He came to my house last night, and I woke up with him sitting on the bed staring at me. He broke down crying and told me everything. He told me he couldn't lie to me. That he didn't want to lose me but refused to have a relationship filled with lies. But I bet you fucking could have." Her eyes glittered with rage.

Sam was truly taken aback. Miri didn't curse, and Sam had never seen her angry. Sam was at a loss for words. This was a side of

Miri in three years she'd never seen, never needed to see. She cleared her throat.

"I don't know what to say. I didn't mean to do it. It just happened. I regretted it immediately."

Miri watched her for a minute and balled up the napkin. She threw it down and slammed her hands on the table, knocking over the old lady themed salt and pepper shakers she'd given Sam a few years back as a joke. One rolled across the table and smashed on the ground.

"Things don't just happen, Samantha. People make things happen. You made this happen. What I don't understand is why? What the hell is wrong with you? Do you hate me that much?"

Sam sat down across from Miri. Jesus, she didn't hate Miri at all. This was the one person she truly cared about. But how could she tell her that, after doing something she knew would tear her apart? Sam never understood why she did the things she did. She felt like she was watching herself through a television screen, acting out life. She was tied to a chair, watching television Sam drive people away and make bad decisions. How could she ever explain that to Miri? Did it even matter? Regardless, her body made the choice. A choice they were all paying the price for now.

"Miri, I don't hate you. I hate myself for this. I'm sure Ty hates himself for this too."

"Don't you dare bring Ty up. What happened between him and me is between him and me. We have to deal with that ourselves. *If* we can. This here is between you and me." Miri pointed at the table between them. "And you don't hate yourself because you're devoid of real emotion. It's all an act."

That felt like a slap in the face to Sam. She thought she'd let Miri see through the wall, but apparently, she hadn't. It was still a show. Just a more comfortable show. Sam got up and went over to the kitchen window, her back to Miri. She hung her head down for a moment. How could she fix this? *Could* she even fix this?

"Do you love him? Did you even want him?" Miri asked bitterly behind her.

Sam shook her head. "No. Fuck, Miri, it was just a lapse of reason. I don't feel anything for him. It was just a stupid mistake. You know, he made it too."

Those are the last words Sam remembers speaking before she felt something heavy crack her on the side of her head. She went to her knees and grabbed her head, trying to keep from falling. Her ears were ringing, and all she could see were red fireworks. Right before she blacked out, she heard the words from what sounded like a different, darker Miri.

"...are no mistakes, you selfish bitch."

By the time she came to, her ears were still ringing, and her skull felt fractured. She laid on the floor, attempting to stop the room from spinning. Miri was gone, and the metal rolling pin she'd swung like a baseball bat at Sam's head was laying on the floor near her. Sam reached out and touched the rolling pin as if to confirm it had actually happened. Her fingers brushed the cold metal, and she groaned as lightning shot through her head. The rolling pin was a gift from her brother and his wife last Christmas. Ironically, she didn't even bake but kept it anyway. Now she wished she hadn't.

When Sam finally was able to sit upright, she rested her head in her hands, her elbows on her knees. She'd never have guessed Miri had it in her. Part of her felt sick, part of her felt admiration for Miri. She rolled over to her knees and placed her hands on the counter to pull herself up. She looked at the clock and realized she'd been out for about fifteen or twenty minutes. She couldn't go to work. She couldn't face Miri again.

She shuffled to the bathroom and peered at herself in the mirror. Her pale gray eyes stared back at her. Shit, her pupils were getting uneven. A concussion, likely. She deserved it at the least. She touched the knot on her head and pulled her fingers away. They were covered in blood. She made her way back to the kitchen and grabbed some paper towels and ice, putting them on the knot. She sat back at the table, where less than an hour or so before she was facing Miri for the last time.

She couldn't or wouldn't call the police. Miri was justified in her anger and having to relive all that with the police would just make it worse. It was time to move on. She peered around the tidy kitchen. Everything was nice, but she felt no attachment to any of it. Except the salt and pepper shakers, and those just because they made her laugh. They'd always joked they'd grow into little old ladies together, toddling around thrift stores and flea markets. She turned and stared at the living room. The same. She'd built a life that was just a television studio set. Everything in the right place. Nothing personal. It was the way her life had always been.

When she was little, her parents had a rule that before holidays and birthdays they'd go through their things and donate a few items to a charity to give back. Being part of the grand circle. Sam's brother would always bargain and try to keep things, never wanting to give up anything. Sam would fill her box with more than she was being asked to part with. She found it easy to move on from things. From people. It was almost a relief to her.

Once she felt steady enough, she got up and grabbed some duffel bags she kept under her bed and started to fill them with necessary items. Clothes, toiletries, shoes. She grabbed her blankets, pillows, some dishes, and pots. She put everything in the back of her car. Sadly, this had cleared out most of her apartment. Nothing personal. She put her hand on the remaining salt shaker to pack it, then decided against it. It would just bring up painful memories. The furniture, as little as there was, was all pretty much second hand. She filled up a couple of grocery bags and water bottles. She had money in her bank account because she rarely spent money. Just the necessities. A couple thousand at least. Maybe even closer to three.

She took one last look around the apartment and felt nothing. She'd lived there for years, and it meant nothing to her. She closed the door, walked down to the landlord's apartment, and dropped the key in the slot with a note that just read *moved out*. On the way out of town, she filled her gas tank and grabbed a few snacks. It was going to be a long night. She passed the *you are leaving* sign for the town she'd lived in for over five years, feeling hollow. Just another place on the map. It wasn't that she didn't care, it was simply how her brain worked. Add another layer to the wall.

She drove through the night. Not knowing where she was going, but heading south and whichever direction she'd turned on the highway. East. She didn't care. She stared ahead and watched the lights blur by her. Town after town, exit after exit. At times she felt like hours passed, but she didn't remember them. She thought about the people sleeping in their homes, wondering why she wasn't like them. Why didn't she feel attached to anything? Even Miri was easier to let go than she should've been. Sam turned off the interstate sometime in the night and started driving back roads.

By the time night was coming to an end, she found herself in a beach town and kept driving until she couldn't drive anymore.

She pulled into a parking lot near a closed restaurant, across from the ocean. She looked at the map and figured she was somewhere on the coast between Wilmington and Jacksonville, North Carolina, in a town called Crestview. She got out and stretched for a moment, listening to the waves hitting the shore. It was soothing, calling out to her. She couldn't see the water but it was familiar as if she'd been there before. The wind was steady, blowing her hair around her like spider webs. She pushed it off her face, twisting it to one side over her shoulder to keep it under control. She climbed wearily back into the car and dragged a blanket over her. She'd wait until morning and figure things out. She had money, so she was okay. She could make a fresh start. She'd done it before. She just didn't think she'd ever have to again.

Right now, she just needed to close her eyes which were dry and sore from driving all night. She couldn't sleep because of the concussion, she reminded herself. Her high school health class teacher's voice rang in her head.

"A person with a concussion must be kept awake or they could die."

Just close and rest your eyes, she convinced herself. Fifteen minutes or so, you won't fall asleep. In the morning you can figure things out. You can start over.

Chapter Three

After she finished vomiting, and a few rounds of dry heaving to make sure everything that was going to come out did, Sam leaned back and closed the car door, wiping her sweaty hair off her forehead. She caught the eye of a blotchy, pale, sausage-shaped woman, glaring at her with an expression of disgust as she unloaded an equally sausage-shaped child from her minivan. The woman's thin lips pursed in a straight line, making them disappear into her face. This caused her cheeks to hang even lower than they already did. Sam stared back with dead eyes, one of her many unique skills. The woman looked away and shook her head, muttering something under her breath.

Sam rolled down her window. "You got something to say?"

The woman glanced over and quickly away, not expecting confrontation. She shoved her child into an already overloaded wagon and started dragging the monstrosity away, shaking her head as she went. Sam heard the lady mutter "trash" as she jiggled away, her flip flops making a disgusting squish sound with every step. Well, it wasn't the worst thing to have happened to Sam in the past twenty-four hours at least.

She sorted through her bags and pulled together a change of clothes, a few toiletries, and her wallet. She headed for the restaurant, sand quickly filling her sneakers. As she got closer, she saw a weathered, hand-painted sign above the door. By the Sea. She imagined the decor would match the name, and it did not disappoint. Dock style posts with thick rope outlined an outside patio with a small bar. Inside carried on the thick rope, anchor, and admiral's wheel theme. The tables were covered in sticky, vinyl, light blue tablecloths with seahorse and sand dollar imagery. The floor had a thin layer of sand she could tell they tried unsuccessfully to keep out. From end to end ran a bar with a surprisingly good selection of liquor and taps. Probably the bread and butter of the place after tourists took their sunburned and cranky children back to the hotel.

It was still early, so only one table was occupied and a young girl was standing behind the bar, flipping lazily through a magazine. Laminated but slightly greasy menus were stacked upright in napkin holders on the tables. Sam grabbed one to see what the fare was. Yup, just as she expected, it consisted of a lot of deep-fried restaurant standards with cheesy beach themed names. Mozz"argh"ella sticks. "Walk the plank" cut fries. Crab cakes served in plastic seashells. The works. She just wanted coffee and toast.

The girl looked up as she approached. No older than eighteen or nineteen with pretty dark blue eyes and sun-bleached golden hair. The name Taylor was printed with a little smiley face next to it on her name tag. She closed her magazine and gave a service industry smile.

"Hey there, did you want to order?"

"Yeah, can I just get a cup of coffee, black, and toast? Oh, but put the butter on the side."

The idea of greasy butter didn't sit right, and she didn't think she couldn't stomach anything more than dry toast at the moment. If that even. Her stomach lurched in agreement, turning a few times before it settled.

"Sure thing, it'll just be a sec on the toast. I can bring it to you unless you want to sit at the bar?"

Sam glanced around the dining area, spying a table in the corner which already had the day's paper sprawled out, left behind by a previous diner. She pointed to the table, wishing she hadn't turned her head which caused the room to warp and spin. She put her hand on the barstool to steady herself.

"Uh, no, thanks. I'll sit over there. I need to run to the bathroom anyhow real quick."

The girl nodded and gestured to the bathrooms, tucked away at the end of the bar. Sam headed that direction and was surprised they didn't have ocean themed names too. Maybe they ran out of ideas. She went into a two-stall bathroom where sand had made its way in as well. The fluorescent bulb flickering above the sink triggered her headache and she rested her hands on the sink, closing her eyes to stop the spots flashing behind her lids. Finally, her vision normalized, and her head settled.

She peered in the mirror and saw her left eye had started to blacken from the blow to her head. The unevenness of her pupils had gone down. Fortunately, she didn't die when she accidentally fell asleep in the car. She appeared tired and gaunt. The knot on her head stood out, creating a misshapen look to her skull. She pulled out a hairbrush and gingerly tried to clean up the rat's nest her hair had become. She brushed her hair over to the left side, attempting to hide the lump. The brush hit the knot, sending waves of pain down through her. Delicately reaching up to touch the bump, she could feel the blood had crusted over at least.

After a change of clothes and little makeup to try and camouflage the damage, she headed to the table in the corner. Taylor came a minute later with her coffee and toast. As soon as Sam saw the pat of butter with its greasy little dots on top, her stomach did a couple of flips and she pushed it away. She covered it with a napkin, so she didn't have to look at it.

Dry toast it was.

The lifeguard guy was right. The coffee tasted like ass, but it was better than nothing. She took large swallows between bites of the toast, and slowly her stomach started to calm down. The small-town paper, the Crestview Chronicle, was about what she expected. Local interest stories, articles about minor crimes, domestic disturbances, break-ins, obituaries, and community meetings. Nothing exciting, even though they tried to make it seem so. She opened the classifieds, which were disappointingly sparse. Under the places to rent there were three. A three-bedroom house outside of town. Nope. A roommate request. Nope. A studio/one bedroom above a garage. Seemed like her only option. She called the number listed and left a message.

Under jobs it was mostly trades, medical, and day-laborers, but then one caught her eye and made her laugh at the circumstances.

By the Sea seaside restaurant and bar looking for an afternoon/evening bartender/floor manager. Must have reliable transportation, driver's license. No job hoppers. Work evenings and weekends required. Come in to apply. By the pier.

Well, then, that was convenient. Taylor was back behind the bar, reading the magazine. She glanced up when Sam approached and smiled, a little more genuinely this time. She looked behind Sam as if she'd forgotten something and then raised her eyebrows in question. Sam pointed at the ad in the paper.

"Hey, I saw in the paper you're hiring for an evening bartender?"

Taylor turned her head, furrowing her brow. She glanced at the paper and shrugged. She tipped her head back towards a small office door behind the bar, which read just the word *office* in stick-on metallic letters.

"Natalie! Are we hiring?"

The door swung open, and a large, older woman came out. Saying she was disheveled was being kind. Her apron was half unstrung, her shirtsleeves rolled up and pushed over her elbows, baring her meaty forearms. She seemed to be red all over, and sweat made her hair stick to the side of her face. Her glasses were perched at the end of her nose, and she peered over the top of them. First at Taylor, then at Sam. Her expression showed she'd sized Sam up immediately.

"Afternoons and evenings. Weekends required. This is a tourist town; we're busy on the weekends. No excuses. You have experience?"

Sam didn't, but she was a quick study and was willing to learn on the fly. Plus, she'd worked steadily for years and could handle it. She couldn't blow this chance. She didn't want to have to go to another town to find work if she could help it.

"Some. Mostly on the other side of the bar. But I worked in an office for the last five or so years and trained new employees when they came in. I catch on fast and am willing to work hard."

Natalie nodded and leaned on the bar, pushing her glasses up on her nose. It was obvious she owned the place and didn't have a lot of options. She was probably working open to close as it was from her appearance, and Sam knew she had the upper hand. Especially being slightly older than the current staff, who all looked to be fresh out of high school or college-aged. Natalie rifled under the bar and pulled out some wrinkled paperwork. Tax forms and a moist application.

"Can you get these filled out? Start Friday? The shift starts at three to prep for the evening crowd. We close at midnight and it takes about an hour to clean and close up. So, ten-hour shifts four days a week. Thursday through Sunday. We're closed Mondays. Tuesdays and Wednesdays we only do lunch and dinner, so don't need you then. It pays twelve an hour plus tips. You'll man the bar and make sure floor supplies are ordered."

Sam's brain fumbled around, trying to remember what the day of the week it was. She went to the bar with co-workers on Monday and fought with Miri on Tuesday. Drove all night, woke up this morning in the parking lot. That made it Wednesday. That would give her a couple of days to get situated, find housing, and hopefully let the knot go down some. She wanted to get the lay of the town and work through all that had happened. Friday would be good.

"For sure. I'll get these done here and leave them before I go. By the way, I'm Samantha Rutliff. You can call me Sam."

If Natalie was relieved, she didn't show it. She nodded and pushed her graying hair out of her face, attempting to put it back in the loose ponytail it was managing to escape from. She reached her hand out, which was both damp and calloused dry.

"Nice to meet you, Sam. Natalie. I own the place. Bought it from a couple of guys a few years back who were more interested in getting super high and giving their friends a place to party, than running a business. Don't know what I was thinking."

Her eyes glanced over the dining areas, and she shook her head. "Taylor, get her a couple of t-shirts and a bartender's apron. You'll need good shoes. We're real busy those shifts. You'll be lucky if you get a chance to sit at all."

Just like that, she disappeared into the back office. Taylor handed Sam a couple of By the Sea t-shirts. They had an image of the restaurant with a smiling starfish out front. One pink, one seafoam green. Sam noted Taylor was wearing shorts and sneakers. Nothing standard except the shirt. Everyone had their hair pulled back in ponytails, and the guy cooking in the back was wearing a hairnet over his long, wavy hair.

She grabbed the paper off the table she was sitting at and took one last gulp of now cold coffee. She slipped a ten under the receipt Taylor had left and headed back to her car. The parking lot was now packed with cars circling, looking for parking spaces. She'd need to see if there was a different place to park for work if evenings were as crowded.

She had a job. Now, she just needed a place to live and fast. She couldn't live out of her car and didn't want to waste the money she had on a hotel. Clearly, the town was set up for tourist stays but not so much for single residents. Just as she was thinking that her cell phone started ringing. It was the number she'd called about the apartment above the garage. She took a deep breath, crossed her fingers, and answered the phone. Her voice sounded a little shaky when she said hello. She had a lot riding on this. The girl on the other end responded cheerfully.

"Hey, you called about the apartment? It's still available. Did you have any questions about it or want to come see it?"

Hopefully, things were starting to fall into place.

Chapter Four

About an hour later, Sam parked her car a street away and walked to meet with the girl she'd spoken to on the phone about the apartment. She assumed it was a younger girl, due to the fact she felt like she was talking to a cartoon mouse on the phone. A high-pitched squeaky voice told her about the apartment. Furnished, ideally for a single person. A few blocks from the beach. Walking distance to the small grocery store and a few restaurants. They preferred a female tenant but would make an exception if necessary. It was available to be seen that afternoon.

Noting where her car was parked, so she didn't have to search for it later, Sam did a quick check in the reflection of the car window to ensure she looked presentable. Parking a street over she thought was smart, as it's one thing to be new in town looking for a place to live and another to pull up appearing like she was living in her car. She needed to make a good impression because this was pretty much her only option.

The walk over was pleasant, each home she passed seeming like a cottage out of a beach magazine. Weathered and simple but charming. As a child, her family had gone on vacations to the beach a couple of times, but it was always them staying in some oceanside hotel and wandering only far enough away to shop at tacky gift shops or eat at the aptly themed restaurants. She'd never thought about the town behind those. Schools, banks, everyday places the people who lived there would go. Walking the back streets of the town brought a new sense of appreciation to a place most people thought only existed fifty yards from the beach.

As Sam approached the home for the address she'd scribbled down, she was pleasantly surprised. A little yellow cottage with pale blue shutters, and someone had a green thumb. The little walkways were lined with flowers of all kinds, giving it an English cottage feel. To the left was a detached garage. Above it, she could see windows for the apartment, each decorated with delicate white curtains. She tried not to get her hopes up, so she wouldn't seem too eager. Or weird.

She walked to the door and saw a small rainbow Pride flag in the garden under the front windows. She raised a brow. She'd not seen such open representation where she was from and wondered if it caused issues for the people who lived here. Especially being a fairly small town in the south. Everywhere she'd lived people had seemed to keep this behind closed doors. She'd had gay co-workers and while generally accepted outwardly, they still presented themselves in the workplace in a very neutral state. Fair enough though, because behind their backs people still made jokes and expressed their discomfort. At best, people only acted enlightened when face to face.

Just as she raised her hand to ring the bell, the door swung open, exposing a small, plump girl who looked no older than fourteen. Her rich brown pixie cut and large, dark cocoa eyes gave her an air of innocence, almost angelic. The girl smiled, creating soft lines around her eyes, showing she was much older than she initially appeared. She pushed open the screen door and stepped out.

"Hey! You must be Samantha. I saw you walking up. I'm Rosie." The squeaky timbre of her voice was almost infectious. She started walking down the path and cocked her head towards the garage, not waiting for Sam to respond.

"The apartment is right over here."

They walked over to the garage and Rosie led the way up a narrow flight of stairs to the right of the building. This ended at a small porch with a wooden chair and round table, decorated with a potted plant and bunny statue. It was almost too much for Sam, who felt like she'd stepped into an alternate reality. Rosie opened the door to a cute but tiniest apartment Sam had ever seen. Rosie walked around, waving her arm like a realtor giving a tour as if everything couldn't be seen from the door.

The door led into a brightly yellow decorated kitchenette with a half-sized refrigerator, small range, and counter bar with two light blue stools. To the left was a similarly decorated living room with a floral loveseat, shabby-chic white coffee table, and a matching stand with a television on it. Floating between the two spaces was a wood rocking chair and matching floral pillow. A partial wall behind the loveseat separated the bedroom from the living room. The bedroom being just that. A space that could only fit the full-sized bed it contained. Two small wooden plant stands acted as end tables on either side of the bed and touched both the sides of the bed and the walls. And as Sam would've guessed, a floral bedspread. The room had a closet with a dresser put inside, she guessed because there was no way it would've fit outside the closet. On the other side of the kitchen was a tiny bathroom with a single sink, toilet, and a shower she wasn't sure she'd even be able to turn around in. All the walls in the apartment were painted bright, beachy colors with what looked like still-life paintings done by a three-year-old.

"Oh, it's very pretty." Sam lied through her teeth.

Well, it was pretty in a coordinated sense, but not Sam's taste in the least. It seemed like someone's grandma had taken acid and decorated the space. But it was clean and what she was looking for.

"Is it available now?"

Rosie beamed with pride. "Thank you! I did the decor. My wife, Ansley, isn't much of a decorator but lets me do what I want. I'm glad you like it! It is available now. First month's rent and security deposit. Utilities included." She paused and glanced at Sam, biting her lip. "Would it be only you? I mean, I guess a couple could live here, but it's pretty tight."

"Just me. I'm new to town and recently took a job at By the Sea as their night manager."

Rosie's shoulders relaxed, and she smiled broadly. "Oh, I know that place and Natalie, the owner. Can get a little crazy for my tastes, but I'm more of a homebody. Locals get rowdy down there in the evenings sometimes. Is that what brought you here?"

"No, I guess I was looking for a change and had never lived near the beach." Sam hoped the line of questioning would stop because she didn't like to lie but didn't want to tell the truth either.

"Well, you'll love it here! I'm from the area and met Ansley while away at college. We moved back as soon as we could find decent jobs here. Hard to do in a beach town. I'm a preschool teacher, and Ansley is the manager at the surf shop on the strand."

Anxious to wrap up and start moving in, Sam pulled out her checkbook to speed up the process. "I can write a check for the rent and deposit. Is it possible to move in today? I've been staying in a hotel." Another lie. "I'm anxious to get settled before I start work on Friday."

"Of course! We're excited to have you! Here are the keys, we keep a spare if you get locked out. I have to go out for a while and Ansley works this evening, but you can come and go as you please. There is only parking for two vehicles in the driveway, but if those are taken you can park out front. I'll let Ansley know, in case she comes home and wonders whose car is in the drive!"

She took the check without looking at it, then was down the stairs and gone. Sam sat on the couch and let out a deep, long breath. In twenty-four hours she'd secured a completely new life. Maybe she should've changed her name too, she thought bitterly to herself. No, no one here knew her anyway, so it wouldn't matter. She ticked off tasks in her head to make sure she hadn't forgotten anything important.

Her family.

She supposed she should let them know she'd moved. It wasn't like they'd ever visited her previous home, but she didn't want to risk any kind of worry or search. Especially since she'd just dipped on her job, and she had her brother as her emergency contact. She dialed her brother's number, as it rang she whispered "don't pick up, don't pick up" over and over. When the recording came on to leave a voicemail, she breathed a sigh of relief.

"Hey Brad, it's Sam. Just a quick head's up. I took a new job, which required an unexpected move. My phone is the same and here is my new address. Hope all is well. Say hello to the wife and kids for me! Let Mom and Dad know when you see them." She read off the address she'd written on the paper for the apartment and quickly hung up. Short and sweet.

It wasn't that she didn't love her family. She did in the way she thought families loved each other. But she just didn't connect, or maybe they didn't connect to her. She wasn't sure. Brad fulfilled her parents' need to have grandchildren and photo ops for the holidays. They were happy that Sam seemed to have a good life, a good job. They never questioned her lack of relationships or desire for children. She called them enough to keep them from worrying and showed up on the occasional holiday to be the dutiful daughter. She figured she'd be sad when her parents passed but also expected it to happen one day. Brad had always carried the conversations around the table when they were kids, making it easy for her to not have to create things to talk about.

The thing was, she couldn't really tell them what was going on because she couldn't explain it in a way they could understand. That sometimes she'd be driving or walking somewhere and look up, not knowing where she was or how she got there. How sometimes she'd take a safety pin and stab herself in the arm because when she looked down at her body it didn't feel real, like a mirage. Even the pain from the safety pin would be more like she was watching someone else feel it. That when she was dealing with other people, whether at work or in a relationship, she was acting out a part, reading from a script for the character of Samantha. That she cared but couldn't bring it to the surface. How she avoided mirrors because sometimes she felt like the person staring back at her was judging her for being such a failure. For being so odd.

Only when she was with Miri did she feel like what she thought other people felt like sometimes. They'd be laughing, and she'd get this warm feeling and think, "Oh, this is what it feels like to be real."

But that was over, and apparently, according to Miri wasn't real either. Miri was gone, and Sam had to go back through life acting a role she knew the world expected. Keep your head down, work hard but not too hard. Be polite, but not overly friendly. Pay your bills on time, get your oil changed. Show interest in people but not too much. Share about yourself but only the stuff they can't use against you. Make eye contact but just for a moment. Keep people at arm's length but not so much they worry and get nosy. Be responsible, but don't take on too many responsibilities. They are a trap.

Sam leaned her head back against the half wall behind the loveseat and closed her eyes. The best way to deal with it was to shut it all down. Her heart hurt sometimes, but she didn't know what to do with the feeling. She started to doze off and shook herself awake. She needed to go get her stuff and get it moved in before Ansley came home. She wasn't ready to interact with another person today. She was tapped out. Rosie was nice, lovely really, but their interaction had worn Sam out. She grabbed the keys, locked the door, and headed over to her car. A light breeze was coming off the ocean, and she could smell the tang of salt in the air. It made her feel nostalgic, but she wasn't sure what for.

After she'd brought the car over and unloaded it, she dug through her groceries to see what she could make for dinner. The stuff had been sitting in the car all night and day, so she threw out anything she thought might have spoiled. She pulled out a small pot and opened a can of soup. She had half a box of crackers to go with it. As it warmed, she glanced around the little apartment, feeling a weird sensation of being home. Not something she'd felt before, except after being at a sleepover as a child and coming back to her room. It was similar to the feeling she'd had on her walk to the car. It was odd and comforting at the same time.

While she ate, she turned on the television, which surprisingly had cable, for some noise in the background. She flipped to a game show, requiring no mental investment. When it got dark, she heard a car pull up and peered out the window. A dark tan, leggy girl with waist-length, kinky-curly blond locks got out of the car and started up the path to the cottage. She glanced up at the window and raised a hand at Sam. Sam waved back. Must be Ansley. She was stunning. Like she'd stepped off a billboard for some exotic island retreat. Sam saw Rosie step out and put her arms around Ansley. They kissed and then were gone into their little home.

Sam washed her dishes and went to lay on the bed, doubting she'd be able to sleep. Hours later she woke to the television still chattering away and got up to turn it off. The street was dark and still. She climbed back into bed, put her head under the covers, and slept another nine hours.

Chapter Five

The next day Sam organized her tiny space, did some grocery shopping, and walked around the town. It was pretty much like every beach town ever. A strip right off the beach with bars, restaurants, ice cream and candy shops, tacky gift shops with an assortment of keychains, glass blown animals, shot glasses and the likes. Being a smaller beach town, the hotels that faced the beach were no more than three stories high, probably due to town regulation. In between were cute, themed homes with names like *Life's a Beach* and *Toes in the Sand*, which had the names of rental companies on signs facing the road. She doubted many people lived directly on the beach unless they were wealthy.

A few streets over, behind the grocery store, surf shop, and gas station were where the residents lived. She saw homes with kids' toys out front, quirky windchimes, and other things saying someone actually lived there. These were the homes she liked. They had character and weren't decorated to fit a certain clientele. People seemed friendly and said hello or waved when she walked by. She wasn't ready to get to know anyone or make small talk, so she waved back but kept moving.

The only school she saw was an old elementary school, which looked like was now being used for offices and had a sign for a health clinic. The kids who lived in the town must be bussed to a bigger town for school. For some reason, that made her feel an emptiness inside. The town did have a library in an old, small church. She was hot and tired from walking, so she popped in to browse. An ancient-looking lady glanced up at her when she walked in and moved her mouth in what Sam guessed was supposed to be a smile. It kind of looked like a creepy grimace.

"Welcome! Bathroom's in the back." The woman's voice crackled as her long wrinkly finger pointed to the back of the library.

She obviously knew the locals and thought Sam was a tourist looking for an easy bathroom. Sam nodded and decided to let the woman think what she wanted if it saved a conversation. She noticed a row of computers to the left with a couple of teenagers giggling behind them. A sign by the front desk said to ask for the password and to limit time to thirty minutes on the internet for other patrons to use. Good to note, in case she needed to use a computer. She didn't own a computer, nor did she want to. She didn't like most people in person, so the idea of having to see their every thought all the time made her cringe. But the world sometimes required it, much to her distaste.

There were about twelve rows of books, about six feet high and twelve feet long, in the main room and a children's section in a front room. Up on what used to be the pulpit was a reading area with magazines and a regional authors section, which contained a surprising number of books. The side walls had shelves about three feet high, on top had books displayed and between them rough clay sculptures done by the local preschool children. Sam wondered if this was the preschool Rosie taught at. At the end of each of the rows of dark wood shelves, was a little plaque, donated in memory or honor of someone from the town.

Sam went to the front and applied for a library card. The old woman peered at her suspiciously and asked for proof of residence. Sam mused that the old lady didn't want some tourist stealing the dusty books. Sam didn't have any but explained she'd rented an apartment from Rosie and Ansley. It dawned on her she didn't even know their last name. The old lady's eyes lit up and she smiled, turning from crypt keeper to kindly grandma.

"Oh! I love that Rosie. She is the sweetest little thing. Her classroom made the clay art over on those shelves." She fumbled behind the desk and slid the form for the library card across the desk. "Once you fill this out, you can check out up to six books and two alternate media at a time for up to two weeks."

Alternate media must've been the creaky spinner rack to the right of the checkout desk, which had some audiobooks and a few DVDs. Sam quickly scribbled her info down and grabbed her license out of her bag. She handed those to the lady and glanced at her name tag. This caused Sam to blush and her stomach to form into knots.

Miriam.

The old lady's name was Miriam. What were the odds? Sam quickly glanced down to hide her shame. If the old lady had noticed, she didn't say anything. She took the forms to the scanner behind her and made a copy of the license. She painstakingly filled out Sam's name on a paper card and handed it to her with her license.

"Real card will come to you in the mail in about two weeks. For now, this one will do."

Sam took the card and slipped it into her bag. She mumbled a thank you and walked over to browse the books. Since she was walking, she didn't think she'd get six but figured a couple should tide over for the next week or so.

Once she checked out, trying to not make eye contact with old Miriam, she went to the side of the library and lit a cigarette. She wasn't a heavy smoker and had been trying to quit for years, but it was still her stress go-to. She leaned against the wall, glancing over at the gas station across the street. A couple of young guys were hanging out on the curb, cutting up and taking turns doing tricks on their skateboards. It made her wonder what teenagers, and people who didn't drink, did for entertainment around the town. Going to the beach had to get old if you grew up there. Everything becomes ordinary when it's always around.

She stubbed out her cigarette and put the butt in the trash can, though from looking at the ground no one else was doing the same. The walk home was quiet, everyone from earlier must've gone in for dinner. Her stomach rumbled, reminding her to do the same. She rounded the corner of her street and saw Ansley getting something out of her car. She didn't want a conversation but knew she couldn't keep putting it off. Ansley was just pulling her head out from her car when Sam came up. Sam was taken aback by her beauty. She had dark tan skin, but coarse, curly, almost white hair and eyes a shade of amber and green Sam had never seen. Sam guessed she was multiracial and the combination was absolutely perfect. Ansley stood up to her full height, which must've been around six feet tall. She looked like a goddess.

"Hey, you must Ansley. I saw you from the window last night. I'm Sam, your new tenant." Sam stuck out her hand awkwardly towards Ansley.

Ansley grasped it and held it firmly. "Sam! Yes! Didn't want to bug you last night, figured you needed time to settle in. We're glad to have you. Rosie should be home shortly from the school. She stayed late to work on setting up a project for the kids. We'd love to have you join us for dinner if you'd like."

Her voice was deep and rich like honey. Sam thought Ansley and Rosie were like yin and yang, a perfect harmony and balance of each other. While she did want to get to know them better eventually, she just wanted a quiet evening to prepare for her new job the next day. The idea of socializing sounded exhausting. From what the position at By the Sea seemed like it entailed, she figured she'd get more than she could stand there.

"I'd love to, but I start my new job at the restaurant tomorrow and need to get ready for that. I was going to go over and scope the evening crowd out, then think I'll turn in early. I'd love a rain check though!" She hoped she sounded appreciative and excited.

Ansley grinned, showing a full set of pearl white teeth. "Offer stands. I work two evenings a week, but anytime you want."

She grabbed the bags she gathered from the car and headed towards the door. She turned back, casting her kaleidoscope eyes towards Sam. "It's really nice to meet you, Sam."

Sam gave a small wave as she climbed the stairs to her home and slipped inside. It was so quiet inside, she could almost hear the buzzing of molecules moving around inside her. She set the books from the library on the counter, next to her phone she'd left behind for her walk. It was blinking for a voicemail. The missed call was from her brother Brad.

"Hey, Sam, it's Brad. Thanks for the head's up. Wow, that's a far move! The job must be a good one. And the beach! Have to admit, a little jealous. I let Mom know when I talked to her last night. She said, 'That's Samantha, always on to the next adventure!' Maybe they will want to visit now, right? Anyway, the kids say hello, and Jess sends her love. Talk to you later."

Even though Sam had moved a lot, she'd never felt anything was an adventure. Everything was just another home, on another street, in another town. What her family saw as her always seeking out new things to explore, was really her not connecting enough to anything to stay in one place. Leaving was the easy part. As for them visiting, she hoped not. Or at least if they did, that they'd stay in a hotel and do their own thing. She hated entertaining.

After a bite to eat, Sam realized the time was getting late. She wanted to go and check out By the Sea before the dinner rush was over, and to see what type of patrons came in after that. Sam had to admit she was nervous about the new job, mostly because she'd pretty much lied her way into it. The more information she could gather on the place and how it ran, the more confident she'd be walking in the next day.

She brushed her teeth and did a quick mirror check. The lump was definitely still there but starting to go down. The black eye had not gotten any bigger, thankfully, and she was able to hide it with concealer. She pulled hair into a loose ponytail and threw a fresh shirt on. She was only planning to spy from the parking lot but still wanted to be presentable, in the off chase she ran into anyone.

The tourists had pretty much headed out for the evening by the time she drove into the lot. Even though the restaurant was hopping, she'd no problem finding a parking space, confirming it was mostly locals in the evenings. A few families were eating on the outside patio, and the inside was full. She pulled in to park as close as she could without seeming creepy and watched the goings-on.

The crowd was fairly young, mid to late twenties and early thirties with some old hippie type beach bums sprinkled in. Everyone seemed to be drinking. A lot. As she suspected, the bar was what was really keeping By the Sea afloat. She glanced over and saw the lifeguard who had knocked on her window earlier, leaning on the rail of the lifeguard stand. He was talking to a few people his age on the beach below. They were laughing about something, and one of the guys in the group was making grand gestures with his hands. Sam tried to remember the lifeguard's name, but she'd been out of it at the time. Something with an S. Scott? No, something odd. Smitty? Maybe that was it. She wasn't a hundred percent, but it stuck in her head, so that's who he became at that point.

Smitty was shaking his head and waving his hand at the other guy with shoulder-length, dark, curly hair, who was making the gestures. Smitty's other hand was on his stomach, and he was cracking up so hard he almost fell over the railing, catching himself at the last second. The curly-haired guy fell back on the sand, laughing and waving his arms. The girls in the group were enamored by the guy on the sand. He was the life of the party, probably the reason they were all there. Smitty threw a water bottle at the other guy and tipped his head back laughing.

Sam had never had a group of friends like that. In a group, she was the quiet one. She was never the life of the party. She'd always had friends and been invited to things but could leave and the party would go on. With Miri, she opened up and laughed more. When she thought about it, though, Miri still was the one leading the way. Sam was no wallflower, but she was never the center of attention, mostly by choice. She was the observer, taking mental notes all of the time. Analyzing people and situations. Picking things apart. Creating upcoming scenarios she thought might happen.

The crowd around the lifeguard stand had begun to disperse, and Smitty was gathering his things for the end of his shift. Sam didn't want him seeing her sitting there again, appearing like she was lying about not sleeping in the parking lot. She'd seen what she'd needed to anyhow for her shift the next day. Tomorrow was going to be tough and take a lot for her to prove. As she'd taught herself in the past, though, she could do anything she set her mind to. Mind over matter.

She turned on the car, giving one last look at the restaurant and setting her resolve. She guided the car quietly out of the parking lot towards home. But not before Smith, who she called Smitty, spied her and watched as her taillights disappeared into the dark.

Chapter Six

By the Sea was between the lunch and dinner crowds when Sam arrived on Friday, which eased her anxiety about jumping in. Taylor was resetting the waitress stand and Jimmy, the cook with the long, dark, wavy hair, was cleaning and restocking the line. Natalie gave her the tour of the back and a key to the office. Sam had worked retail in her earlier days, so was familiar with counting tills, making change, and cashing out once the drawer got too large. Natalie showed her the safe and showed her where they hid the current combo. Sam would be the only one on shift who had it, and she made a mental note of where the code was hidden.

  She knew basic drinks from being a consumer and had checked out a bartender's guide from the library, which she'd been studying. She was relieved to see they also kept a copy behind the bar. Natalie told her beer was the drink of choice for the locals, and beer and wine for the tourists, making it simple. Most liquor sales would be shots and two-ingredient drinks, so they only used the guide when someone, usually a tourist, asked for a fancy drink. Beer and shots drove the sales and were the easiest pours.

The kitchen closed at seven, and Jimmy was the only chef on the days she worked. Natalie ran it the other days they were open. Since it was mostly fried foods, salads, and sandwiches, the term chef was loosely used. Taylor was the waitress Wednesdays through Sundays, and Tuesdays were so slow Natalie handled it by herself. She talked about closing that day, but with summer upon them, she was holding off deciding as business was starting to pick up during the weekdays.

Sam would be the only bartender, but since most drinks were taps and pours any other staff could jump in. The dishwasher, Chris, came on after the lunch service and was on until ten, but after that, she'd be by herself. She wasn't thrilled by being alone to close up but felt it was doable. She'd only have to count the deposit and shut down the bar. Police started patrolling right around the time the bar closed to make sure there were no stragglers. She could wait until she saw them come through to walk to her car.

As the dinner and evening crowd started to filter in, she didn't have much time to be nervous as she was pouring drinks steadily. The music overhead was a mixture of reggae, sixties surf music, and anything with a beach theme. Once the crowd filled in, the music was pretty quickly drowned out by constant chatter. Natalie stayed behind the bar with Sam to make sure she got the hang of things. Taylor was the opposite of the girl reading a magazine behind the bar in the morning, and was flying through the tables with trays of food and drinks like she was on skates. It was a well-coordinated dance.

Jimmy bopped to music on his headphones, as did Chris, and Sam was a little envious as the beach-themed music she could see very rapidly getting on her nerves. Jimmy was a large, tan dude in his early twenties. He was friendly but not overly chatty. Chris looked to be nineteen or twenty years old, very slim and pale, with thin, light brown hair. He seemed friendly but painfully shy, never initiating conversation. On his breaks, he read on the patio. Always with headphones on. They seemed to be in their own bubble in the back of the house, but both were willing to jump in behind the bar to help when things got crazy.

Natalie wasn't kidding; Sam never got a chance to sit. They were allowed one free meal, so during a slight lull, Sam stood beside the bar to scarf down a grilled cheese sandwich and fries. Outside on the patio, clear strings running from the roof to the rope wall caught her eye, and she tried to figure out what they were there for. They were every inch or so, creating an almost invisible curtain across the patio. Taylor saw her looking at them and answered the question.

"Keeps out seagulls. If we didn't have them, they'd swarm the patio, stealing people's food and crapping everywhere. It's fishing line," she explained matter-of-factly.

As if called into question, a seagull landed on one of the pier posts on the outside patio and scowled in. Sam felt as if it was scoping things out, figuring out the design. It cocked its head and glared at her, or at least seemed to. On cue, a patron was leaving the restaurant with takeout and made the mistake of pulling a French fry out of the bag to eat. Out of nowhere, a flock of seagulls descended on the person, trying to get the fry out of their hand. The person screamed and threw the fry at the swarm as they started to run. The flock split, half chasing the person and the other half fighting over the single fry. Taylor started to laugh.

"Amateur. Must be a tourist. Wait until you get to your car before you open any food. I've seen them snatch whole sandwiches out of people's hands. Every few weeks they figure out a new way into our patio, and we have to add more fishing line. Rats with wings, I tell ya."

Sam watched the hoard steal the fry from each other, eventually dispersing in search of easier prey as the fry was whittled down to almost nothing. She admired their tenacity. Humans would likely starve without grocery stores and restaurants. Here the birds always had a good selection of food to steal from all the wagons and coolers filled with snacks being dragged over the boardwalk. Always a new sucker to prey on.

As dinner wrapped up and the crowd switched to solely drinkers, Taylor and Chris finished cleaning the dining room and dishes. Patrons became louder and more obnoxious, making Sam's head throb. Natalie waved at her to take a quick break, so she stepped out to smoke a cigarette. She walked towards the ocean, letting the crowd noise fade behind her. She approached the lifeguard stand and lit her cigarette, inhaling deeply.

"Hey, anyone ever tell you those things can kill you?" a voice from above joked.

A glance up revealed Smitty leaning on the lifeguard stand rail, peering down at her.

She laughed and shrugged. "A lot of things can kill you. Smitty, right?"

"Haha, no. Smith, actually. Samantha, right?"

Smith, that's right. She knew it was something odd.

"Yeah, or just Sam. Sorry about the wrong name. I was a little out of it that morning."

"No worries, I kind of like Smitty. My parents thought they were being unique. They were really being like, 'hey no one will ever remember my kid's name'. Can I grab one of those from you?"

Sam laughed. Her name had always seemed so generic. There were at least three Samanthas in her school growing up. Luckily, one went by Sammy, so she chose Sam to be different from the other two. She pulled a cigarette out of the pack and put her hand out towards him with it.

"Doesn't seem very lifeguardish to be smoking on duty."

"I'm coming down. Actually off duty, waiting on a friend."

He jumped over the rail down to the sand, landing in front of her. He took the cigarette and lighter she was handing him, expertly lighting the cigarette with one hand and one drag. He blew out smoke and handed the lighter back.

"So, just hanging out, or still living out of your car?"

"No. I work over at the restaurant now. First day. And I was never living in my car."

The bite to her voice was apparent, causing him to blush and look away.

"I moved into a place that day. I need to get back to work. Enjoy the cigarette, Smith."

She stubbed hers out, shoving the butt in her pocket. As she turned to leave, he put his hand on her arm, stopping her. She glanced up into his sincere face, noticing his eyes had a unique golden amber to them.

"I'm sorry, that came across shitty. I was trying to be funny; it fell flat."

She shrugged and stared at her feet. She nodded, glancing back at the restaurant. It was busy and Natalie was at the door, gesturing for her to come back. She could hear the crowd noise accelerating and sighed.

"Okay, gotta go. Natalie needs me."

Smith looked over, giving Natalie a wave and she waved back. They obviously knew each other, working just yards apart. Sam still felt like an interloper, and even that rubbed her the wrong way. She started the trek back through the sand towards the doors.

'Hey, Sam!" Smith called out. "I'm really sorry. Thanks for the cig, and I don't mind if you call me Smitty. I'd prefer it, truth be told."

Sam gave a small smile and wave. "That was going to happen anyway, Smitty."

Before she ducked back into the chaos, she gave one last glance back and saw Smitty smiling at her, as he turned and waved at someone walking up to him on the beach. Natalie looked relieved to see her come back in and handed Sam her apron. The rest of the night was a blur of beer after beer pour, wiping counters, cleaning glasses, and leaning in to hear what people yelling at her were ordering.

By the time they kicked out the last patron, her ears were ringing and her head was buzzing. Thankfully, as soon as the door closed Natalie turned off the music and began straightening the chairs and tables. Sam counted the till and was shocked they'd cleared a few thousand that night. Natalie counted out the tips for the day, handing Sam her stack. It was over three hundred dollars, and that was after Natalie had sorted out the rest of the staff.

"Whoa. That's a lot." Sam stared at the stack of bills.

"Friday and Saturday are our big nights. You'll earn your tips. Thursday and Sundays are definitely more chill, but you'll still clear over a hundred or two in tips those days most times. Winter is much less, but since locals drink year round we do okay," Natalie said, giving the last wipe of the counters.

They put the till in the safe, and Natalie took the deposit with her. She'd be there to help Sam the next night as well, but after that Sam would be on her own. After tonight, she wasn't confident she could handle it but it was just for the last two hours. They walked quietly to their cars. Natalie smiled and nodded appreciatively, pausing at her car to fish her keys out of her bag.

"You did good tonight. I'll try to get a barback for you soon. It's picking up, and I think we can afford it for the summer. That will limit all the restocking and lifting on shift. Maybe keep the kitchen open a little longer too. We'll see."

She heaved herself into her car and pulled out. Sam stood for a few minutes, taking in the quiet night and gentle sloshing of the waves. Without people there, she felt like it was there for her. Her very own part of the earth. Right on time, she saw a police car slowly pull in and drive silently through the lot. She still had on her bar apron and work shirt, so they glanced at her but kept moving. She knew if she was still there when they came back around they'd likely question her, so she got in her car and left.

Driving through a beach town late at night has a ghost town feel. All the sunburned tourists back in their cool hotel beds, sleeping or watching late-night television. Locals turned in, as their lives were the same day in and day out. Going to jobs, kids going to school, running errands, doing laundry, cooking dinner. Two different worlds, both coexisting and on different planes of existence. One the reason for the other but not reciprocated.

Sam stopped off at the only twenty-four-hour gas station for a pack of cigarettes and chocolate covered pretzels. She knew she wouldn't be able to sleep for a while, the adrenaline from the evening still coursing through her veins. The sleepy clerk barely looked up from what he was reading before mumbling the total. Sam paid in cash since she was going to have a lot of it now and grabbed her things. A little bell chimed as she left. No one else was around, and she felt sorry for the night clerk. Being alone was nice, being isolated not so much.

Grateful for the little porch at the top of her stairs, she sat and stared at the night sky while she munched her pretzels and smoked. Here she was. The same Sam, but different. New people around her, a new home, a different town. Even though literally a week ago she was sitting in her kitchen chatting and drinking wine with Miriam, talking about work and weekend plans, that seemed like months ago. A memory she'd conjure up from a time long past.

Four days ago that life ended, thrusting her into this unfamiliar world.

Why then did it feel so right?

Chapter Seven

As summer progressed, Sam all but forgot her previous life. The days she worked were just that, a blur of work. The ten-hour shifts took their toll, she pretty much only slept and worked those days. The other three days she ran errands, read, and explored the town. Rosie was out gardening most evenings after she got off work and often asked Sam if she wanted to help. Sam enjoyed this, as Rosie would chatter away as they pruned and dug in the dirt. Sam could just listen and plug along without having to think. Rosie reminded her of Miriam, but less insecure and more worldly. Ansley would join them sometimes, but like Sam, was typically quieter and Rosie would run the show. Because of all their varying work schedules, Sam hadn't joined them yet for dinner but kept promising to.

Natalie hired a barback to help on Fridays and Saturdays, an older, tattooed guy by the name of Gus. Short for Gustavo, as he told everyone he introduced himself to. He was a talker but a hard worker, so Sam didn't mind. Not to mention, he filled in chatting with the customers when she didn't want to. A few times she caught him eyeing Natalie, and he was always at the ready when Natalie had her arms full or was trying to get through the door. Sam thought it was sweet, even more so because Natalie didn't seem to have a clue. A part-time waitress and another kitchen helper were hired before the Fourth of July. Even if Natalie questioned buying the restaurant, it was slammed and paying for itself, plus some. Natalie finally was able to take days off and work normal length shifts.

Sam and Smitty exchanged pleasantries when they were working and in passing. They usually shared a cigarette at her seven o'clock shift break, as he was getting off work. She wasn't looking for friends, and he seemed to have more than his fair share. People dropped by the lifeguard stand his whole shift. This set-up worked fine for Sam and gave her all the socializing she wanted. She was busy enough to not need anything else in her life. She heard after Labor Day it slowed down and got quiet, but she'd cross that bridge when she got to it.

One afternoon in mid-July, while she was setting the restaurant up for dinner service, something moving in the waves caught her eye. She stepped out and walked closer, crossing the boardwalk to see a group of surfers riding the waves. She recognized Smitty immediately, his tall frame gracefully dipping in and out of the waves, his feet braced, knees slightly bent. He was looking back to the left of him, laughing at another surfer who was crouching on his board, riding the same wave. She recognized the other guy as the one who had been gesturing wildly at the lifeguard stand, the night she'd come to scope out the restaurant before her first shift. Slender but muscular, with shoulder-length, curly, almost black hair. He was laughing and jumped off his board, flipping over the wave, surfacing a few seconds later. Smitty rode the wave until it died off, laying on the board and riding it into the shore.

They grabbed their boards and came back to the beach, pointing out at waves that were coming in. There was something so delicate, yet powerful, about how easy they made it look. She envied how natural and confident they were with the waves. She also couldn't help but admire their lean bodies, carved by growing up at the beach, swimming and surfing almost their whole lives.

Later that evening, she was cleaning up some napkins that had blown all over the outside patio. The sunset was remarkable and she stopped, mesmerized by the purples and oranges which lit up the sky. The sunsets were always pretty, but this one was damn near magical. Tourists often were heard saying how beautiful it was, and how they should move to the beach. They never would though. They'd get home and get sucked back into their monotonous lives and responsibilities, afraid to take the leap, afraid to move away from everyone and everything they knew. But Sam had done it. Granted not intentionally, but still, here she was, watching the most amazing sunset.

"Pretty ain't it? Never gets old." A voice jarred her out of her thoughts.

She looked over and into the brightest blue eyes she'd ever seen. It was the curly, dark-haired guy who had been surfing with Smitty earlier. He was tan with black eyebrows, making his eyes stand out even more. He grinned with a mouth full of perfect white teeth, seeming like he'd stepped straight out of a movie. He took her breath away for a moment.

"Yeah, it really is. Like the best painting you'd never get to see in a museum," Sam concurred.

"For sure. Hey, I'm Casey. I see you around sometimes. You work at the bar, right?"

Sam nodded. "Sam. Yeah, you're friends with Smitt-, Smith?"

He glanced over at the lifeguard stand and grinned again. "Something like that."

Casey was almost as mesmerizing as the sky. Sam could see why the girls that night were all huddled around him. He had a way about him that drew one in. She could see the night waitress peering out at him from inside, and she chuckled. Guys didn't usually have that effect on her, but like the night sky, he was a beautiful painting she wouldn't see in a museum.

"Nice to meet you, Casey. Well, I have to get back inside and deal with the madness. See you around!"

"Same, Sam. I may pop in and say hey every now and then. Maybe catch a sunset." He raised a hand and walked towards the parking lot.

She watched him go, simply because he was really nice to watch, his slim jeans and striped tank showing off his physique. Damn, that boy is going places, she thought. She wouldn't be surprised to see him on the big screen one day. She headed back in, raising her eyebrows at the waitress who was still watching Casey. The girl blushed and hustled back into the crowd.

Over the next couple of weeks, Casey seemed to be around more and more. He'd show up at the lifeguard stand during Smitty's shifts for a little bit, stop into the restaurant, have a soda, and then head out. He was quick with a joke and laughed all of the time. Sam started to look forward to his company, as did every girl around. Even middle-aged tourist women would eyeball him and get a little hot when was around. Sam liked his open nature and ability to make conversation seem easy. There was something about him she was drawn to, and she found she didn't automatically have to put up internal walls when he was around.

Sam told him he should be a movie star. He winked and replied, "Maybe I will someday."

Sam would even just greet him as "movie star" when he came in, and he'd take a little bow or do a little shuffle dance. She started hoping he'd come in because he'd brighten the little window of time he was around. She asked Smitty about him once on their nightly smoke break.

"Man, that Casey," he replied, shaking his head. "He's a trip. On his own level."

Something in the way he said it, though, made Sam uncomfortable. Like something was floating under the surface. She didn't ask, didn't really want to know. She liked things the way they were. She just laughed it off and changed the subject.

Sometimes Casey wouldn't come around for a week or so. Or maybe she just didn't notice, but she felt like she would if he did. Then he'd be back every shift, doing his bow and cutting up. He never seemed to have a girlfriend, or stick around for more than just a bit. He didn't drink or smoke, just ordered a soda, sipped on it, and then left. He clearly knew Smitty well because he'd always go to the lifeguard stand first, they'd joke around for a bit, and then he'd come by the restaurant. But Sam noticed when Smitty was leaving with other friends, Casey was rarely in the group, even though they seemed to hang out almost every day.

One day in August, Sam came in early to pick up her check before her shift, and Casey was sitting at the end of the bar.

Taylor was circling around him, doing menial tasks, trying to catch his eye. He was staring out at the ocean with an expression Sam hadn't seen on him before. Wistful? Pensive? Something like that. She set her bag down near him and cleared her throat.

"Hey, Casey. Not used to seeing you here so early."

He gazed at her, and for a second it was like he didn't recognize her as a shadow passed over his face. Then it was gone, and the old Casey was there with his big grin.

"Sam! Yeah, had to run an errand and stopped in for a bite. What are you up to?"

Sam noticed he had no food in front of him and wasn't looking at a menu. Something was just off. She couldn't place it but something about the way he was acting struck a familiar chord in her.

"Just stopping in for my check before my shift and the bank closes. Need the dough, you know?"

Actually, she didn't. She was living almost solely off tips and banking the rest. She'd no idea what she'd do with it all but figured she'd keep saving as long as she could. It was always good to have a nest egg. Never knew when it might come in handy.

He nodded and perked up. "Hey, could I grab a ride from you into town? I kinda walked here. Well, I was out walking and ended up here."

He drifted off again, something was obviously pulling his mind elsewhere.

"Sure thing! I'm heading out now. Were you waiting on an order?"

He looked at her blankly and shook his head, forgetting he'd told her he was there to grab something to eat. She dropped it and went to the back to get her check. By the time she came out, h was standing by the door and Taylor was pouting behind the bar, not having gotten the attention she was seeking.

They walked quietly to her car, and Sam shoved items she had in the passenger seat to the floor, making room for him to sit. They made small talk on the ride to town, but this wasn't the Casey she knew. He seemed tired and distant. But they all had tough days, so she didn't press. They pulled up in front of the bank. She ran in to make her deposit. When she came out he was out of the car, leaning against the door. She cocked her head.

"Hey, I can take you to where you need to go. You don't have to get out here."

He stared at her silently, his eyes dark, and put his hand out. She was totally confused and just stared at it. Did he want something from her? He again gestured his hand to her, so she took it. It was warm and soft. He sighed heavily and met her eyes.

"You're not like everyone else, are you, Sam?"

It was like he could see through her facade, to see she was buried behind door after door. Casey made her feel safe with his presence, and she was tired of hiding. She wanted to tell him, to tell someone. To finally let out the deep secret she carried with her. But it scared her and made her feel vulnerable. She couldn't shut that door once it was opened. She stared at the ground and shrugged.

"I don't know," she muttered.

"Me either." His voice was quiet. "Everybody just wants a ticket to the show. Ya know?"

Sam knew. She'd known her whole life. She looked up at Casey and he stared at her. For the first time behind his eyes, she saw a sadness she hadn't seen before. A heaviness. She felt if she didn't look away, she'd get sucked in. She gave a little smile and attempted to cheer him up.

"We all have bad days, Casey. It'll get better. Is something going on?"

He shifted his eyes away and gazed off into the distance. He shook his head. "Nah. I suppose you're right. Hey, I can walk from here. I don't mind. Not exactly sure where I'm heading anyway."

He dropped her hand and touched her shoulder for a second. Something passed between them at that moment. He stood up off of the car and smiled. "You're not like everyone else, Sam, even if you won't admit it. Neither am I. It's like we were dropped here from out of the sky."

Smitty's comment of Casey being on his own level surfaced in her mind. She kind of liked that level though. Maybe Casey was someone she could get to know better; someone she could talk to about the mazes in her brain she got trapped in sometimes. She had a feeling he'd understand. Maybe he could help her figure it out.

"With feet of lead, trying to walk through mud," she replied.

Casey laughed and nodded, his eyes lighting back up. "Couldn't have said it better myself."

He leaned in and let his lips brush gently against her cheek. Her skin tingled where his lips had touched. "See you around, Sam. Thanks for the ride."

She didn't have a chance to reply before he headed down the road with his back towards her, the wind catching his hair in the breeze. She started to call out to him but the words caught in her throat.

Little did she know at the time, she would never speak to Casey again.

Chapter Eight

The smells coming from Rosie's and Ansley's kitchen made Sam's stomach grumble, making her glad she finally took them up on their offer to come over for dinner. She was greeted at the door by their small white and gray fluff of a dog, Spork. Spork danced around in circles and wagged his tail at Sam, barking incessantly. Ansley came down the hall and scooped him.

"Shhh, Spork. Come on in, we're back in the kitchen."

Sam had never actually been inside. Going into people's homes without purpose felt claustrophobic to her. It was cute, similar to her own apartment, but with more touches of Ansley, who was minimalistic and drawn to solid colors and simple patterns. Florals were limited more to accent pieces and certain decor had a modern art vibe. It worked well together. The kitchen was towards the back and was bright and open, painted a butter yellow with turquoise blue accents. The island had stools around it, so Sam grabbed one, not sure what to do with herself.

Rosie was dancing around, chopping veggies and tasting things. Ansley took her station at the stove and kept things from burning. They were drinking wine, while eighties alternative music played in the background. Sam took a small glass of wine, more to be polite and hold something in her hand. She asked to help, but they waved her away. Spork ran back and forth; his nails tap-dancing across the floor. Whatever they were making smelled divine.

"I hope you like Cuban food. We're making tamales, maduros, and seasoned rice," Ansley said as if she'd read Sam's mind.

Or maybe she heard Sam's stomach rumble.

"Wow, that sounds great. I usually eat what's easy for one. Soup, sandwiches, premade dinners. This smells amazing."

"You know, you're always welcome here. We tend to make too much for the two of us anyhow. We're always asking people to come dig in," Rosie chimed in.

This was true. Sam noticed they had a good solid group of friends that came over weekly. She was invited as well to these gatherings but couldn't talk herself into going. They'd sit on the back deck eating, listening to music, and talking. Sam wanted to be able to join, but as soon as she'd think about going down her stomach formed in knots, and her mouth would get dry. Starting with just the two of them was all she could do.

Once dinner was made, they took the platters of food to the back porch, which was covered to keep out the beating sun. A ceiling fan had been installed and was going at high speed, as was a floor fan that rotated over the sitting area. There was a small yard off the porch, which unlike the front yard was just grass and a small fountain. Spork sprinted out into the yard and did his business, which Sam guessed was why it was left just grass.

They sat around the table and handed the platters around, filling their plates to the brims. They dug in and Sam couldn't believe how good the food was. Better than any restaurant she'd eaten at. The tamales melted in her mouth, and the rice was delicate and spicy. Maduros were fried sweet plantains, which was a perfect contrast to the savory dishes. They had sangria to go with the meal, and Sam sipped on a small glass. There were lots of fresh-cut vegetables to add as desired. Sam wondered if they'd let her take a plate after they were done, to stick in her fridge for later.

"So, Sam, how are you liking living here?" Ansley asked between bites.

"It's been a blur, but I really like it. Benefits of a small town and excitement of a beach town. So far it hasn't gotten dull."

"Exactly! That's why we wanted to come back and settle here. Buy a home. Ansley is from Miami and was ready for small-town living. I didn't want to leave in the first place but wanted to see the world and get my degree in Early Childhood Education," Rosie said, beaming.

"Miami? I've heard the food is amazing there," Sam directed at Ansley.

"Born and raised. My father is Cuban, my mother is from Norway. Interesting upbringing. Then I left for college to get my BA in Fine Arts, where I met Rosie and fell in love. The rest is history."

Cuban and Norwegian. That made sense for her striking features.

"Well, part history," Rosie interjected, squeezing Ansley's hand. "We finished school, got married and started looking for work back here. I was able to with my degree but Ansley not so much, which was a bummer. She is in the process of opening a small gallery in the back room space at the Sea Glass Emporium downtown."

"Oh, wow, that's really neat!" Sam was envious.

She figured she'd spend her life working just to pay the bills. She peered through the porch window at the art in the home, which was much better than the art which decorated her tiny space.

"Ansley's," Rosie affirmed. "Isn't she so talented? Sorry to say the art in your place was me trying my hand at it. Obviously, the talent is one-sided."

They all laughed; Sam was relieved the art in her place wasn't Ansley's because she didn't think she'd be able to fake being impressed about it. The art in their home was amazing, and Sam was sure the gallery would be successful once it was up and running. She might even see about acquiring a piece. Her thoughts shifted to Rosie growing up here, and why she wanted to come back.

"Rosie, so you grew up here? What did you do for fun?"

Rosie's eyes lit up, excited at the chance to talk about her hometown. "Yes! My father was a teacher at the old school. It was my sister, my father, and me. My mother passed away from cancer when we were little, so my dad took the job here, thinking it would be a good environment for us. For the most part, it was. We loved the beach. I was also a book nerd, so I pretty much spent my days in far off lands."

"Does your sister still live here?" Sam asked.

"No. I love it here, but my sister not so much. She struggled more as we got older. She got in with a bad crowd, drinking and partying, and left as soon as high school was over. She lives in Atlanta now and never comes back. My dad lives over on the far end and is retired, which was basically required once they closed the school here. I guess that was when I was in college. Now, it's just offices and a small health clinic. Kind of sad really. All kids are bussed to the next town over, even the kindergarteners. I hate that when my little ones graduate from preschool, they have to ride the bus so far away. I've been in talks with a group who has suggested reopening a charter school for kindergarten through second grade here."

Rosie's passion for the children of the town was apparent, and Sam wondered if they planned on having children of their own. She didn't always have a filter on what was appropriate to ask and what wasn't.

"Not to be nosy, but do you want your own children?"

This is where Ansley came alive. "We do! We had looked into sperm banks or friends who might be willing to help out, but in the end, we decided we wanted to adopt. One of the benefits of North Carolina is they don't have laws prohibiting gay couples from fostering or adopting. Once the gallery is up and running, we are submitting our paperwork to foster and hopefully adopt."

Sam didn't have a desire for children but appreciated their strong relationship and determination to add to their family. When her brother had children, her inclination was that's just what people did. Got married, had kids. While his kids were cute, she never looked at them and wished for any of her own. She imagined having Ansley and Rosie as parents would be a loving and cultured experience.

"That's really awesome. You seem to have it so together. I can't even decide what to wear most days!" Sam laughed.

It was true. She found herself staring into her dresser most days, trying to decide what went best with the weather. That was about it. She hated shopping and saw clothes functionally. Hot, cold, clean, dirty. She couldn't imagine having to care for another being. Caring for herself was hard enough.

"So, Sam," Ansley said softly. "What's your story? How did you end up here? Who are your people?"

This question caused a wave of shame to wash over Sam, and she could feel her ears get hot. Who were her people? No one, because she pushed them all away. Her family. Miri. She was truly alone in the world, and it was of her own design. It wasn't a topic she wanted to think about, much less discuss.

"I don't know. I'm still trying to figure that out. I guess it's just me."

Rosie reached out and touched her hand. Her big, dark eyes were expressive with caring and a layer of determination. "No, you're not. You have us. I don't know what brought you here, and you don't have to tell us, but you are our people."

This kindness, after what happened with Miri, almost made Sam tear up. But she refused to do that in front of people if she could help it. She cast her eyes down until she bit back the tears, blaming the sangria. Once she composed herself, she glanced up and both of them.

"I made a stupid mistake, and it really hurt people. Specifically, someone I cared about and who trusted me. It was easier to just drive away than to face it. I drove until the land ended and wound up here. So, I stayed."

Rosie nodded knowingly, peering at Ansley. Ansley was the one who spoke.

"You know, Sam, we all have pasts. We've all done things we've been ashamed of, and were afraid people would hold against us. We've all feared the hard hand of judgement, but that's when we're at the end of our rope, and give in to our journey to find the place that accepts us. Rosie and I've had our fair share of people that didn't want us around, who hated us for who we are. But for every one of those people, there are two who will wrap their arms around you and accept you for who you are. Despite what you have done."

"You're not here by accident," Rosie added. "You were brought here to find a place where you can find yourself, and get out of the prison you have built around you. I came back here because I knew it was the place for me. Ansley came with me because she knew I was the place for her. You drove until you got here because there is something here for you. You just have to allow yourself to discover what that is."

Sam listened and wanted to believe them, but she'd been to so many places and didn't feel they held anything for her. Even Miri, who she thought she valued and had opened up to, she destroyed for no reason. Somewhere deep down she'd cared for Miri but still drove her away. Maybe to protect herself, maybe to keep the wall. Sam believed true connection, being able to let her guard down and breathe, were all just make-believe. An unattainable lie sold by society. Ansley sighed and leaned back in her chair, her cat-like eyes cutting through Sam's soul.

"But, Sam, first you have to accept you are your own people. Only until then can you let anyone else in and find your place."

Chapter Nine

It probably started out like any other day in late August. Sam was behind the bar when she heard screaming coming from the beach. Screaming wasn't all that unusual, considering little kids and teens screamed as they chased each other around, throwing each other in the waves, or snapping each other with wet towels. But this time was different. This was the scream of someone who had encountered something horrific, the scream of the mind trying to run away from itself. It made the hair stand up on Sam's arms. She cut her eyes around, searching to find the source and saw a crowd forming over the boardwalk on the beach. Someone was frantically waving their arms. Was someone drowning? Every few weeks or so they'd have a scare, but in the end, it would be alright. This time something felt different.

Sam met Taylor's eyes and mouthed for her to watch the restaurant. She ran out the door towards the boardwalk. Hopefully, it wasn't a kid. Parents often forgot how powerful the ocean was, and unsupervised kids would end up far from shore. She pushed through the ever-growing crowd and strained her eyes to see what the lifeguards were pulling through the water. As they got closer to the beach and found their footing, they dragged what they'd been swimming with towards shore onto the beach. To Sam's horror, she realized what it was, just as the sound of sirens came blaring into the parking lot. Maybe it would be okay. Maybe it looked worse than it was. Maybe there was still hope.

Smitty and the other lifeguard, Ryan, were the ones at the shore, having come out of the ocean with the body. When Smitty peered up, scanning for the EMTs, he met Sam's eyes and she knew it was really bad. The EMTs pushed through the unforgiving crowd and down to the shore where Ryan and Smitty were kneeling. They knelt in the sand, surrounding who had been pulled from the ocean, and went to work. It seemed like forever. Nothing was changing.

"What happened?" a man asked from her right.

She shook her head. She couldn't tell what was going on and was afraid to say what she thought it was.

"They dragged some guy out of the ocean. A body. Some lady saw it floating out by the pier," another person responded.

The crowd murmured in response. The word *body* was passed around between them like a donation plate at church on Sunday morning.

"Oh man, hope they're okay. Water's choppy today," the first man said. He stood on his tiptoes to try and get a better view. He couldn't and sighed in frustration.

This type of conversation ran through the crowd, but Sam stayed out of it and tried to see what was going on. Smitty stood up and went to the lifeguard stand. He grabbed a radio and started talking on it. He glanced over again, his eyes landing on Sam as if for reassurance. His eyes were dark and scared, giving the impression of a small child. Sam tried to read a message in his eyes but couldn't. Lifeguards often got a bad rap of being there for eye candy and to nag people into doing the right thing, but Sam couldn't imagine what it must be like to try and save someone who might not make it. To do their job, and still not be able to save someone's life.

Police came through, attempting to disperse the crowd, which was like herding cats. The crowd would move slightly but just to a different area, then quickly push back in, ignoring the severity of the situation. Wanting juicy bits to share around. The police responded in kind, pushing back on the crowd. Sam moved away and watched from the boardwalk. She could see the paramedics loading the person on a gurney and painfully moving them up the beach, their feet slipping around in the sand. As they drew closer, she could see the person was pretty much covered, confirming her worst fear.

Had they drowned? The waters were choppy but not that bad. The lifeguards were fast and grabbed people if there was even a risk of them drowning. She felt terrible for Smitty and Ryan. She knew they would've done everything in their power to save the person. She could see the two of them grimly following behind the paramedics, talking with the police who were furiously taking notes in their small notebooks.

As the paramedics came closer and the police created a path for them to pass, Sam saw a shoe sticking out from the sheet on the gurney. A sneaker. That was weird. People didn't swim with sneakers on. Maybe they fell off a boat? The crowd excitedly squeezed in again, trying to get a closer look, which made it hard for the paramedics to pass. This caused the sheet on the gurney to get yanked to the side, exposing the body, much to the crowds' sick delight. Sam tried to look away but her eyes caught something familiar, and she jerked her eyes back.

Her heart clenched into a fist. She recognized the jeans and striped tank top. The face was turned away, but she'd know that curly, black hair anywhere. She started to feel faint and instinctively took a step back away from the sight. In a panic, she turned away and searched for Smitty, the only other familiar face around. He immediately saw her freaking out and made his way through the crowd to her. He grabbed her, drawing her away from the crowd. She couldn't focus and started hyperventilating. He put his arms around her tightly, as if to keep her from falling over.

"Casey." She kept saying his name over and over in disbelief.

She shook her head and tried to make it go away. It couldn't be. She hadn't seen him in a couple of weeks, but that was how Casey was. He came and went as he pleased. Casey was going places; he was too big for this town. Nothing could hold him down. None of this could be real. Bile rose in her throat, and she pushed it down. She'd finally wanted to let someone in and now they were gone, just a lifeless body. She thought of the last time she saw him, and how she should've told him she felt like he did. That they were alike.

Alone.

She pushed away from Smitty and sat on the sand, resting her head in her hands. She heard a strange sound and realized it was the sound of her own sobbing. She wiped snot away from her face with her sleeve, shaking her head. She felt Smitty sit down next to her. He didn't try to touch her or make it okay. He just sat next to her in solidarity. Or maybe for his own need to not feel alone in this.

"Sam, I'm sorry." That's all he said.

There were no words to say. There was nothing that would make it better. She heard a police officer ask to speak with him again. He rested his hand briefly on her shoulder, then he was gone from her side.

She didn't know how long she sat there. She could hear the crowd conjecture on what happened, not too kindly, and eventually move on. She couldn't even look up. The sun was still shining as if nothing was amiss. Finally, she lifted her head to look around. The police had blocked off an area of the beach and were also up on the pier. They had flashing lights everywhere and it hurt her head. Her head was swimming like she'd come full speed off a merry go round. She tried to stand up but had to sit back down quickly. She'd never seen anyone dead. She couldn't wrap her head around seeing someone she knew in life empty like that. It didn't seem possible. A scene out of a movie.

Her mind kept replaying seeing the back of Casey's head, the way his head was cocked unnaturally to one side. His arm hung off the gurney lifeless as they passed, his finger splayed towards the ground. The same hand she'd held for a moment outside of the bank. The same warm soft fingers that had wrapped around hers when he said how they were alike. Casey, full of life and humor. Except now he was dead.

She burst into tears again and stood up. She couldn't stay here. She should get in her car and drive. Just run as far as fucking humanly possible. She should never have come here; she should never have started to let anyone in. She stumbled up the boardwalk and into someone. She went to push on and felt the person grab her. She peered up into Smitty's face. He looked like he'd seen, well...a ghost. He didn't say anything and led her down the beach under the pier. Again, he wrapped his arms around her, but this time she let him. She was mentally exhausted and leaned her head against his chest. Finally, she found her voice, crackly and tired from crying.

"What happened?"

He let out a long shaky breath before responding. "They think he fell off the pier and drowned. But Casey grew up surfing, he knew the ocean. Hell, I think he even jumped off the pier more than a few times."

Casey was fully clothed. He hadn't gone for a swim. As Smitty said, he knew the ocean. It just didn't make any sense. She leaned away and stared out at the ocean. Kids here knew everything about the ocean, it was their second home. Casey probably could swim by the time he could walk. It just didn't add up.

"My head fucking hurts," Sam replied miserably.

She peered up at Smitty and could see his thoughts were a long way off. He glanced down at her and nodded, his mouth in a grim line. He cast his eyes back towards the end of the pier.

Sam knew she needed to get back to the restaurant, but there was no way she could work the rest of her shift. She had to get away. To escape this reality. She tapped Smitty's shoulder to let him know she was heading back to the restaurant. He stared at her hard like he wanted to say something, but then just gave a small wry smile, his eyes sad and heavy, and looked away.

She would just drive. She still had money in her account. She could go and forget all of this. She could start over anywhere. Bury her head in the proverbial sand, like she always did when things got tough. She'd nothing keeping her here.

As she neared the bar, she saw Natalie standing outside, staring at the beach. Natalie had been crying, her eyes red-rimmed and red spots on her cheeks. Word about Casey had spread like wildfire. Sam guessed Natalie knew everyone well, she'd seen them grow up as kids. She always asked Casey about his mother and gave him good-natured ribbing when he stopped in. As Sam drew closer, Natalie opened her arm and hugged her.

"Honey, you can head out. I'm going to close up early. I can't stand hearing the tourists talk about what happened to Casey like it was some episode of a crime drama. I might seriously hurt someone."

Sam went in and made an effort to not make eye contact with anyone. Taylor was already gone, and Jimmy was gathering his things. She grabbed her purse from behind the counter and mentally said goodbye to everyone since she couldn't in person. Natalie was shooing customers away and locking up. Gus was by her side like a doting hen, attempting to help and comfort her at the same time. Sam headed for her car and crawled in. She sat there, trying to stop her head from spinning, to ensure she was fit to drive. It might be a long night. She felt bad for not letting Rosie and Ansley know, but she just couldn't face them.

She started the car up and backed out. As she put it into drive, she glanced at the pier. Police had placed caution tape across the entrance, giving it an eerie carnival feel. She shuddered in her seat. Her mind imagined Casey falling off the pier, reaching out to grab a hold of something. It just didn't make sense.

The memory of the last time she saw him filled her thoughts as she started to drive. They weren't like other people. On the outside peering in. Was he alone that night, feeling disconnected like she always did? The day she gave him the ride he seemed so far away, so heavy. Did he feel that way that night on the pier? She felt guilty for not digging deeper that day, but she didn't know how to. She couldn't even get herself out of that trap.

She wasn't sure how far she'd driven by the time she pulled off the road. She stopped at a gas station and got out to stretch. She didn't know where she was going yet. She smoked a cigarette and went in to grab coffee to stay awake. She filled the tank and glanced around. It was dark, so she must have driven for a couple of hours already. She really couldn't remember. It's like her brain would fracture and a different part of her would take over for a while. It had happened as long as she could remember when she was stressed. She'd just come to and be somewhere random.

Climbing back into the car, she caught a glimpse of the green resident beach parking pass hanging from her rearview mirror. The word resident struck her as odd. Like a string she couldn't cut, stretching out behind her from her car, back down the road to the little beach town she'd left. She removed it from her rearview mirror but could still feel the pull. She glanced behind the car, fully expecting to see a string stretching out into the dark in the direction she'd come from. There wasn't and she wasn't sure if the feeling was relief or sadness, or a mixture of both.

Casey's face appeared in her mind. His big, beautiful smile, his crystal blue eyes, and dark curly hair. He was a movie star now. Someone she could picture but would never be able to touch, or speak to, or laugh with. He was part of the big screen she could only watch from afar.

She began to cry again. Her inability to connect kept everyone at arm's length, but somehow he'd broken through a little. She thought of Natalie, Rosie, Ansley, even Gus, Taylor, Chris, and Jimmy. They would forget her. Just another transient who passed through their small town. Her thoughts landed on Smitty and his haunted expression the last time she saw him.

He and Casey had grown up together. Casey had been a few years younger, but they knew each other and after school hung out with the same crowd. The ones who never left. Sam couldn't imagine never leaving the town you grew up in, and what that might do to someone's psyche, but she could see how everyone in the town had this invisible line that connected them. Like the fishing line at the restaurant. Naked to the eye, but there, creating necessary connections and boundaries. Now, that same line had connected her too. She could feel it pulling her back.

"Fuck," she whispered to herself.

She started the car and turned back in the direction she'd just come from. She didn't know why, but she had a place there and had to go back. She took a big sip of coffee and headed home.

The town was dark when she drove through. The library illuminated by a light old Miriam had forgotten to turn off when she closed up. Sam could see the clerk at the gas station hunched over a book, trying to pass time and smiled sadly to herself. The familiar pull kept calling to her and leading her down the streets to her tiny place above the garage. She climbed the stairs of her apartment, looked down at Rosie and Ansley's place, and ducked through her door. It was right there waiting for her, in all its floral glory. Even it knew she was coming back. As her head hit the pillow, she realized no one probably even knew she'd left. Just another day in the life.

Except it wasn't.

Even if the town didn't know it yet, a bright light had been extinguished, and it would never be the same again. A darkness had descended over all of them. The innocence of this small beach town had vanquished in the surf, along with a boy who had fought so hard to get to the surface more than once in his life.

Chapter Ten

A funeral is an uncomfortable, somber event at best. A funeral for a young person is a heartbreaking trip through vulnerability and reflection. Those older, wonder how someone so young could be gone too soon, those the same age or younger are hit in the face that not only old people like their grandparents die. So many questions are mentally asked, so much backtracking and scenarios played out. Could things have been changed, what if they just took a different course? Sam had only ever been to funerals for elderly family and even then had been shielded by her parents from the grim reality. As she glanced around the room, she could see the faces of those there trying to grapple with the death of someone so young.

She was surprised at how few people were in attendance at Casey's funeral. She assumed it would be packed out the door since he was so well-liked and young. But while the rows had people in them, they were in no way full. She'd ridden with Gus and Natalie, while a couple of others from the restaurant came in another car. They slipped into the back row and sat awkwardly, as music, which could only be described as funeral music, played. People shifted in their seats, unsure how to behave in an event such as this. The room seemed too bright, considering what it was used for.

A small, caramel-skinned woman sat in the front row crying, her long, black hair fastened in a tight bun at the nape of her neck. Casey's mother. She was surrounded by a handful of younger women, maybe sisters or cousins, and a boy about fifteen or sixteen sat in the row behind her. He had not grown into his long limbs yet and was wearing a suit he'd grown out of the previous year. Did Casey have a brother? The boy favored him but with dark eyes and smooth hair.

Sam didn't see anyone she could recognize as Casey's father, but an older gentleman sat near the boy. They looked like father and son, and the way the man put his hand on the mother's back in front of him, Sam knew they were husband and wife. Casey's father must have been different. Casey had been older than the boy by about seven or eight years. Maybe the child of a first marriage. She realized she didn't know anything about Casey's life. He hid it well. Always joking and making light of situations, but never showing what he was going through.

The gregarious, charismatic guy she knew wasn't the person who walked around inside that skin. He hid his torture well and fooled just about everyone. She was ashamed she hadn't seen through it. Maybe she hadn't wanted to. He brought her joy, and her darkness lifted when he was around. She felt like she'd used him to escape her own hell for a bit. Her cheeks flamed as she came to grips with this and tears pricked her eyes. She should've been a better friend. She should've stopped him from leaving that day. She was too damn wrapped up in her own shit to have reached out.

A picture of a younger, teenage Casey sat by the closed casket. Shorter hair. A plastic smile. She recognized it as a senior high school picture. His eyes cast off at a random spot the photographer had told him to focus on, giving him a thoughtful, full of hope expression. Lies kids were told about life. Dreams they were sold, they couldn't pay on. Push them out the door into the world, then pull the rug out. Whatever it takes to collect payment on their lives. What was there even to hope for?

Casey didn't stand a chance.

The same photo had been used in the paper with the headline, *Local Man Loses Life in Fall from Pier*. The article was a cross between a police report and an obituary, written by someone who didn't know Casey. Stated his age, that he was part of the debate club in high school six years previously, and he was an avid surfer and skateboarder. It listed his surviving family and what the police thought had happened, pending an ongoing investigation. That he had lost his balance, fallen into the ocean, and drowned. It came across like it was rushed to be able to plaster on the front page and feed the town's need for something to gossip about. It totally negated who Casey was, or what he was going through.

Sam resisted the urge to stand up and scream, "This is bullshit!"

She dug her fingers into the fabric on the bench beneath her. She bit her lip and shoved the feelings deep into her stomach. The music had shifted, and a man had taken a place behind Casey's casket. He cleared his throat softly as he started to speak. He spoke on the unfairness of a life gone too soon. About how this was just part of our journey, and how all would be reunited on the other side. He spoke of a mother's love, and a brother left without the guidance of his older brother.

Sniffles filled the room, and a low painful moan came from Casey's mother as she tried to come to grips with the loss of her older boy, her first child. The baby who had reached up to her with his bright blue eyes and wide smile. Her little boy who drew her pictures and asked for bedtime stories. The young man who disappeared for days on end, but would always call to tell her he was okay and kiss her on the forehead when he returned. A parent wasn't supposed to outlive their child. It was an unbearable pain with no release.

The boy put his forehead against the back of the row in front of him. Casey's pain would now become his. He'd be that kid. The one whose brother died in strange circumstances. The boy other kids wouldn't know what to say to. He'd walk the halls of his school, kids moving out of his way and staring, whispering things about him. Some true, some not. It wouldn't matter to them. To him, it was just a larger bubble that shut him out from the rest of the world. He would curse Casey, but as he got older he'd wish his brother was there to talk to. To confide in. Like Casey, he'd live feeling no one understood him and like he'd been dropped out of the sky, with lead feet trudging through the mud.

A few more people spoke. A couple of songs were played. Behind the podium on a screen pictures of Casey's life played on a reel. Baby Casey, playing at the beach, Halloween, prom, holding a surfboard. All smiling, happy pictures. All the Casey he presented to the world.

All the memories they wanted to keep.

Sam began to feel like she wasn't in the room anymore. She touched the bench in front of her to feel real. It didn't help, she could feel herself slipping outside of her body. Panic bubbled up inside of her, and she dug her nails hard into the palms of her hands. She couldn't do this here. She excused herself and rushed out of the room. The room led to a larger room, which was decorated with flowers and pictures with hopeful sentiments. Her hands started to tingle, and the room elongated. She darted out the closest door and found herself standing in front of a hearse. Tears rolled down her cheeks, and she knew she was about to lose it altogether. She made her way around the side of the building and lit a cigarette. Her hands were shaking so badly that she dropped her lighter in the bushes.

She resisted the urge to just start walking. Mostly because she'd no idea exactly where she was. Gus had driven, and she hadn't paid attention to how they'd gotten there. After what seemed like forever, she could hear people leaving the funeral home. Just family was going with Casey's body to the cemetery and other people were getting in their cars, after paying their respects to the family.

She slipped back into the crowd and ended up in the line to pay respects. Panic started to rise back up, and she pushed it down hard. She was suddenly in front of Casey's mother. She mumbled a condolence and took the extended hand. Soft and warm like Casey's. A scream caught in her throat, and she moved on. Next was Casey's brother. She met his eyes. So much like Casey's, but dark, almost black like their mother's. She tried to pass a message to those eyes, to let him know he wasn't alone. But he was, really.

"I'm sorry. Casey was a good guy," she whispered.

The boy nodded, swallowing hard, and looked away. Good guys didn't leave, right?

Sam squeezed his hand, then was moved forward by the crowd to the end of the line. Natalie and Gus were waiting for her and they headed towards the car, silent and worn out. No one spoke on the ride back. There was nothing left to be said. Sam had left her car by the restaurant, so they dropped her off there. Natalie decided to close the restaurant for a few days after the funeral, giving them all time to grieve and the gossip to hopefully die down a bit.

After they drove off, Sam made her way across the boardwalk to the beach. It was overcast, so there weren't too many people there. She walked over closer to the pier and sat down. Her body was heavy and still felt disconnected from itself. The waves continued their reassuring beat against the shore. They'd done this long before she'd been there, and would do it long after she was gone. She didn't know if that was comforting or depressing. It made her feel inconsequential.

Seagulls called out to each other above her, as she laid back against the cool wet sand. The sky was gray, clouds moving slowly across her view. The funeral was over, Casey's body was being put in the ground. That was his life. He'd never leave this town. Maybe if he'd been born somewhere else, things would've been different. Maybe he would've changed things. Maybe he would've shared his lovely smile with the world. But they would never know him. Only a handful of people would remember Casey. His laughter, his soulful eyes, his kindness, his potential. Potential that would turn to dust in the ground, and only held in the memory of a few.

Sam sat up and wrote his name in the sand. Like him, it would be washed away by the waves. She stood up and turned around, facing the lifeguard stand. Ryan was the only lifeguard on duty. It had not escaped her notice that Smitty had not been at the funeral. It irritated her, seeing as how he and Casey had known each other most of their lives. If she could go to it, after knowing Casey for only months, he should've been there. It dawned on her, not many people of Casey's age had been in attendance. It was mostly older people, friends of the family, teachers, and neighbors. No girlfriends, nobody who had been on the beach that night. Anger ran through her at their callous selfishness. Casey had felt alone in life and now was so in death.

She picked up a rock and thrust it into the sea. How fucking dare they? They couldn't spare a couple of hours for him? For his family. The longer she lived here, the less she understood. For a town where everyone knew each other, they sure had a weird way of showing it. This wasn't just some random person who had died. This was one of their own. Raised here from a baby. She headed back up the beach and over the boardwalk. It crossed her mind if she died not a whole lot of people would care. Her family and a handful of people who felt they should show up. Maybe she and Casey were a lot more alike than she'd realized. He'd seen it immediately, but she'd been so in her own bubble she hadn't noticed.

She stopped and picked up another rock and put it in her pocket. She'd put it on her counter as a tangible reminder of this day. She aptly named it Casey's rock, for no other reason other than a way of not letting him go. When she got home, she was relieved to not see Rosie or Ansley around. They'd known of Casey but didn't know Casey, him being quite a few years younger than them. She was bone tired and just wanted to sleep the rest of the day away.

She put Casey's rock on the counter and stared at it.

"Casey, I'm sorry I didn't say more that day. I should've made you stay and talk to me. I should've gotten to know you better, shown you the real me. Your brother seems sweet. You need to keep an eye on him. I have a feeling life is going to be tough for him. He needs you. Damn it, I need you. But I don't have that right. We barely knew each other, right? What was going on with you? I'm just so sorry. About everything."

She sighed and put her hand on the rock. It was still warm from being in her pocket. She couldn't talk to people in real life, but here she was talking to a dead guy through a rock. She shook her head. Not a dead guy. Casey. Beautiful, sparkling, sensitive Casey. From the sky Casey. He deserved her thoughts and her words. He deserved her to carry him on, even if others wouldn't. So, if it meant she talked to a rock the rest of her life, then so be it.

She slipped off her shoes and her funeral garb. She climbed into a way too hot shower and leaned her head against the wall. She let the body wracking sobs overtake her. She sobbed for Casey, and his mother. She sobbed for his brother, who would now carry the weight of the world on his slim shoulders. She wept for the heartlessness of the town, and how quickly they'd move on and forget one of their own. She bawled for the kids like Casey, who would grow up here and feel isolated, even though everyone knew their names and could recognize them on the street.

As her tears finally came near an end, she let a few fall for the girl she'd been and the woman she'd become. The woman who couldn't recognize herself in the mirror or understand why she was even here, other than to pass the days. That was all she'd cry about it. She'd cried more over the last week than she could ever remember in her whole life. She felt a small crack cut through the wall she'd built between her and the rest of the world, but didn't know what to do about it. She stepped out of the shower and dried her tears.

One small crack, but the wall was still standing. She took a deep breath and straightened herself out. She wouldn't break that easily. Casey was on the inside of the wall with her now, so she wasn't totally alone. She could protect him along with herself.

Chapter Eleven

After a couple of weeks, the town chatter started to die down, then skyrocketed again when the toxicology report which was run on Casey's body came back. He'd been on drugs, they all whispered, with a nasty air of condescension. Ketamine. They found ketamine in his system. He 'deserved what he got'. Wasted his life.

Suddenly, the nice boy on the front page became a back-alley junkie, whose life had no value. His mother was irresponsible, he was a bad kid. It made it easy to hold themselves above, to believe they were unaffected. They turned up their nose at a person who had spent his whole life around them, growing and interacting with their children and grandchildren. Now his life was nothing more than a decision he'd made on the last day he was alive. He was discarded like yesterday's trash.

Sam had grown up in the suburbs with people moving in and out, as jobs brought them and took them away. She knew some of the same kids throughout school, but most were there for a few years and then were gone. There was no real neighborhood talk. Perhaps just neighbors musing over who the new neighbors were, or who was getting divorced. But there was no real commitment to the talk. Just conversations in passing.

Not like the vitriolic gossip which drove small-town minds. She was genuinely shocked at how openly people would destroy the credibility and life of those around them. It was hatred, driven by the lack of value they'd given to their own lives. Easier to sit over coffee and spew venom toward others, than to turn energy inward and fix what was going on inside of them.

More than once Natalie removed patrons who let the talk get out of hand and permitted Sam to do the same. Sam didn't have Natalie's confidence, so often just stepped outside to smoke a cigarette to calm her nerves. Natalie reminded her it would pass once something else came up. But it takes a lot to come up in a small town, and the talk dragged on for weeks, making Sam resent the people and town she'd come back to. She felt for Casey's family, and how hard it must be to hear the whispers and endure the stares. School had started back, and Casey's brother had to face kids, who even on a regular day weren't kind to each other. It made Sam's stomach hurt, and she wished she could make it better.

One day, as she was smoking, she looked out towards the lifeguard stand. Smitty had avoided her, and just about everyone else, since pulling Casey out of the ocean. She'd see him sometimes standing by the railing, but he made no effort to reach out to her, and she just didn't have it in her. She respected how hard this all was for him and figured the time would come when they'd talk.

Until then, she'd keep her distance. She didn't see him on this day, but that wasn't what caught her eye in the first place. She recognized a familiar shape sitting in the sand. It was Casey's mother.

She was sitting by herself staring out over the ocean, her shoulders slumped in despair. Sam imagined she was trying to figure out what had happened to her boy, how it had all come to this. Having had no children, or anyone she really connected with, Sam didn't know how Casey's mother felt. But she could see the physical pain her emotions were causing her. Her body was in a tight knot, her head down close to her chest. Sam's heart ached and went out to her, knowing she was suffering. Sam put out her cigarette and headed back into the restaurant.

A couple of patrons must have recognized Casey's mother, and it had spurred more gossip and cruelty. They sat loudly talking about Casey's death, his drug use, and his family, so casually as if it was on a show they watched. Everyone just wants a ticket to the show. Sam took a deep breath and something in her snapped. She walked over to the table and slammed her hands down, causing plates and glasses to go into the air and clatter down. The group all jumped and stared at her, their eyes big and wide.

"Shut the fuck up!" she yelled at the group.

They were utterly shocked, one of the lady's mouths kept opening and closing like a fish. A man got beet red and started to sputter, pointing his finger at Sam.

"You can't speak like that to us. We are customers!"

He said customers like it was royalty.

"I don't give a rat's ass who you are, you hateful, petty, small-minded pieces of shit."

The man stood up and got in Sam's face. She hoped he'd try something, so she could beat the hell out of him. She'd never been so angry. The weeks of hearing people talk crap about Casey and his family had finally made her lose it. The restaurant went dead quiet. Gus came around the other side of the bar in case he needed to step in. Natalie emerged from the office and was watching with what seemed like a mixture of satisfaction and maybe delight. The man glanced around nervously, and Sam clenched her fists. She could almost feel her fist hitting his cheekbone. The lady beside him stood up and put her hand on his elbow, whispering they should just go. He took a step back and looked from her to Sam.

Sam didn't budge.

"Get the fuck out," she hissed between closed teeth.

The group quickly got up and got their things together, heading for the door. The man turned at the last minute and stared at Sam, then toward Natalie.

"This is how you treat your loyal customers?"

Natalie shrugged. "You heard her, get the fuck out."

This made the man turn a deeper shade of red than Sam had ever seen. He glared incredulously at Natalie for a moment and stormed out. Natalie gave Sam a quick wink and made a gesture for her to come to the office. Sam let go of the breath she'd been holding and made her way back. She noticed eyes on her from other patrons, some in horror, some in admiration.

What she didn't notice were the eyes of Casey's brother, who had come in just about the time the group had started talking about his family. He'd seen the whole incident and was frozen by the entrance to the patio. He watched as Sam disappeared behind the bar, and turned his eyes out to his mother who was sitting on the beach. He forgot about the sandwich he was going to order and slipped out to go to her.

Natalie was sitting sorting papers when Sam came back. She peered up at Sam with a knowing look.

"You alright?"

Sam plopped down on the chair across from her. She nodded. She hadn't known she'd had that in her. It was like years of rage had formed into a bullet and shot out of her.

"It's good to let things out, Sam. You always push everything down inside. You have to express yourself. Maybe not so...well, violently. I thought you were going to clock that guy." Natalie laughed and made a fist as an example.

"Me too." Sam laughed, feeling the tension drain from her body.

She really had wanted to and part of her regretted she didn't get the chance. "Do you know him?"

"Enough. But not enough to care," Natalie replied earnestly.

"So, am I in trouble?" Sam bit her lip. She couldn't afford to lose this job.

Natalie leaned back and chuckled. "Over that? Of course not. I'm glad to see you finally speak up. Maybe now people will know they can't talk all that shit around here."

Relieved, Sam put her head down on the desk.

"Thanks, Natalie."

A little while later, Sam glanced out and saw Casey's mother gathering her blanket. This time his brother was there and helping. The mother went towards the parking lot, as the brother headed towards the restaurant. He came in and walked up to the bar, placing an order with Gus for some sandwiches and fries. Sam watched him, wanting to say something but was too afraid to approach him. Luckily, she didn't have to. He met her eyes and came over to her. Like Casey, he had dark but short, smooth hair and dark eyebrows which sat over his almost black eyes, making him appear more serious and older than his years. He was wearing long board shorts, a plain blue t-shirt, and skate shoes, like pretty much every other teenage boy in town.

"Hey, I'm Aidan, Casey's brother. I saw you at his funeral?" He stared at her with such intensity, she needed to glance away.

"I wanted to thank you."

Sam cocked her head at him, confused. Why was he thanking her? The funeral?

"I was in here earlier and saw what happened," he went on. "So, thank you."

Sam realized he'd seen the altercation between her and the group who'd been talking about his family. He'd probably heard, then, the horrible things they'd said. This reignited her anger towards the group, and now she wished she'd punched the guy. She met Aidan's eyes and nodded.

He cleared his throat and spoke softly, "My family has been going through a lot. Casey. And now everything else. Not many people have our backs."

"Aidan, I'm sorry. I truly liked Casey; he was such a bright spot in this town. We didn't know each other long, but he meant a lot to me." She fidgeted with a straw on the bar, realizing this was the truth. He meant a lot to her. "I miss him."

Aidan stared hard at her and then nodded, tapping his fingers on the back of the stool he was standing by. "Yeah. Me too."

His order arrived and he went to pay for it. Gus refused to let him and pushed the food towards Aidan. Aidan thanked him and gathered the bags, turning to leave. He paused and looked back, seeming so much like Casey the last time Sam had seen him. She wanted to tell him to wait, to not go. That he mattered. But the words caught in her throat.

"Um...my name is Samantha. Sam. If you or your family need anything-" she trailed off, feeling stupid.

Aidan smiled that smile, big and clear just like Casey's and tipped his head. "Thank you, Samantha."

He headed out the door to the car where his mother was waiting. His mother's eyes watched him closely, her only living son, until he climbed in beside her. He gave her a peck on the cheek and they left.

Sam felt Casey's presence around her so strongly, she turned expecting to see him. He wasn't at his usual seat at the bar. He was still just gone. But she could feel him regardless. She sighed and started wiping the bar down. The rest of the evening, thankfully, went without further event. She closed up and headed home, just as the police were starting their patrol. It made her wonder how the toxicology information was going to affect the investigation into Casey's death.

Ketamine. She didn't even know what it was. She heard something on the news about it having something to do with veterinarians, but that was about all she knew. She couldn't think what the hell he was doing with that in his system. She'd go to the library tomorrow and see what she could find on it. Obviously, he was taking it to feel something. She just didn't know what.

On her drive home, she thought bitterly about people who worked all year to save up to come for a week to the beach, all the while those who lived here couldn't get out. They were trapped behind the scenes. No good jobs, limited opportunities. Stuck creating a fantasy for other people's vacations. So, they found different ways to escape. Some through drinking, some through smoking, some through gossiping, some through drugs. Whatever their vice.

Some escaped permanently.

Chapter Twelve

Before long, people moved on from talking about Casey. Summer came to a close and the town shifted from its focus on tourism, more inward towards community activities, and restoring and repairing from the heavy summer season. The restaurant laid off its seasonal employees, leaving just Jimmy, Natalie, Sam, and Taylor. Chris still helped on Friday and Saturday nights, but he went on to college, limiting his time. Natalie closed the restaurant on Mondays and Tuesdays, cutting service on Wednesdays and Sundays to close at nine. Sam was relieved because the ten-hour shifts took their toll, and she didn't need the extra hours on Sunday.

Along with businesses cutting their hours, the town reduced the lifeguard hours to middays and weekends. Smitty had not made any effort to reach out since Casey passed, and Sam started to feel their friendship slipping away. It bothered her a little more than she thought it would, but she was accustomed to making the break. Rip the bandaid off. Makes it easier. Still hurts, but makes it faster to move on. She stayed focused on her work at the restaurant and made plans for her next steps. Would she stay in the town, or was it time to think about her next journey? She thought she was needed here, but now it seemed like everyone had just gone their own way.

On a Sunday at the beginning of October, she locked up a little early because after about eight they had no more customers. She waited a bit, then made the call. She wiped everything down and locked up the till in the safe. She stepped out to smoke a cigarette, enjoying the warm breezy evening. It was so quiet, just the splashing of the waves filling the void. It was perfect. She'd a little time to enjoy before the police started to patrol, so she made her way across the boardwalk and stood watching the ocean. The moon cast a beacon over the water towards her, encasing her in its light.

About the time she turned to go, a quick flash of light caught her eye and disappeared. It came from the lifeguard stand she thought and strained to see what it was. It stayed dark. Maybe kids hanging out in the stand. Sometimes they'd sneak up there at night to smoke and drink. She decided to go move them on, so they didn't make a mess.

As she drew closer, she could make out the outline of a figure sitting on the outside porch of the lifeguard stand, their feet dangling over the edge. She could smell cigarette smoke and came around the front to tell them to leave. She circled to the ladder of the stand, and as she was about to speak she recognized the figure.

"Hey, Smitty. I thought you were kids up to no good."

A soft laugh cut the dark. "Nope, just me. Up to no good."

Sam climbed the ladder and sat down next to him. He offered her a beer, one of many he'd been drinking. She took it and set it down next to her. Neither spoke for some time, staring out at the water. Sam sipped the beer and fought off the drowsiness the waves were causing in her. She glanced over at Smitty who was very still, occasionally taking a drag of his cigarette or a swallow of his beer. She could make out the outline of his face in the moonlight. He appeared as if he hadn't smiled or laughed in months. He caught her watching and side-eyed her. She needed to break the silence.

"I haven't seen you around much. You doing okay?

"Nope," he said, and they fell back into silence.

She knew Casey's death had to have been a blow for him, and being the one to pull his body out of the ocean must've been horrifying. She had to get through to him somehow.

"Yeah, I guess not. Stupid question. I'm really sorry. I know you were friends. I met Casey's brother a while back."

"Aidan? Yeah, he's a good kid. I remember when he was a little kid. He loved Casey, man, he was always trying to keep up with him." The tip of his cigarette lit up as he took a deep drag. "Never could though and he'd cry and cry being left behind."

Picturing this made Sam's heart hurt. Imagining a little kid chasing after his big brother, who was too out there to slow down. The Aidan she met had hardened with never being able to catch Casey. He was tough, a little angry, and yet still just a kid who wanted his brother. It made her angry at Casey for not being there for him. But she knew better, she knew Casey meant no harm and would've never wanted his brother to hurt. Aidan was hurting though. He'd spend his life chasing a brother he couldn't catch.

"I worry for him. This town can be really mean," she said.

Smitty laughed, a bitterness coming through. "That's an understatement. These fuckers would hang you out to dry if it would give them a story to tell. God, I fucking hate it here."

Sam sat in utter silence. She didn't know how to respond to that. Smitty was honest and a little sarcastic, but he'd never been hateful. She suddenly felt out of place, deciding it was best to leave. He was avoiding her for a reason and now she could see why. He'd changed. He was immersed so deep in resentment, it was preventing him from getting to the surface. She cleared her throat and started to gather her things.

"Look, Smitty, I know Casey was your friend and losing him must be terrible. I didn't know him for long, but I miss him too. I'll leave you alone. You clearly want it that way."

She started to climb down the ladder when he spoke, almost a whisper.

"That fucking day. The lady started screaming. Ryan and I were off the stand and down the beach in a flash. She was pointing at something out in the surf. I thought it was trash at first. But then I saw skin. We jumped in and I don't even know how, but we got out there so fast. We grabbed it...him. I didn't even think. But I knew. My brain wouldn't let me really look, but I knew. We got close to shore, and when I stood up I had to look to get through the waves. I kept telling myself we could do CPR once we hit the beach, but he was so cold. Like, so fucking cold. Like nothing I'd ever felt. I wouldn't let myself accept it was him. Then the paramedics came, and I thought they could fix it, right? I saw you standing there and wanted to call out to you. But it was like I was stuck in slow motion. Nothing made sense."

He paused and finished his beer, cracking open another one. Sam stood at the bottom of the ladder, afraid to move.

"They pronounced him dead at the scene. All I could think was, who is going to fucking tell his mother? They kept asking me questions like I'd fucking know. Dude, I got there just minutes before them. I didn't know anything. And the people were just standing around. Like, like-"

"Like they wanted a ticket to the show," Sam repeated Casey's words.

"Yeah, like they wanted a ticket to the goddamn show." Smitty slammed his beer down and it fizzed over the top onto the wood.

"I've been a lifeguard since I was eighteen and had never seen a dead body. A few years back some guy had a heart attack at the beach, but he died in the ambulance on the way to the hospital. He was alive when I saw him. The coast guard has pulled a few bodies from the ocean, but I didn't see them. This was the first time, and it was fucking Casey."

Sam climbed back up the ladder and sat down next to him. He lit another cigarette and handed it to her, then lit one for himself. The events of that day played over and over in their minds. Sam didn't want to intrude on his train of thought, so she sat and listened.

"Then they took his body away and I was just there. Just sitting there. People came and went like nothing had happened, and the police kept asking questions like I had a fucking clue. I wanted to grab their gun and blow my brains out. Or their's. Or someone's. I don't fucking know. I was stuck in this hellish circle and have been ever since. There is no way out, no way forward. I'm a goddamn hamster on a wheel until I die."

Sam sighed. It was one of the conversations where nothing can make it better. Reality was reality. You can't get from A to C without going through B, one of her teachers used to say. You have to go through it. She didn't want to make light of his pain by trying to say something to make it better. The last time she saw Casey she'd tried that, and now she lived with that regret. So, she said nothing. Smitty stopped talking and for the next while they drank beer, staying silent.

When the police started their nightly patrols, they hid their cigarettes behind their hands, so the light couldn't be seen from the parking lot. The police rarely got out and came to the beach. Her car was in the lot, but it wasn't unheard of for drunks to get a ride home and leave their cars. If her car was there in the morning the police would put a citation on it, but that was about it.

Around midnight, Sam ran over to the restaurant to use the bathroom and make a couple of sandwiches. She wrote up a receipt and put the money for them on the counter with a note to Natalie. Natalie would come for the deposit in the morning, and Sam wanted to make sure she paid for what she'd used. When she got back to the lifeguard stand Smitty wasn't there, but his bag still was. He must have taken a walk to clear his head. She laid back to look at the stars and dozed off.

"Hey, Sam." Smitty was shaking her awake. "Sorry, I ran down the beach to work some things out. You were asleep. You should head home."

Sam sat up and shook her head. "No, I'm ok. I made us sandwiches."

Smitty chuckled and sat down beside her, taking one of the sandwiches she was pushing towards him. "Thanks, Sam. I don't know when I last ate. I don't think beer counts."

"It doesn't."

They ate in silence and noticing Sam shivering, Smitty grabbed a blanket out of the stand and put it over her back. She pulled it tightly around her. They'd run out of beer, and Sam started to think about her nice warm bed. She wondered if Smitty was staying in the lifeguard stand overnight.

"Smitty, if you need a place to stay you can crash at my place."

"Nah. I just don't want to go back to my place. I think I'm tired, then I lay in bed and these thoughts and images start racing through my mind. Then I'm wide-awake staring at the ceiling, fighting off panic. I just can't get Casey's face in the ocean out of my head."

Sam knew exactly what he meant. For her, it was when the paramedics had taken his body past and the sheet had fallen off. Also, the made-up images her mind created about the night he drowned. Him grasping for something as he fell, him hitting the water disoriented, not knowing which was up. Him fighting to get to the surface, eventually giving in to the realization he wouldn't, letting go while his lungs filled with water. She shuddered hard as these images played in her head. Smitty tucked the blanket around her tightly.

"Still cold? I think I have another blanket in there."

Sam nodded, the lie being easier than the truth. Smitty grabbed another blanket and put it over the two of them.

"I'm sorry I haven't come to talk to you, Sam. I've been trying to come to grips with my own demons."

"I understand. Trust me. I understand." Sam leaned in against his warmth.

They'd both come out of that day different people and she wasn't one to judge. It started to sprinkle, so they moved inside the stand, which had a medicine cabinet, bench, radio, and odds and ends. The floatation devices, normally locked up inside, were put out on the porch to make room. They leaned against the wall and talked into the morning, avoiding any more conversation of that day. Before daylight hit, Sam laid down on a blanket on the floor. Smitty laid next to her to stay warm, covering them with the other blanket.

Eventually, the conversation dried up and they drifted off to sleep, as the sun made its way up into the sky.

Chapter Thirteen

Sam sat up and peered around, the sun hurting her eyes. She was still in the lifeguard stand, but it had to be close to noon. She could hear the gulls screeching as they circled overhead. Smitty wasn't there, but coffee in a paper cup was. She gratefully gulped it down, her head pounding from the beers and lack of sleep. They'd dozed off around sunrise, but sleep was uncomfortable on the cold wooden floor. She stood up and stretched her arms above her head, feeling a catch in the middle of her back. She saw the medicine cabinet was unlocked and grabbed a couple of aspirin. At least the restaurant was closed today, so she'd be able to take a nap.

Smitty was standing outside with his back towards her, leaning on the rail. He heard her come out and turned.

"I see you found the coffee."

"And aspirin. My head's pounding. Thank you."

"I hear you. Luckily, it was my midday shift today because we would've had some explaining to do."

Sam laughed and leaned on the rail next to him. It would've been awkward if Ryan had shown up and they were sleeping in the stand. The beach was quiet with a few beach walkers down aways, and a mother picking up shells with a couple of small children, but no one else was around. She realized how much she preferred the offseason beach. A light breeze blew her hair around, making loose strands tickle her nose. She glanced at Smitty who was off in his own world.

"You hungry? I can pop over to the restaurant and make us something." She was a little queasy, but he was looking thinner than usual and it worried her.

"Nah. I'm good."

He wasn't, but she couldn't force him to eat. He turned and stared at her, his face serious. She could tell he had something on his mind, but they'd talked so much the night before she couldn't think of anything left to say. He bit his lip and let out a deep breath.

"There's something you need to know. About me, about what happened-" he trailed off, trying to form the words. "I don't have a lot of good friends and I consider you a friend. I need you to know the truth."

What the hell was he talking about? What truth? She waited for him to go on, a knot forming in the pit of her stomach. He cleared his throat and looked away.

"I knew Casey since we were kids. We weren't like best friends, but in a town this small, you're pretty much close to everyone your age. He was a couple of years younger but lived the next street over, so we spent a lot of time playing together. After I left school, we ended up in the same crowd. Not a great crowd. People who liked to get fucked up a lot. Like, really fucked up. You know that Casey was on ketamine. I mean, I guess everyone knows. You know what that is?"

Sam knew a little. It was a horse tranquilizer people liked to take to get high. A different kind of high. From what she read, it made them feel dreamy and disconnected. Some people hallucinated, some people didn't. Depended on the person and how much they took. Too much could be super disorienting, causing a disconnection between body and mind. She could see the appeal to an extent, but it also sounded like how she felt at times when she didn't want to. The idea scared her. She had a hard enough time feeling like she was in her body completely sober.

"I read up on it after Casey died but that's about it."

"You ever do drugs, Sam?"

"Not really. Smoked weed in high school, but it made me feel even more detached than I already do. I...I have this thing where I feel like I'm not in my body sometimes. Well, most times. Like I'm watching myself from another body, or outside my body. I can't explain it. But anyway, I avoid anything that makes it worse."

Smitty nodded slightly, taking in what she said. He didn't look at her weird or act uncomfortable like she was expecting. "So, yeah, you know the feeling anyway. Ketamine can do that. Some people like to party with it. I like to party with it. Casey started out that way but then began using it more as an escape. He struggled, man. Even as a kid, he said things that were dark or really out there. Like he saw the world differently than the rest of us."

Sam knew exactly what Smitty was saying. That's where she and Casey were alike. Even though it seemed like they felt things less, it was creating barriers because they felt them more. It was like they wore their skin inside out. Maybe that's why she disconnected so much, her brain was trying to protect her from overstimulation and pain. He wanted to feel things, but on a level he could tolerate.

"So, he took ketamine to deal with life?"

"I guess so." Smitty ran his hand through his hair. "At first we all kind of did it and just got fucked up. Had a good time and went on with our lives. But he kept using, more and more. Before long he wasn't coming to parties with us to use it, he was just using it. By himself. He started to pull away from the crowd. I don't think a day went by where he didn't use ketamine. He was always like, not there, you know? Like he could be talking to you and still not be there."

Sam thought of her last conversation with Casey, how he was there for a moment and they connected, then with a snap of the finger was behind the wall again. She wondered if that was how other people saw her.

"Did you talk to him about it?"

Smitty laughed, but it was a hopeless, angry laugh. "You know how it is. We were all using. I didn't have a place to come from. I had my own issues."

"Do a lot of people here use ketamine? Is it rampant?" Sam was curious. Small town. A drug used by veterinarians. Where was it coming from?

"I don't know if it's rampant, but a lot of the kids use it. Like I said, mainly to party. It was originally acquired by theft from vet offices, shipments, and vets looking to make an extra buck. Now, it's just a street drug, pretty easy to get. It's not the most popular fix, but the demand is going up. It's becoming more regular in the town. It's made available based on demand," Smitty answered, too knowingly.

"So, you use it?"

He sighed and nodded, slightly ashamed.

"And where is it coming from? Like how are you, how are these kids getting it? Where did Casey get it from? They should be held accountable," Sam said angrily.

Smitty stared at her for a long time. Too long. He made a sound crossed between a bitter laugh and a sob.

"I sold it to him."

The world started spinning around Sam, and she grabbed the railing to keep from falling. She didn't hear that right, she couldn't have. Smitty was the shady drug dealer that took Casey's life? Took Aidan's brother from him? The sound of rushing filled her ears, and her head filled with rage. She threw herself at Smitty, knocking him against the wall. He didn't fight her as she pounded her fists against him.

"You fucking asshole!"

She screamed so loud the lady with her children jerked her head over. She shooed her children down the beach away from them as quickly as she could, not looking back. Sam smacked Smitty as hard as she could across his face, leaving a red handprint in her hand's wake. He didn't flinch or move. Just stood there and took it.

"I fucking hate you!" She seethed at him and moved quickly down the ladder.

He didn't try to stop her or say anything back.

"You deserved to be the one who died. You fucking piece of shit."

Hot tears ran down her cheeks as she ran up the beach to get as far away from him as possible. She trusted him. *Like Miri trusted her?* She thought he was her friend and Casey's. *Like she was Miri's friend?* She wanted to physically hurt him. *Like Miri physically hurt her?* These thoughts raced through her brain. She'd traveled so far up the beach, she could no longer see the lifeguard stand. She leaned over and vomited, the smell of stale beer and coffee coming back up to hit her in the face. She collapsed on the beach and raged angry tears. When she finally cried what she could, she stared out at the ocean. Her thoughts calmed, and she started to consider the other side of the coin.

Smitty was just as much a victim of this town as Casey was. She knew that. She could see it in him, and almost every other young person around. All the dreams and beauty of the place belonged to the visitors. The locals just plugged away, keeping that dream clean and sparkling year by year for other people. Kids here were raised in basic poverty, for the most part, their parents being service workers and blue-collar to keep the town going. They rarely went to college, unless they earned scholarships or worked their way slowly through, like Chris the dishwasher was doing. They ended up in the same dead-end cycle as their parents. Even if their parents had money, the town had little to offer to the kids growing up there. No wonder they got fucked up. It was the only way to find the dream. She wasn't giving them a pity party. She'd seen it firsthand.

Smitty said he used ketamine as well. To party. But she knew better. He was also trying to escape. She thought over the times they had talked, the expressions on his face. His ability to isolate himself for long periods of time. The way people were around him but only briefly. He could disconnect himself so easily.

It dawned on her he wasn't a shady drug dealer, making money off the suffering of the people of this town. He was suffering. He was probably selling to cover his own habit. From the way he lived and worked, he was no more than just a guy selling to his friends so they could all use together. To escape together.

She didn't want to make the same mistake she'd made with Casey, by not pushing further and being there as a friend. Smitty was at risk, maybe at a slower rate, but she knew he was on the edge about to push himself over. The guilt of Casey's death was making that happen a lot faster. She got up and began the trek back, hoping he'd still be there. As she drew closer, she could make out his outline on the porch and started to move faster, breaking into a run. He caught a glimpse of her and came down, his brow furrowed, just as she reached the bottom of the ladder.

"Sam, I-"

"No, stop. I'm sorry. I was wrong. I know you didn't want what happened to Casey to happen, and you wouldn't have sold it to him had you known he was going to take it too far."

She was out of breath from running but had to get it out. "You said you were using. You were selling to use?"

He nodded and stared away, his face red with embarrassment. She went over to him and wrapped her arms tightly around him. She couldn't lose another friend. She had to break through her own shell and get to him before he drowned too. He was tense but relaxed against her as she held him.

"It's not you, Smitty. You didn't cause Casey's death. He had his own demons, and this town wouldn't let him get away from them. He didn't want to leave his mother or brother here to deal with this shit alone. He was doing the best he could to get by. You didn't do this."

Smitty put his arms around her and let his head rest against hers, as sobs shook his body. She could now see the torture he'd been putting himself through over this last month. He was carrying the weight of Casey's death on his shoulders when in reality the whole town was responsible. As children they were sold the idea of a better life, to be anything, and then were trapped by reality into being nothing as adults. There had to be a better pathway out.

Rosie had found it and had come back to help, bringing an army of Ansley with her. She did have certain advantages over other town kids though, her father being a teacher. They loved the town for what it could be and were determined to stay to make it something for the residents. Sam was used to running, but now she knew she had a purpose to stay.

She leaned back and peered up into Smitty's eyes, which were red-lined and exhausted. The boy he'd been and the man standing before her, both apparent through the pain in his face. She could see it clearly now, past the light-hearted persona he put out. He'd been fighting alone for a long time. She brushed his hair away from his brow. He was her friend, and she wasn't going anywhere without him.

"You have me. It may not be much, but it's something." She promised.

He laughed softly. "It's more than you'll ever know."

Chapter Fourteen

The wind was whipping across the pier, causing the overhead lights to sway. Seawater sprayed across the weathered wood as waves hit the posts below. She could see him in front of her, stumbling and wavering as he made his way down the planks. He had one hand clutched close to his chest, the other out to try and catch his balance. The curls of his hair were black with moisture and hanging below his shoulders. She tried to run to catch up to him, but her feet wouldn't move. He fell to his knees and picked himself up again, staggering as he rose. He was getting dangerously close to the end of the pier. She needed to get to him before he got there.

"Casey!" she screamed, the words getting lost in the wind. She willed her feet to move faster.

He stopped at the end of the pier and stood. She was getting closer. He was looking over the edge. She was almost there.

Please, just wait. As she got to where she could see his face, he climbed over the rail and held on with one hand. He leaned out over the ocean, swaying back and forth in the wind. She was just about within arm's reach to grab him when he turned to her and shook his head slowly. Blue eyes locked on gray.

"Sam, there are no mistakes." He let go and disappeared into the black ocean.

She screamed and ran to the edge, peering over for a sight of him. He was gone into the abyss. She climbed over and jumped in. She could save him this time. She hit the water and was tossed around helplessly by the force of the angry, cold waves. She put her hands out searching for him, feeling her fingers brush against skin. She moved towards it and his hair ran through her hands. She grasped for him and grabbed his shoulders. She could save him. As she pulled him towards her, his body rotated and she came face to face with his blue eyes, empty and dead. Suddenly, she felt his weight pulling her down, deeper and deeper. He was dead and was taking her with him. She needed to let go. She reached out and touched his face as he slipped away from her, down into the blackness. His crystal blue eyes stared up towards the surface, his lifeless hand reaching upward.

Sam sat up in bed screaming. It took a second to catch her breath and realize she was in her apartment. Sweat made her sheets stick to her skin and she kicked them off, feeling the water in her dream still pulling her down. Panic gripped her and she took shallow breaths until she could feel its heaviness passing. It was almost two in the morning, but she knew she wouldn't be able to sleep anymore. She went to the kitchen, put coffee on, and turned on the television for distraction. It was still quiet and dark outside, and she was feeling scared and shaken from the dream. Turning on the lights helped. As the coffee finished brewing, she began to feel a little better. She poured a cup and sat on the stool by Casey's rock.

Rubbing her fingers across the cool smooth surface, she tried to make out what the dream meant. Was it a message? Why couldn't she just save him? He'd told her in the dream there were no mistakes. Was his death not an accident? He was on ketamine, that much had been proven. Had he not stumbled and fallen over the rails? In the dream, he'd climbed over and let go. His words were similar to Miri's last words to her. There were no mistakes. Was this a message to her about that? She sighed and put her head down. Maybe she was reading too much into it.

She knew Casey was dealing with things and started using ketamine more, possibly to cope. He was alone that night, and the amount of ketamine in his system was enough to make him feel disoriented, out of touch with his own body. But in the dream, he climbed over the railing with no problem and held on. He chose to let go. He'd been clutching his other hand to his chest like people do when they are in great emotional pain, such as grieving. He'd said there were no mistakes.

Sam knew what the dream meant, even though she didn't know if that was what happened. In the dream, Casey had taken ketamine but it wasn't easing his pain, so he took it away the only way he knew how. He didn't stumble and fall. He let go. The ketamine didn't kill him, it just helped numb him enough to have the courage to do the only thing he felt he had left to do.

"Damn it, Casey," she whispered as she put her hand on the rock.

There were no mistakes. Of course, people make mistakes unaware at times, but she knew what he, and Miri, meant. Once something is put into motion and not stopped, it isn't a mistake.

It's a choice that becomes a reality. Casey knew what he was doing that night, she knew what she was doing the night with Ty. Whether or not she was aware at the time, she was pushing Miri away because she was feeling vulnerable. Ty was just a pawn in her plan.

She truly didn't think it at the time, but looking back she could see how she was creating a wall, even if Miri had never found out. Sam would've always known, and it would've allowed her to keep Miri that much away. By betraying Miri's trust, she'd secured a wedge between them, which would keep her from ever needing her too much.

She dug in the drawers and found paper and pen. It was time to put the past to rest and do what she should've done, to begin with. She scribbled out a long overdue note.

Miri,

You probably don't want to hear from me, and I can't blame you. I was a horrible person to you and don't deserve your consideration. I don't blame you for hitting me, I deserved worse. I'm not asking forgiveness, but want to let you know how sorry I am for destroying our friendship and betraying your trust.

There are no excuses and I'm ashamed for saying it was a stupid mistake. I did this. I can't say the reasons why and they don't matter, but I own what I did.

You were the kindest person I'd ever met, and I want you to have every happiness in your life. I'm sorry I tried to take that away from you. I know you think I'm devoid of emotion, but I promise you, it breaks my heart that I was such a shitty, callous person.

I hope you and Ty were able to move past this and just forget me. I won't write again. I just felt I owed you a real apology.

I truly am sorry.

Sincerely,

Samantha

She reread it a few times, hoping she conveyed her true feelings. She wouldn't blame Miri if she just ripped it up and cursed Sam's name. She scribbled Miri's address on the envelope and her return address without her name, so it had a chance of Miri opening and reading it. So she wouldn't chicken out, she slipped out down to the mailbox and put the letter in with the flag up. A weight lifted from her shoulders, and she breathed in deeply. She couldn't make Miri forgive her, but she could own her part in what happened. The only way she was going to climb out of the well was to build steps underneath her.

By the time the sun was in the sky, she'd showered, dressed, eaten breakfast, and packed a lunch. She wanted to get out and think about things. As Rosie said, Sam had built a prison around herself only she could take down. Writing Miri was a start, but she needed to dig deeper. The part of her dream she couldn't resolve, was why when she jumped into the water Casey was already gone. She felt he was trying to send her a message in that. What was he showing her?

Then it hit her like a brick. She couldn't save him, because long before he hit the water he was already gone. She'd felt it coming off him on the pier when he stumbled and fell to his knees. The utter loneliness that encapsulated him. He was only making his body match what he felt inside. He was setting himself free. He

121

knew she was getting trapped and was trying to save her, not the other way around. Casey had known it all along, he knew it the first time he spoke to her. He could see it in her eyes. This whole time she was mad at herself for not saving him, not realizing he was lightyears ahead of her.

She slipped Casey's rock into her pack. There was a state park not far from the town, and she wanted to go hiking and clear her head. As she drove to the state park, like Tetris, pieces started to fall into place. Casey thought he was too far gone but wanted to help her. She was there to keep Smitty from slipping away. They were all holding a rope at different stages of a black hole. Aidan. Where was Aidan standing in this black hole? She could see he was connected to the rope but wasn't sure where. This town was an abyss, sucking the life out of certain people. People like Rosie and Ansley were lighthouses, guiding people ashore. But for the rest of them, they were struggling to get to the surface. If there even was one.

Sam hiked most of the day, pushing until her muscles wanted to give out. Wooden pathways cut through wooded marshlands and led out to the beach. It was the complete opposite of the town beach. Tall grasses and dunes edged a rocky shoreline, untouched by humans trying to fit nature into their ideals. The few people there were walking and appreciating the pristine landscape. It felt so much rawer to Sam and gave her a sense of humbleness. Most things were best left undisturbed. She sat and ate the sandwich she'd packed, slipped her shoes off and dug her toes in the sand.

She pulled out Casey's rock and held it for a long time. He was the wild one, raised in a manmade reality. He was like this untouched beach, not meant to fit into society's box. She pressed

Casey's rock against her cheek for a moment, then went and placed it near the tideline. He was unfettered now. Not bound by the aspects of this earth. She needed to figure out how to help Aidan but didn't know where to start. As she made her way back to her bag on the beach, a breeze kicked up, blowing her hair away from her face. She knew Casey was in that breeze, she could feel it. Light as a feather.

Later that evening, after hiking all day, she eased her car into the drive and saw Smitty sitting at the top of her stairs. A bag of groceries beside him. He cocked his head at her and smiled, motioning to the bag. She tipped her head, confused, and climbed up to him. He watched her come up, his eyes locked on her.

"Hey, wasn't sure if you were coming back soon. I brought some stuff to cook for dinner if you'd like?" he asked, unsure.

"Yeah, I went for a hike. Needed to think and work some things out," she replied, peering in the bag.

Smitty seemed to know his way around cooking. It appeared he had a fancy Italian meal planned. Ingredients she'd never seen before and ingredients she'd never cooked before, even though she was familiar with them.

"Nice. So, you want me to cook you dinner and you can tell me about it?" He squinted up at her, his eyes catching glints of gold in the sunlight.

Sam took his hand and helped him up, while he grabbed the bag. He smiled crookedly at her as she stood watching him for a moment. She nodded and moved past him to open the door.

"I'd love nothing more."

Chapter Fifteen

The next time Sam went to dinner at Rosie's and Ansley's, Smitty was in tow. They'd started to spend most of their free time together, and it only seemed fitting for her friends to get to know each other better. Smitty was a natural in the kitchen and joined right in, preparing food with Rosie and Ansley, while Sam with her canned soup skills watched from the island. Rosie had a way of making everyone feel right at home, and Smitty was bopping to the music while cutting herbs. Sam had never felt a real sense of family, even though her family was good to her. So, the warm feeling she had observing the three of them move around the kitchen was unfamiliar but welcome.

"So, Sam calls you Smitty, but I swear I knew you as Smith in high school. You were a couple of years behind me, right?" Rosie directed at Smitty.

He laughed and winked at Sam. "Indeed. You know Sam. She gets her way, so she renamed me. Like a shelter puppy."

Sam threw a fabric napkin at him. "Hey! You told me you liked it!"

He turned his puppy dog eyes at her and smiled. "I do."

"You two. Are you sure you're just friends?" Ansley asked over her shoulder from the stove.

Sam blushed fiercely. They were. She'd never been successful in the relationship department and wasn't willing to risk ruining the blossoming friendship she had with Smitty. She'd learned not to fuck that up through her own selfish actions. Not that she wasn't attracted to him. It just wasn't worth it. Smitty came behind her, wrapping his arms around her and giving her a big dramatic kiss on the cheek.

"Just friends. Soulmates of the fraternal kind," he replied.

Sam smacked his arm away, laughing.

Ansley raised a brow, looking doubtful. "Okay then."

Rosie giggled from across the room. "Ignore Ansley, she's always trying to matchmake. She thinks everyone should be together."

"Can you blame me?" Ansley went over and kissed Rosie on the back of the neck.

Sam was envious of their relationship. They had it figured out. Space, support, love. They gravitated around each other with such precision, it almost seemed flawless. Rosie grinned and turned around. She glanced at the stove and her mouth formed an O.

"Ansley! Your veggies are burning!"

Ansley hopped over to the stove and gave everything a quick stir.

"Stop distracting me," she teased Rosie.

Rosie chuckled and turned her attention to Smitty. "How many years apart are we? I know you were in school while I was, but you were a skinny little kid then."

Smitty nodded. "You were a senior when I was a freshman. I sprouted up in tenth grade. My mother was freaking out about me being so small, then was freaking out about having to buy new pants every month or so, once I did grow."

Sam couldn't imagine Smitty not being so tall. He had to be at least six-foot-three now. She stared at him trying to see it. "I'd love to see a picture of you back then."

"Just picture me about a foot shorter, with braces and acne."

"Wait, Rosie, you're thirty years old, right? So, Smitty, you're twenty-six?" Sam tried to do the math. She'd never thought to ask.

"Yep. Twenty-seven next month. About time to grow up, right?"

"Well, if it is, I'm a late bloomer." Sam laughed. "I don't know if I'll ever get my shit together and I'm thirty-one."

Smitty eyed her for a second seriously. He shrugged and smiled. "I took a job as a lifeguard at eighteen. Just a summer job, right? Here I am over eight fucking years later, still wandering around lost."

"Fair enough. But there isn't much else to do here," Sam reassured him.

"I could've left. My parents left after I was done with high school and I stayed. It was fucking stupid. Didn't want to leave my friends, and they all ended up leaving anyway. Or dying."

Silence fell over the group.

Rosie, not one to let silence sit for too long, spoke up. "I'm sorry about Casey. I didn't know him. I mean, I knew who he was, but we weren't in school together or anything. Sam speaks highly of him."

"Yeah, Casey should've left too. We all thought we were being temporary. That life was just over the horizon. But that horizon kept getting further and further," Smitty said quietly.

"You couldn't have known then, you were just kids," Sam responded, meeting his eyes.

"Smitty, how do you make ends meet? I mean lifeguarding isn't full-time, is it?" Ansley asked in an attempt to redirect the conversation.

"I really don't. During the summer it's okay because I work full-time as a lifeguard, but the rest of the months are tough. I don't tell them, the town, I mean, but I sleep in the lifeguard stand a lot to avoid paying rent. Until it gets too cold. Then I usually rent a room wherever I can find it. I do odd and ends here and there to make ends meet. Day labor jobs, selling stuff-" he trailed off and glanced at Sam.

Selling stuff. Ketamine. She shook her head at him and furrowed her brow. Don't go there.

"Your parents, what did they do?" Sam asked, curious as to how he ended up in the town.

"My father was the hospitality manager for the White Nautilus, that upscale hotel at the far end. My mom mostly stayed home and volunteered at the school. Probably just to keep herself from sheer boredom once I was in school. We moved here when I was like one or two, I don't really remember. Then my father was offered a high paying job elsewhere the summer after I graduated, and they moved. I could've gone but didn't. Obviously." He waved his arms comically around him to show he was still there.

Sam snickered. "Well, if you had, you wouldn't have gotten the privilege of meeting me."

He placed his hand on his chest like he'd been shot. "Devastating."

"Seriously, you two!" Ansley eyed them and laughed. "Alright, food's ready, let's eat."

They took everything to the table outside. Rosie sat next to Ansley, with Smitty and Sam sat across from them. Smitty's leg brushed Sam's under the table, sending little shockwaves up her leg. Just friends. The most important thing. He sheepishly grinned at her, moving his leg away. He felt it too.

"Oh, so great news!" Rosie exclaimed. "Ansley is doing an art opening at the gallery next month. November seventh. I hope you both can come."

Smitty chuckled softly. "Also my birthday. November seventh. I'd love to come."

Sam stared from Rosie to Smitty. "Seriously? I wouldn't miss either of those. I get you for your birthday *day*, though."

"Wouldn't have it any other way." Smitty grinned at her and squeezed her hand under the table.

"How fun! Why don't we all grab a bite to eat and then head over to the gallery after? Ansley will be there all day getting ready, but we can steal her for an hour to eat. Right, Ansley?" Rosie's eyes were hopeful.

"Of course," Ansley responded. "The opening is at seven, so why don't we meet for dinner at five-thirty. There's a fancy little place a couple of doors down. I think it's called The Chain. I assume an attempt at being sardonic. The menu looks good."

"It's a date!" Rosie grinned, her big, round eyes sparkling.

"Rosie has news too," Ansley announced. "They got approval to use part of the old school for charter classrooms. The funds look like they're going to come through, so next year they can open it for grade kindergarten through second."

"Oh, wow, Rosie! That's amazing. No more bussing little kids to the next town. That's great news!" Sam meant it. The kids of the town needed a warrior to fight for them and tiny Rosie was stepping up to the plate. A five-foot-tall, high-pitched warrior.

Rosie beamed with pride. "Thanks. It's my dream. Well, part of it. I'd like to add classes until it's a full elementary school, so they don't have to leave until middle school. We had that growing up and I want to bring it back.

Smitty nodded. "We did. Being little here was the best. After that, not so much. We had to get up so early to go over to the next town, the school day ended up being like ten hours with that ride. I hated it. Started getting into trouble around then."

"Not to mention, there is just nothing here for older kids to do," Sam agreed. The teens she saw hung out at the gas station and on the beach, but it seemed like by middle school a lot of them were already drinking and smoking. By high school, some were into much harder stuff. Sometimes having sex and getting pregnant, continuing the poverty cycle of the area. She couldn't blame them, they weren't being given a lot of other options or opportunities.

They ate in silence for a bit, enjoying each other's presence and the good food. The conversation picked up, turning lighter and was filled with laughter. As the evening wore on, they moved inside to have drinks. Sam sipped on hers, knowing better than to have too much. She started to get sleepy, her eyes wanting to close but not wanting the evening to end. Once she could no longer keep her eyes open, she began saying her goodbyes. Smitty agreed and they headed for the door. Part of his conversation from before stuck in her mind and she turned to him.

"I don't know if you're sleeping in the lifeguard stand but you're welcome to stay over. It's getting cold."

His golden eyes stared at hers. They knew the risks but also were determined to protect their friendship. He nodded and they climbed the stairs to her place. Once inside they stood awkwardly for a moment. They were both tired, but moving to the bedroom seemed like such a big step. Sam put her hand on his arm and laughed.

"It's okay. I sleep on the edge anyway. I think I can resist."

He broke into laughter. "I don't know. I'm pretty damn irresistible."

"Shut up!" She shoved him lightly and walked to the bathroom. She dug through the drawer and pulled out a pack of toothbrushes, handing him one.

"What is that? Garlic breath?"

"Probably." He winked at her, taking the toothbrush.

After brushing their teeth, they went to the bedroom. Smitty stood at the end of the bed for a moment. Sam quickly changed into pajama bottoms and a tank top in the bathroom and slipped under the covers.

"You don't have to sleep in your jeans. I assume you have something on under there?" she teased, trying to hide her own embarrassment.

He blushed and nodded. He slipped off his jeans, climbing into the bed in boxers and his t-shirt. His warmth carried through the covers to her, and she questioned her decision. She breathed out deeply.

"I would've offered you the couch but it's a loveseat, and your legs would've dangled over."

"Sam." He rolled over and put his arm over her. "There is nothing in the world I'd do to risk our friendship. I promise. I can't say I don't feel things for you, but you're my friend and that's what matters most."

She met his eyes and whispered, "Then, dude, you'd better move your arm because I can't promise the same."

He laughed deeply and moved his arm. The heat between them was indisputable. He nodded and turned over, his back to her. She turned the other way and tried to quell the electricity running through her body. Once she heard his patterned breathing of sleep, she turned back over and watched his back rising and falling gently. She could trace his spine through his shirt down to his slender hips. Damn. She reached out to touch him and knew better.

She let her hand drift down between them, feeling the heat coming off his body. Just friends. She needed him in her life, and there was only one way to make sure of that. She matched her breathing to his until she felt herself slip through the layers and fell into a dreamless sleep.

Chapter Sixteen

November seventh was there before they knew it. Ansley's art opening and Smitty's birthday. Sam fretted over what to get Smitty for his birthday. He didn't have a place of his own and didn't need stuff he was going to have to haul around with him. This made it harder, but she didn't want to get him nothing either. She perused gift shops and came up empty-handed, everything there seemed so trite and uninspired. The day came and she was still left with no good ideas.

She got up early and packed a backpack picnic for them to take to the state park. It was a place she'd come to love and wanted to share it with him. They agreed to meet at the restaurant to head out from there. She wasn't sure where he was staying but didn't question because she knew he was embarrassed by his lack of stability.

When she pulled up, he was leaning against the *no overnight parking* sign, and he pointed up at it with a smirk. She pushed the door open.

"Haha, very funny. Get in."

He slid in beside her, grinning. She leaned over and kissed him on the cheek.

"Happy birthday, Smith."

He raised his eyebrows and laughed. "That sounds the weirdest coming from your mouth."

"Trust me, it felt weird."

They drove out of the parking lot and headed out towards the state park, the sun still low in the sky. The air was crisp, and Sam was glad she'd brought a sweatshirt with her. Smitty was wearing a jacket over a t-shirt and jeans. She'd packed some hot coffee in a thermos for when they got to the park. The days warmed up, but the mornings and evenings were still cold.

Smitty was staring out the window lost in thought, so she took the chance to appreciate watching him. He wasn't the kind of guy one would necessarily stop and stare at on the street, other than for his height, but he'd his own unique beauty. Long tan limbs, muscular but very slim. He had light brown eyes that when the light hit them right, glittered gold. Long straight nose, shaggy brown hair, always bleached out from being in the sun. He had a slightly goofy smile, which she found endearing. He was very attractive in a relaxed, subtle way. Sam was so entranced in thought staring at him, she hadn't noticed he'd turned his attention to her and was saying something.

"Sorry, what?" She flushed.

"I asked you what you were thinking about, and to watch the road."

"Oh, uh. Honestly?" she replied, looking back at the road. "I was admiring you."

"That so?" He turned a little red and stared back out the window. "Sam, you aren't making this easy on me."

"What?"

"You know what. You told me how important protecting our friendship was, and then go and say stuff like that."

He wasn't wrong. She was being unfair. He'd respected all of her boundaries, and she found herself slipping over them. She didn't want to upset him and understood where he was coming from. She'd set the line and needed to not cross it.

"I'm sorry. You're right. I'll be more aware."

He nodded but didn't look her way, keeping his eyes out the window. The rest of the ride was in silence, Sam feeling ashamed for her actions. Once they pulled in the park, tensions had eased and Smitty grabbed the backpack out of the back seat. They started across the marsh, careful to stay on the wooden path. It had rained a bit in the last few weeks, causing the water to come up to the edges. At places, the water had come over the path and they had to hop over to stay dry. The path winded in and out of densely wooded areas, with carved wooden benches to stop if needed along the path. At one of the benches, they stopped and had coffee.

Sam still felt guilty about not finding a present for Smitty's birthday. She didn't want him to think she hadn't tried. "Hey, Smitty? I don't have a present for you. I'm sorry. I tried to find something, but everything seemed so cheesy, and I knew you didn't just need stuff. But I honestly tried."

He laughed and turned to face her. "Seriously? You brought me here, you're spending the day with me. You know what I did last year? Walked around town by myself and drank a couple of beers at the lifeguard stand. That was it. No one else even knew. I didn't get anything and did the same shit I do every day. I've lived here most of my life and have never been to this park. So that's enough."

"Okay," Sam said, relieved. "But I really wanted to get you something."

He peered around where they were sitting and gestured his head behind them. "So, get me something. Walk back there and the first thing you see that makes you think of me, give me that."

Sam laughed and then saw he was serious. She got up and started walking in the woods, scouring the area for something special. Now, she really couldn't come back empty-handed.

"If I get poison ivy, I'm giving you that," she yelled back at him and heard him chuckle in response.

She came across ferns and mushrooms, stopping to admire them. Nothing said Smitty to her. Rocks, sticks, while cool to look at, just didn't jump out at her. Then she saw it. A small, gnarled piece of wood with a knot. She picked it up and moved her hands around it, feeling all of its edges. It was both smooth and rough, smelling like saltwater. It was small enough to fit in the palm of her hand, so it was easy to slip in her pocket. He was laying on the bench, with one leg over the arm and the other stretched out beside it, staring up at the trees. When she came back, he sat up to make room for her. She reached in her pocket and drew out the wood. He peered at her and took it from her hand, turning it around in his own.

"So, why?" He met her eyes.

"You show this side of you to the world, but you're so much more intricate than that. Smooth, rough, with areas that no one sees. Deep crevices you hide yourself in. Besides, it smells like you."

He put it to his nose and breathed in. He laughed and put his arms around her in a big hug. When they pulled back, he put his hand under her chin and kissed her. The lightest, soft kiss where their lips just touched. She breathed in and looked at him, again smelling salt from his skin. His eyes had a twinkle to them.

"Thanks, Sam. I'll cherish it. And that."

Sam was dumbfounded, nodding like an idiot. Smitty stood up and put the wood in his jacket pocket. He put his hand out to her.

"You want to keep moving?"

Sam took his hand and got up. He picked up the pack and they walked in silence for a long time, each in their own thoughts about what happened. As they came out of the marsh, the sun and the ocean greeted them. It was magnificent, and they stood staring at the water. It contained a level of awe, which the ocean they lived by somehow lacked, even though it was the same body of water.

"Wow." Smitty's eyes moved from one side to the other, taking it all in. "Who knew?"

"I did," Sam replied from his side.

"Yeah, you did. And you gave it to me."

They spread the blanket she'd packed out on the sand and took food out of the backpack. She'd managed to snag a cupcake from the restaurant, and she bought a singular green candle she pulled out to stick in it. Smitty saw it and his eyes lit up. She lit the candle, handing the cupcake to him

"Fuck yeah," he whispered, as he took the cupcake and closed his eyes to make a wish.

Then he yanked the candle out, shoving the cupcake almost whole into his mouth. Sam laughed and plucked the candle from the sand where he'd put it, slipping it back into her bag for safekeeping.

"Good thing I didn't want any, huh?"

He turned slightly pink and put his hand out, the last little bit of cupcake in his palm. She took the small, mangled piece and ate it. As they finished up, Sam caught the time, knowing the hike back would take a bit.

"Shoot, we better go. Ansley's opening is tonight. I was going to grab a shower and get changed."

"Today has been very nice, Sam. Thank you." Smitty took one last look around at the virtually untouched beach and nodded, satisfied.

They hiked back to the car. By the time they got there, both were tired, sandy, and sweaty. On the car ride home, they talked about how different the tourist beach was from the protected state park beach. The state park beach had large dunes, rocks, and shells. The tourist beach was always so picked clean and the dunes worn down by people walking over them, even though there were boardwalks, and signs forbidding it. Even the wildlife had been different at the park beach. More than just seagulls. Larger birds and more creatures scurrying across the sand. They promised to go back more often.

Smitty had to get changed too, so asked Sam to drop him off at the restaurant. When they pulled in, he didn't get out right away and they sat with the car idling. Finally, he turned to her and took her hand. He cleared his throat.

"I don't regret kissing you, but I do honestly respect your boundaries. I won't do it again, but I *will* remember it with the present you gave me. I want you to know what you've done for me. What you have given to me."

Sam could feel a tightness in her throat, emotion bubbling up and pushed it back down. She let him continue.

"When you showed up here in town, here at the beach, I was in a dark fucking place. Like no way out of here, you know? I thought you were funny right off the bat and liked taking breaks with you. Thought you were pretty." He smiled, blushing. "After Casey died, I felt like you were the only other person I could talk to. Everyone else just made it about themselves, or worse, turned on Casey. You didn't. You were fierce and kind. You listened, but also held me accountable for the stupid shit I'd done."

He paused and stared out the window, measuring his words. Sam squeezed his hand for encouragement. He gave a small smile and met her eyes.

"Sam, I want you to know that since that night, the night we stayed in the stand, I haven't used. I haven't been selling either. I stopped."

Sam had wondered but hadn't known how to bring it up. Relief washed over her. "So, you haven't taken ketamine? Or anything?"

"Nothing. I mean, I have a few drinks here and there, but that's it. It's because of you."

"No, Smitty. It's because of you. You don't give yourself enough credit."

He nodded and smiled at her so genuinely, she felt her heart break a little. He leaned in and put his arms around her.

"You really fucking are my best friend," he whispered in her ear.

Sam didn't think she was worthy of this but leaned back and brushed his hair out of his eyes. She felt the same but was scared to go out on a limb. "Happy birthday, Smith."

This time it sounded a little more natural.

They went their own directions to get ready for the opening. Sam drove to her place and took a quick shower, slipping on a light pink dress she'd pushed to the back of her closet. She dabbed a little makeup on and pinned her hair up in the front, letting the back cascade over her shoulders. She looked at the mirror and smiled. She was a little surprised when it didn't feel so foreign to see herself smiling back.

Realizing she was running late, she grabbed her bag and ran out the door. She had a hard time finding parking in the town, due to all the bars and restaurants, ending up a street over. She ran as fast as she could in her sandals, whipping around the corner to see Smitty, Rosie, and Ansley waiting for her outside the restaurant. Smitty caught her breath. He'd changed into a button-down shirt, fitted jacket, and dark jeans. His hair was clean and brushed back a bit, making him look older, or at least more his age. He kept his eyes on her as she rushed up. He put his hand out, which she took gratefully.

"So sorry. I was running behind and couldn't find parking," Sam explained breathlessly.

Smitty put his arm over her shoulders as they walked into the restaurant. He leaned in and murmured, "You clean up pretty good."

She laughed and pushed him off. "You aren't too bad yourself."

Dinner was fresh and delicious, better than the fried food Sam served at work. They chatted while they ate and made it just in time to the gallery for the opening. Ansley disappeared into the growing crowd, greeting people as she went, Rosie beaming in hand. Smitty and Sam walked around admiring the art. Ansley was incredibly talented, bringing something other than seashell and beach art to the town. Her bold lines and modern approach popped against the white walls. Sam eyeballed a piece she wanted and paid for it at the front, planning to pick it up after the opening.

Once they'd made the rounds, Sam started feeling claustrophobic and gestured to Smitty that she was heading outside for air. She slipped back through the crowd and outside. The air was refreshing but chilly, and she shivered. She lit a cigarette but put it out after a few puffs. She made her way down the street towards the water, letting it call to her. The night was clear and this end of the beach was much more lit up by the town.

She sat on the edge of the pier post wall, separating the town from the beach, and let her feet hang off, kicking them back and forth like a child. The gentle lapping waves were having a calming effect on her. She could hear laughter, the clinking of glasses, and music in the distance, which was strangely comforting. Footsteps came up behind her and Smitty plopped down next to her.

"You alright?" he asked, slipping his jacket around her shoulders. It was warm from his body and smelled like the ocean and whatever aftershave he'd used. It made her want to draw closer to him.

"Yeah, I was just starting to feel a little trapped in there. So many people, so little space. I kind of panic in that type of situation."

"Well, now it's just you and me and the stars," Smitty said softly.

It was. The stars were bright, and the moon created a large swath of light across the water, creating a magical glittering illusion. She leaned her head against Smitty's shoulder and sighed. He rested his head on hers. No matter what the future held, at this moment, sitting here with him was absolutely perfect.

"Hey, Smitty, I'd love it if you'd come and warm the other side of my bed tonight. I don't want to be alone."

She could feel his chest shake with laughter.

"You got it."

Chapter Seventeen

Natalie and Gus surprised everyone by getting married in a private ceremony at the end of November. Gus was clearly head over heels for Natalie, but she never publicly showed she'd even had a clue, much less felt the same. Sam didn't find out until she went to work and there was a reception announcement behind the bar. She stared at the announcement confused when Taylor passed behind her.

"No joke. It's for real," Taylor said and shook her head. "Who knew?"

The announcement had the date for the reception as the following week. The restaurant would be closed to the public and it was a catered event, open bar. Music was to be performed by a local classic rock cover band and the attire was casual. Request in place of presents was donating money to a sea turtle research fund.

It was for a Sunday evening, probably to give everyone a chance to recover prior to their next shift. A note scribbled at the bottom said all staff were off that evening and invited to attend. Sunday nights had been painfully slow, so Sam was glad to have the evening off.

On her break, she went out to the lifeguard stand to see if Smitty was still up there. He was and leaned over the rail to talk to her.

"Hey, Sam, how's business?"

"Slow. But did you hear about Natalie and Gus?"

"I did. Crazy, right? Good for them. You going to the reception?"

Sam didn't relish the idea of being at her workplace when she didn't have to, or how crowded it was sure to be. But Natalie had been like family to her and she needed to go. She nodded reluctantly.

"You?"

"If you are, I am. Open bar too." Smitty laughed and wiggled his eyebrows.

"Yeah, that'll be interesting. People around here do *not* know how to moderate their drinking." Sam chuckled, shaking her head.

Images of people stumbling out on the beach, glasses in hand, came to mind. At least she wouldn't be the babysitter that night. It would be the first time she'd be at the bar as a guest, not slinging drinks, since the first day she arrived in town.

"No, they do not," Smitty agreed. "Don't worry I'll stay by your side and if it gets to be too much we can always escape to the stand."

"True. I appreciate it. Alright, gotta get back. See you later?"

"You bet!"

The rest of her shift, the chatter was around Natalie's and Gus's big news. Patrons were patting him on the back and offering to buy Gus drinks. He didn't drink but was polite anyway about it. Natalie stayed in the back not wanting the attention, only popping her head out now and then to ask questions about receipts or orders. Sam congratulated both of them and called Natalie a sly fox. Natalie laughed and shrugged. She wasn't one for pomp and circumstance.

The night of the reception Smitty walked over to Sam's place to meet up with her. He grabbed a shower and got dressed there. As the announcement had requested, they dressed in casual attire. He wore jeans, skate shoes, and a long-sleeved shirt. He brushed his hair into a more kempt style but it quickly unkempt itself, making Sam laugh. She put on a short red boho dress and tan boots. She braided her hair over one shoulder to keep it out of the way. Considering the weather, she grabbed a sweater and tossed Smitty his zipper hoodie.

By the time they got to the restaurant, both the patio and inside were packed. Sam took an anxious breath as they walked in. She didn't have the bar to separate her and everyone else tonight. As promised, Smitty didn't leave her side and kept her hand in his to make their way through the crowd. They found Natalie and Gus near the bar and gave their congratulations, kissing them each on the cheek. Natalie was glowing in a flowing purple two-piece skirt set, her hair uncustomarily down. Gus wore a button-down shirt, jeans, and cowboy boots. They looked like completely different people than when they were behind the bar. The crowd was pushing in towards them, so Smitty and Sam gave a quick goodbye and moved to the other end of the bar. They grabbed drinks, heading out to the patio where the band was playing.

They found a corner to sit for a bit while they sipped on their drinks. As foreseen, the crowd was beginning to spill out onto the beach, not very sober and pretty loud. Sam's anxiety was climbing and she gripped Smitty's hand hard. He nodded and they set their glasses down, moving out to the lifeguard stand. They climbed up and sat on the edge in the moonlight. Smitty had stashed beers inside and grabbed one for each of them.

"Thanks." Sam breathed out and relaxed her shoulders.

The crowds went in the opposite direction of the stand, so they were pretty much alone. After a beer, she felt the tension slip away and enjoyed hearing the band play, even the noise of the crowd in the distance. She was glad she grabbed her sweater and slipped it on. Smitty was humming along with the band low and soft. She found it incredibly soothing and leaned against him. The waves were heavy with an incoming storm, crashing against the shore. It made her feel vulnerable and small but in a good way. The band started playing a song she remembered from her childhood, one that always made her feel good. She couldn't remember the name, but it had a nice melody and words she could sing along to.

"Oh, I love this song!" she exclaimed.

Smitty smiled at her and put his hand out. "May I have this dance?"

Blushing fiercely, she shook her head.

He persisted. "Sam, please?"

She peered up at him and couldn't resist his soft pleading eyes. She nodded and they stood up on the balcony of the stand. Still holding her one hand, Smitty wrapped his other arm around her waist, pulling her close. The heat of his body caused her to relax against him. She put her hand up and placed it behind his neck. He bent his head down next to hers, his breath tickling her skin. They swayed to the music and Sam wished the song was longer than it was, so they could keep dancing. As it ended, the band started to play a super upbeat song. They laughed and separated. Sam looked up at Smitty, meeting his eyes. She wanted to kiss him, to feel his lips on hers again. He wasn't going to make the move as he'd promised. She considered it but then doubted herself and glanced away. He let his arm drop from her waist and turned towards the water.

"Sam, have you ever considered we could be both?" His voice sounded frustrated and dark.

She had. Every single day. But if things fell apart in that way, it would destroy their friendship. She knew her rebuff was hurting him, and she didn't want to do that either. She went behind him and put her arms around him, laying her head on his back. His back was warm and firm against her cheek.

"Smitty. I destroy things. There are things about me you just don't understand. I'm fucked up and drive people away. I can't lose you. If I did, it would kill me inside. I think about you, us, all the time. But when I do it always ends badly. I lose you and I lose myself."

He turned back around to face her. He put his arms around her, and they stood like this for some time. He rested his chin on her head, his voice was gentle when he finally spoke.

"You have to let me in."

Sam sighed. If she let him in, he might leave.

"I've let you in more than you can ever understand. More than anyone in my life. But, Smitty, I'm scared. I've been alone my whole life and I don't really know why. It's like there are two of me. The me tucked away in the back of myself and the me standing guard. I've never told anyone, and I want to tell you about these things, but it's weird. I just don't think I can explain it."

Smitty tipped her head up towards his face to meet his eyes. They were kind and non-judging. "Sam, I'm not going to push. But you can tell me anything. I've opened up to you and you accepted me for who I am. I can do the same. I won't hurt you."

Sam wanted to crack but she just couldn't. She reached up and placed her hand on his cheek. "When the time comes I will. I just can't right now."

He placed his hand over hers and smiled. "You know where to find me when you can."

The party had started to wrap up as the police were making their rounds. Due to Natalie's standing in the community, they were being more forgiving on their timeline but were making their presence known. The crowds dispersed to their cars. Smitty and Sam climbed down and headed to her car. He'd agreed to sleep at her place to make it easy, so they drove that direction. She pulled into the gas station to grab a pack of cigarettes and some snacks. As she got out a flash of something caught her eye, then disappeared behind the gas station. She gestured to Smitty silently. He cocked his head, furrowing his brows. She pointed to the side of the gas station and mouthed the word.

"Aidan."

Smitty nodded. It was almost one in the morning, so Aidan shouldn't be out. He got out of the car and slowly made his way around the side of the gas station. Sam followed and by the time she made it around to the back, Smitty had his hand on Aidan. A group of other kids were disappearing into the neighborhood behind the gas station. As Sam approached Smitty and Aidan, the expression on Smitty's face gave her shivers. It was a mixture of devastation and rage. Looking from him to Aidan, her heart fell. Aidan was clearly fucked up. His pupils were dilated, and he was swaying back and forth. Smitty had his hands on Aidan's shoulders, trying to steady him.

Aidan was attempting to push Smitty away, mumbling something unintelligible. But out of it, Sam caught the words "know what you did" and "Casey". The color drained from Smitty's face, as he took a step back away from Aidan. His hands dropped to his side. Aidan knew he'd sold Casey the ketamine.

Sam took a step forward to reach out for Aidan. He turned his head towards her, his dark eyes glazed over and unfocused. Suddenly, he smiled.

"Hey, Samantha."

It was all he said before he started to pitch forward. Smitty jumped into action and grabbed Aidan right before he hit the ground. Aidan collapsed in Smitty's arms. Smitty scooped him up and headed for the car. He climbed into the back seat with him, and Sam got into the driver's seat. Smitty was leaning over, whispering something to Aidan. Aidan was nodding, his head wobbling on his shoulders. Smitty glanced up at Sam in the rearview mirror, and she could see he had tears running down his cheeks.

Aidan tried to right himself in the seat, flopping to the other side. He laughed and pulled himself to a sitting position. Smitty mumbled an address, motioning for Sam to drive. She started up the car, peeking repeatedly in the back seat to see how Aidan was. He was definitely fucked up but seemed to be coming out of the worst. She drove the backstreets to the address Smitty had given her. He ran up to the door and knocked. Aidan's mother came to the door, her face twisted with concern as Smitty spoke to her. She looked past him to the car, where Aidan was attempting to exit. Smitty came back to the car, grabbing ahold of Aidan to steady him. The back door was still open and Smitty leaned in to speak to Sam.

"I'm going to get him in and stay with him. I think he's going to be okay but needs to ride this out."

"Ride it out," Aidan mimicked from behind him and clapped his hands for effect.

Sam nodded, understanding. "I'll leave the door open in case you come in while I'm sleeping."

Smitty grimaced, trying to steady Aidan as he tumbled to the ground. He slammed the door and guided Aidan up the pathway to his mother waiting at the door. They both escorted him inside. Glancing back, Smitty gave Sam a small wave as he disappeared into the house.

She sat gathering her thoughts before leaving. Aidan had taken something. It wasn't booze or weed; she was familiar enough with those to know the signs. He was disoriented and didn't have control over his body. Like Casey. Ketamine? Fuck. But how was he getting it? Smitty had stopped selling. His words rung in her mind. Where there was demand. So, someone had taken up where Smitty left off. Someone else was selling to the kids of the town. It was a never-ending cycle.

Once she was home, she smoked a cigarette on the porch and thought about the night's events. Didn't Aidan see what had happened to Casey and know better? Or had he seen what happened to Casey and thought there was no other way than to follow in his footsteps. Like when he was a little kid and would chase after Casey crying?

She climbed into bed, wanting to shake the image of Aidan's glassy eyes out of her mind. Him swaying uncontrollably behind the gas station. He was a sharp, intelligent kid. She didn't want to see him lost to this town. It was like the line which connected them all was dragging him down. Dragging him under.

It was almost daylight when she heard Smitty slip in. She rolled over, watching as he climbed into bed. He looked at her and nodded. Aidan was okay, for now. She went to reach out to him, he flinched and pulled away. She let her hand drop, hurt but understanding. He'd stayed with Aidan to make sure he was okay, even though Aidan knew about Smitty and Casey.

"All my fault," he muttered as he laid down, his back to Sam. Guilt was pouring off him like steam.

"Smitty, you didn't-"

He cut her off sharply.

"Sam, don't."

Chapter Eighteen

Smitty's weight dropped dramatically over the next couple of weeks. Sam tried to make him food and reach out to him, but he was shunning her. He was polite but stopped coming over, avoided eye contact, and kept his responses short. She didn't think it had to do with her rebuffing a romantic relationship. It was something deeper in him that started the night with Aidan. His whole personality had shifted, and he'd become harder, more abrupt. He was wasting away in front of her eyes, but she'd no way of getting through to him.

One night, as she was helping clean up after dinner, she set aside a plate of food for him. On her break, she walked it out to the lifeguard stand. He was standing with his back to her, and she could make out his ribs. As she approached, he turned and watched her but not with his normal smile. She handed the plate up to him.

He took it, balancing it on the railing. His face was almost impossible to read.

"I brought you some food. You're getting thin, Smitty."

He stared at her and sighed. "I'm not your problem anymore, Sam. Or your charity case."

"I wasn't saying that. I'm just worried about you." Sam was hurt and confused. Why was he being so cold to her?

"You don't need to. I'm fine." His words sounded like he was biting off the end of each one of them. He turned, leaving the plate and went into the lifeguard stand. He closed the door behind him.

Sam stood staring at the unopened door for a moment and walked back to the restaurant, defeated. What the hell? She knew Aidan calling him out about what happened to Casey was shocking and embarrassing, but why was he taking it out on her? She'd stood by him through all of this. She glanced back at the stand once she got to the restaurant doors. He was back outside, his arms braced on the railing with such tension, it looked like he was going to snap the rail right off. This wasn't Smitty. He was fighting something inside of himself, and not necessarily winning.

Her mind played over every scenario she could think of as she worked the rest of her shift. Her mind kept landing on the worst case. Around eight o'clock she was washing some bar glasses when a voice called out to her from the end of the bar.

"Hey, Samantha?"

She glanced over and caught her breath, dropping the glass she'd been drying, shattering it on the floor. Casey?

"Shit!" She bent down to scoop the broken glass and looked back up.

No, it was Aidan sitting in Casey's seat, but his expression matched the one on Casey's face the last day she saw him alive. Aidan probably had no idea he was sitting in the same seat Casey would always sit in when he came in. By sheer dumb luck, he'd just picked the same stool.

"Aidan? What are you doing here? It's late." She peered around for his parents, but he was alone.

"I needed to talk to you. About...about what happened. You know, that night?"

She nodded and came down to the end of the bar where he was sitting. "You ok?"

He smiled sheepishly, splotches of red forming on his cheeks. "My parents were so pissed. I don't even really remember much about that night. I was pretty high. This is the first time I've been allowed out, and I told them I was running to a friend's house to grab some school assignments I missed."

"Lying probably isn't a good start to regaining their trust," Sam said softly.

He laughed and bobbed his head. "No, you're right. But I wanted to let you know that we're leaving. My family, I mean. I think I was the straw that broke the camel's back."

Sam reached out and squeezed his hand. He almost seemed like he might cry and cut his eyes down. He was still just a kid needing guidance, despite the tough exterior he walked around with.

"I don't know why I fucking did that. I was hanging out with some friends, and they had K. I was missing Casey and thought if I took it, I'd maybe feel closer to him. Or at least try to understand what he felt. It didn't help. I guess you know that, right?"

He glanced up, meeting her eyes. She nodded and tried to smile to reassure him, but her mouth just wobbled at the sides.

"I'm sorry Aidan. You've totally been handed a shit deal. I'm just glad you're okay. We were really worried about you that night. Smitty stayed with you until he knew you were going to be fine."

A flash of anger crossed his face. "Smitty, Smith. Do you even really know him? Did he ever tell you he got more fucked up than the rest of them? He'd get so fucked up, Casey would sit with him to make sure he wouldn't die."

Sam didn't know that. He said he used to party but not how much he used. He made it sound like it was just occasionally. She had a feeling it was going to get worse. Aidan went on.

"Smith started K right out of high school, maybe before. I don't know where he got it, but he brought it into parties and got so many people hooked. He was dealing it to pay for his own habit. Who knows what else? It got so bad they found him barely breathing a couple of times on the beach. He was fucked up most of the time."

Sam felt cold and empty. Smitty had never told her any of this. The hair on the back of her neck stood up. He was as bad as Casey, if not worse. He had to be selling a lot to cover using so heavily. His sleeping in the lifeguard stand and on the streets was beginning to make more sense now. She wondered if he'd even stopped and was still selling.

"Where did you get it? The ketamine?" she asked Aidan.

"It wasn't Smith if that's what you're asking. He stopped selling after Casey died. Some other dude just picked up where he left off. There will always be someone selling, you know?"

So, that much was true.

"Do you know if he was, or still is using?" Her hands gripped the bar so hard her fingers started to ache.

Aidan shrugged. "I have no fucking clue. I don't think so because he isn't selling, and he has eyes on him."

Eyes on him? Like the police, or dealers? She didn't want to drag Aidan further into this nightmare, so she changed the subject.

"Where are you going?"

"My dad took a job in Washington state. Basically, as far away from here as they can possibly get. They put the house up for sale and we already have a buyer. So, we're leaving over the holiday break. Fresh start, my mom says."

"Do you have family here?"

"Nah. My mom moved here when Casey was just a baby with Casey's father, who she'd met when he was in the military. They couldn't make it work, so he packed up and left and she stayed. She has nobody here. She met my dad a few years later when he was working as a freelance accountant. They got married and stayed. I showed up a couple of years after that."

"Damn, well, I'll miss you. You're a good kid, Aidan, just don't get sucked into the abyss. Wait, let me give you my address. I want to know how things are going in your life."

She scribbled her address on a napkin. "By the way, what is your last name?"

"Osher."

She made a mental note. Casey's had been Duncan; she remembered from the funeral. Aidan stood up, then reached into his pocket.

"Oh, hey, I thought you might want this." He pulled out a strand of dark wooden beads. "They were Casey's. I came across them hanging on his mirror when we were packing his room. Some kind of prayer beads."

He stuck them out towards her, and Sam took them appreciatively. They were warm and the beads had a good weight in her hands. Each bead was hand-carved with a symbol on them. She wiped a tear away, which was threatening to roll down her cheek.

"Thank you, Aidan. You don't know how much this means to me. I'll cherish them."

"Sam, thanks. I'm glad to have met you at least, despite the circumstances. I'd better go before my mother sends out the police."

She watched him walk to the door and he gave her a quick wave. She hoped he'd find a new life and a second chance by leaving. Staying here would be almost certain disaster. She walked to the door, watching him head towards the lot. He got on his bike and rode away. Turning, she caught a glimpse of Smitty watching Aidan as well, as he was leaving the stand. He waited for Aidan to leave before heading to the parking lot.

Sam saw him passing the restaurant and went out after him, anger flaring up about what Aidan had said. She ran up behind him and shoved him. He spun around, eyes blazing.

"What the fuck, Sam?"

"You fucking lied to me! You told me you only took ketamine to party every now and then. You were a goddamn addict! You fucking got Casey hooked to pay for your own addiction."

Smitty looked like he'd been punched in the gut.

"It wasn't like that. I-" His words just stopped. His eyes darted around, looking for a place to land.

"Fuck you, Smitty. You're right, it was all your fault," she spit the words out, hoping to hurt him.

She did what she intended. His shoulders dropped and he stared at the pier. The muscles in his jaw clenched, his mouth forming a grim line.

"You don't know anything," he said quietly. "You weren't here. You have no idea what I was going through. You know, Sam, you hold yourself on a pedestal above everyone, but you forget to remember we all go through shit."

Sam stared at him, waiting for him to go on. He didn't. He turned and walked away from her, disappearing down the beach into the dark.

She was shaking when she got back into the restaurant. She finished cleaning up and closing down the bar. The last customer left, so she took her time putting the chairs up and sweeping. She clicked off the music, letting the silence settle her thoughts. She didn't know what to think. Smitty had been one of the kindest people she'd met in the town, but he had a dark side he refused to talk about. He obviously had dealt with addiction but had brushed off the possibility when she'd mentioned it before.

He'd said his parents had moved right after he'd graduated high school. Was that the whole story? He'd said he could've gone with them, but now she was thinking that wasn't the whole truth. He was an only child to older parents. Had they just kicked him out when he graduated, to fend for himself? He never talked about them. Granted she rarely talked about her parents either, but they came up now and then. He *never* talked about them unless asked. His birthday had passed, and they didn't send him anything. He'd been alone.

She tried to piece together the things he'd told her. He was on his own at eighteen, he worked but sold ketamine to cover his habit and other stuff. He didn't have any close friends but hung out with Casey because they grew up together and both liked to get fucked up. But that wasn't all of it, there was more between Casey and him. Smitty was basically homeless, crashing in the lifeguard stand and other places he could find. He didn't talk much about himself, but he seemed to know when Sam needed him most.

The image of Casey letting go of the railing on the pier flashed through her mind. The loneliness coming off him. If he'd been using heavily to deal with his pain, Smitty must have been suffering greatly to take so much ketamine. Enough to stop breathing. More than once too, it wasn't an accident. There are no mistakes. They were both trying to kill themselves, whether unintentionally or intentionally. Casey had succeeded, which only made Smitty feel even more guilty and worthless. Then Aidan at the gas station. Fuck.

Sam locked up the doors, pausing to light a cigarette as everything began to make sense. She didn't see the shadowy figure leaning against the building until he stepped forward. Her eyes adjusted and recognized the tall outline coming towards her.

"Jesus, Smitty! You scared the shit out of me!"

He took the lit cigarette from her hand and took a deep drag. He eyeballed her, nodding his head.

"We need to talk."

Chapter Nineteen

They agreed it was best to go back to Sam's place for privacy and because it was getting very cold, close to freezing. They walked silently to her car. Once inside, Sam pulled the prayer beads out of her bag and hung them on the rearview mirror. They swung back and forth in a semi-circle. Smitty reached up and touched them, running his thumb over one of the beads.

"Casey's?"

"Yeah, Aidan gave them to me tonight to remember Casey. His family is moving to Washington to get away from everything here."

Smitty raised his eyebrows and nodded. "Damn. Probably for the best though."

"It meant a lot for Aidan to give them to me. He is such a good kid. I see a lot of Casey in him. Do you recognize the beads?"

Smitty laughed bitterly. "Yeah, I was actually with him when he got them. He rode with me one day to get a pick up of, well, you know, that shit, from Jacksonville. There was this little hippie shop there, and he wanted to go in and check it out. I didn't want to with that shit in the car, but he was persistent. We went in and it had incense, crystals, metaphysical books, things like that. He was so at home there, as if it was made for him."

Smitty pressed his hand against the cold window glass and sighed. "He found these prayer beads and was so excited. He offered to buy me a set too, but I laughed and blew him off. He wore them sometimes but was always afraid he'd lose them. They hung on his mirror in his room if I remember. I wish now I'd let him buy me a pair. I was just so fucking caught up in my own shit all of the time. Casey, he was spiritual, though. Not like religious but connected to other worlds, you know?"

Sam nodded and started the car. They were both quiet in their own thoughts on the drive to her house. She put on a pot of coffee once they were inside, knowing it was going to be a long night. She had a knot in her stomach, not wanting to hear what he had to say but knowing it was time. Smitty stood by the window, staring out while she made coffee. She clicked on the only lamp in the place, giving a soft glow to the room. She sat on the rocking chair. He stood awkwardly, not sure where to start. Sam cleared her throat.

"So, Aidan told me you started taking ketamine heavily after high school?"

He turned and sighed, shaking his head. "Actually, well before then. But let me backtrack a bit for perspective."

He came and sat on the loveseat, placing his elbows on his knees, leaning slightly forward to make his body fit. He was so tense, she could make out the lines of his muscles through his shirt.

"'I've lived here pretty much my whole life, as long as I can remember. I was a weird kid. Always looking for shit to get into. I had this bizarre need to thrill-seek and would jump bikes over ditches and skateboard off things I probably shouldn't have. I had this drive to feel things intensely. Other kids would chicken out long before I would. I'd get so many injuries, my dad took a hammer to my bike and smashed it into pieces. It didn't stop me. I'd climb to the top of trees just to jump out. I was small for my age, usually one of the smallest kids in the class, so I liked the look the other kids would give me when I'd do something crazy, stupid really. They'd look at me with a mix of admiration and fear. I guess it was my first high." He laughed softly but with a tinge of sadness. He went on.

"So, you know how I told you my dad was the manager at the White Nautilus? He and my mom would go to conferences sometimes for around a week or so. They'd pay this girl who was late teens or early twenties to keep an eye on me and the house. She always had friends over, and when they thought I was in bed they'd party, getting fucked up. I started watching them from my room, intrigued by the shift I'd see. The stern, serious girl who made me dinner would turn into the laughing, stumbling girl who was everybody's friend. I wanted to feel like she seemed to. I always felt alone being an only child and probably scaring off other kids with my antics. She and her friends just seemed so connected when they were high. They'd listen to music and dance without a care. I wanted that. I'd wait until she'd pass out and her friends would either leave or pass out, and I'd sneak in to do what I saw them do. They snorted white stuff off the table, so I did too."

"Jesus," Sam whispered, her mind reeling. "How old were you?"

"The first time, maybe ten or eleven. It was the best thing I'd ever felt. Like the high of jumping out of the trees but without hitting the ground. Just staying in midair. I'd lay in my bed and feel the whole world spinning around me. I loved the feeling."

Sam sat back and stared at him. At ten or eleven she was still hanging out with her friends, playing in the backyard, listening to the radio, and having sleepovers. She was angry at the girl for putting a child at risk, then realized that girl probably didn't have a clue what Smitty was doing. Tucked away in his bed safe and sound.

"She never knew?"

He laughed and shook his head. "No, I guess not. She left her stuff out every night she was there. At first, I'd just sneak in to use it, then I started stealing a little at a time, so I had my own stash. She came around for a couple of years, then I guess my parents thought I was good on my own by the time I was thirteen. I didn't have access for a while and got pretty depressed. I was into surfing and other crazy shit, but nothing came close. Jesus, I used to jump off the end of the pier. I was a good swimmer and would swim back through the pier pilings, just missing them as the waves pushed me through, just to feel the adrenaline. Then one day when I was surfing, I recognized this guy who would always come over and party with the girl when she watched me."

He paused, lost in memory. Sam got up and poured them each a cup of coffee, pulling the rocking chair closer to the table. He took a swallow of coffee and met her eyes for a second, a moment of shame passing over his face.

"Anyway, I approached the guy to ask him if he knew the girl. He said he did and stared at me like I'd stepped off the moon. I was a brazen kid and flat out asked him how I could get that stuff. I didn't even know what it was called. I just described it and how it made me feel. He didn't answer me at first, looked around to see if I was setting him up. When he decided I wasn't, he talked to me like he would anyone else who was looking to score. He told me the shit I'd snorted was ketamine, gave me prices and said he could sell me some. I told him I'd be back and went home to steal money out of a bowl my dad had on top of his dresser. I never took enough for him to notice. So, I suppose that's when I got hooked."

Sam wanted to cry, picturing thirteen-year-old Smitty hooked on ketamine. She took a deep breath and let it out. How do you respond to that? She clutched her coffee cup in her hands to steady them. She had no words. It was all so surreal. Smitty took a sip of his coffee and set the cup gingerly down on the table, more so to steady his own hands.

"Since I'd always been that crazy kid, no one saw me differently. As we got older other kids started getting curious about trying things, and I became their source. I didn't intend to. I just had access. By the time I was eighteen my grades were shit, and I barely graduated. My parents had pretty much given up and who can blame them? I'd no prospects. So, when my dad got a job offer they had stipulations for me to go with them. I had to go to community college and try to get my life on track. I didn't want to. Staying here getting fucked up sounded much better, so I got the job as a lifeguard and stayed when they left."

He stood up and went to the window, staring out into the blackness. He didn't speak for a bit. Sam saw him clenching and releasing his fist, over and over. When he turned around his face was dark and tense. He looked in her direction but was seeing right through her, caught up in the past.

"That's when it got bad. I didn't have anything to hold me back, so I went full force into it. I don't even remember most of that time. It's a blur. The fact that I was supposed to be watching out to save other people is scary as hell. I was always fucked up. Everything I did was on autopilot. That's about the time I reconnected with Casey. I guess I was nineteen. We both surfed and he was about sixteen then. He started hanging out in the same crowd I was in and naturally just started doing shit too. I didn't push it on him, but I didn't stop him either. Honestly, at the time I didn't see a problem with it. Casey was different. He used to connect to some other world. Like it was a way to go back home. I used to obliterate everything. I almost died, more than once."

Sam nodded. "Aidan told me they found you barely breathing on the beach a couple of times?"

"Those were the times they actually found me. Sometimes I'd wake up and not remember anything. It happened a few times a week. I don't know how I survived. I don't know how I kept my job. I guess people kept their mouths shut about it. It worried Casey. We'd get high, and he'd be afraid to leave me alone if I blacked out. He was so damn sensitive. Fuck." He sighed and sat back on the loveseat.

"I think the last time I almost died, and Casey found me, I was like twenty-three. He wanted to bring me to the hospital, but I made him promise not to tell anyone because I didn't want to lose my job. He stayed with me and would scream and shake me if I started slipping away. I pulled through, obviously. After that, it was a wake-up call and I chilled a bit. I still used all of the time, but not so much I blacked out. I stopped using while working, and as time passed it has been a lot less. By the time Casey died, it really was only after work in the evenings and not every night. In the end, I do honestly believe Casey was using more than me."

He stood up to put his cup on the counter. Sam came up to him, wrapping her arms around him tightly. He sighed and put his arms around her. She knew it had been a lot to talk about. He'd probably never told anybody any of this, and the only other one who had known, Casey, was dead. Other people in the town knew some of the fucked-up Smith parts, but it had been a few years and they moved on quickly to new gossip. They also didn't know his struggles with it.

"Smitty, I'm sorry. I have a bad temper and am quick to judge. That was unfair. You were right, I don't know anything or what you went through. It hurts my heart to think about you going through so much. Your parents? Do you talk to them?"

He shook his head. "No, I'm the great disappointment. I think after they left, they got word about me going off the deep end and wrote me off. I mean, justifiably so, I guess."

"No!" Sam replied angrily. "Parents don't get to just write off their kids. You were going through shit. They should've been there for you."

"Yeah, in a perfect world. But people get to do what they want to live their perfect existence, including parents. I didn't fit in with their ideals. The magazine cover, happy family."

"That's not fair! If they didn't want to be a parent to a real person, they shouldn't have had a child." Sam's parents could be distant at times but always checked in on her and supported the decisions she chose. They never made her feel unwanted.

"Sam, it is what it is. It's like when we're little, and they go around the classroom, asking each kid what they want to be when they grow up. Every kid says like an astronaut, doctor, or movie star. No kid says they want to bag groceries or pick up people's garbage. Adults get to hear what they want, parents get to believe that their kid is something special. Kids live the lie for them, then grow to be grocery baggers, garbage men, even drug addicts. Disappointments. Having kids is all fantasy for adults to try and mold little images of themselves, or what they want them to be. No regard to who the kid is, what they are going through, or what the kid wants. It's okay. I've accepted it. It's just me out here."

"No, it's not," Sam insisted.

He stared at her, understanding and hugged her close. "Fuck, I love you," he whispered.

The words resonated through her. No one had ever said it like that, so raw. Her parents did but it was different. Boyfriends did when she was younger, but seemed like a timing thing, not a feeling thing. This was love for her as she was, with no obligation or expectation.

She rested her head against his chest and felt home. "I'm tired, can we just go and lay down for a while?"

Smitty took her hand and they went to the bed. He laid on his side on top of the covers, facing her. She laid next to him and put her legs over his, their knees interlocking. She pushed herself as close to his chest as she could, her hands on her stomach. He put his arm over her. She could feel his heart beating through his chest, which was soothing. She rested her head against his shoulder.

"I love you too," she said easily. Her eyes wouldn't stay open and she drifted off.

But not before she heard him sigh with relief.

Chapter Twenty

The sun woke Sam up. She had not moved from the position she fell asleep in with Smitty. He was still asleep on his side with her tucked under his arm. Her legs were going numb, so she gently eased them off of his and stretched them out. She thought about everything he'd told her hours before and felt a deep sense of shame for being so harsh towards him. He was battling a beast no one could really understand and didn't have anyone on his side. Especially not since Casey died. She was determined to be that someone, and be the friend she'd promised to be.

　　She slipped out of bed and went to the bathroom to brush her teeth. She ran a brush through her hair, peering at herself in the mirror. The sense of not being was getting better, but she needed to be honest with Smitty about it. About everything. He'd bared his soul to her, and she could've judged him or turned away, but she didn't. Now, he needed to know her truths.

He was still sleeping when she climbed back into bed. The sun shining on his face, showing light freckles she'd never really noticed. His eyelashes were golden brown and long. She wanted to brush them with her fingers but thought better of it. She watched his chest rise and fall softly; his ribs too noticeable. His mouth was slightly open, just barely exposing his top teeth. Instinctively, she reached out and ran her finger over his full bottom lip, which was slightly chapped. His eyes squinted open at her, flecks of gold in a sea of brown. He smiled a little and mouthed the word "hey".

That was it. The dam broke and she leaned in to kiss him. His lips were so warm and welcoming, she moaned a little. How had she waited for so long? He put his hand around her back, drawing her close to him. His mouth closed over hers, his tongue grazing her lips. She slid her leg between his and put her hand on the back of his neck, pressing her to him. Electricity shot through her body, and she knew it was time. She pulled back, meeting his eyes. She started to slide her clothes off, as he watched frozen.

"Sam-"

She put one finger to his lips and stared hard at him. Fully unclothed, she laid down next to him. He furrowed his brow. Was she sure? She ran her hand down his side, kissing him again. She was sure. He slipped off his clothes, bringing her in towards him. She glided her hands over his shoulders and down his back. He leaned in, pressing his lips to her shoulder. She couldn't wait any longer and drew him to her. She met his eyes as she allowed him in, her walls crumbling. As they rose to the heights of their joining, Sam knew she didn't have to keep him out anymore.

They laid intertwined for a while afterwards, soaking each other in. Smitty pulled the sheet over them, and they laid face to face on the pillow.

"Damn, I've wanted that for a long time," he whispered. "I've wanted you more than I've ever wanted anything. I mean it, Sam, anything."

Considering what he told her last night, that meant a lot. She smiled and kissed him softly, resting her head on the pillow and closed her eyes. She didn't realize she'd fallen back to sleep until she woke up a couple of hours later, hearing Smitty rooting around in the kitchen. She slipped on her nightgown and went in to see what he was up to. He was standing with the cabinets open, appearing befuddled. He didn't realize she was there, so she watched him silently. He was wearing only his jeans and no shirt. His ribs stuck out and his collarbones were too defined. He still had a muscular build but absolutely no fat. She yawned and sat on a stool.

"Sam?" He turned around. "You really don't cook, do you?"

"No," she replied honestly and laughed.

"Well, I was going to make you breakfast but there is literally nothing in here to cook. You don't even have spices."

"Nope. No, I don't. If it doesn't come in a can, or I can't slap it between two slices of bread, I don't eat it."

"Okay, I'm going to run to the store and grab a couple of things. I'll be right back." He went to the bedroom to grab his shirt and shoes.

He put his arm around her as he passed, giving her a deep kiss on the mouth. She reciprocated and before they knew it, they were back undressing each other in the bedroom. It was a little less gentle this time, more fierce. Afterwards, Sam felt a little sore.

"No more of that until after you eat something," she teased.

He threw his clothes on and grinned. "I'm going. And if you actually had food in your house..."

She threw the pillow at him.

Once he left, she hopped in the shower. As she stood letting the hot water cascade down her body, she thought of how thin he'd become. It truly worried her. Was he not eating? If not, why? He had to have dropped twenty to twenty-five pounds. Was he using? He couldn't be. He'd told her wasn't and she believed him. Or at least she thought she did. Addiction was hard to break, and he'd been using right up until the night at the lifeguard stand, even after Casey had died. Maybe the situation with Aidan had pushed him over the edge. That was when he started losing weight.

By the time she got out of the shower and dressed, he was in the kitchen cooking. He saw her come in and pointed at the pan on the stove.

"See this thing? It's called a frying pan."

"Oh, is it now? Wait, where did that even come from? I don't have one of those."

"I bought it. So, now you do," he answered smartly and went back to cooking, as she admired him from one of the stools.

He moved around the kitchen like a dance, chopping, stirring, tasting. She chewed the side of her thumb before speaking, measuring her words carefully. They'd just rebuilt trust, and she didn't want to say anything which might damage that.

"Smitty, can I ask you something and you won't get offended?"

He looked over at her with raised eyebrows. "Shoot."

"I know you said not to worry, but you *have* lost a lot of weight. Are you, I mean, have you taken anything?"

He leaned back against the counter and chewed his lip thoughtfully. "I can't say it hasn't crossed my mind, but no. I was going to last night when I saw Aidan leaving and you confronted me. I left to go do that, but something stopped me and let me know I needed to let you know the truth. I've wanted to every day since we found Aidan at the gas station, but have fought it off. Probably why I've lost so much weight. The idea of food has made me nauseous and eating seemed pointless. Everything seemed pointless until last night."

Sam was relieved but understood how precarious this all was. Smitty would always be an addict fighting off urges. It had been much of his life, and as she knew, weeks, months, even years could pass and an addict could relapse.

"Okay. I'm sorry for asking. It's just things had gotten so bad, and you told me you hadn't, but that was before finding Aidan fucked up. I just didn't know," she rambled, feeling foolish.

"Sam, if you're going to be with me, get used to asking. Hold me accountable. I don't want to use until I do. I don't know what's going to trigger it. I want my life back but this is in me. Seeing Aidan has made me more determined to deal with it."

He turned back to flip things on the stove. Sam understood what he meant. She wouldn't do him any good if she turned a blind eye and wished for the best. He needed a support system, someone who wouldn't buy into his shit. She came around the counter to put her arms around him. He moved to face her and smiled down at her.

"Food's ready. Unless you want to let it burn?" he teased, tipping his head towards the bedroom.

She pushed him off, laughing. "Deal's a deal. No more of that until you eat."

"Fair enough, I'm famished anyway."

He grabbed plates, scooping pancakes and hashbrowns on them. He cut up an orange, placing a few slices on each plate. They sat at the counter and ate. As promised, he devoured his first helping and went back for seconds.

She washed the dishes as he showered. She was off work that day, so they agreed to take a walk to the pier. He had to stop first at a friend's house to grab a change of clothes. She let a thought turn over in her mind. When he came out of the shower, she caught a glimpse of him and started to feel hot. They had to get out of there before they spent the whole day in bed.

"Hey, Smitty? I was thinking. You were spending a lot of time here anyway, and I need a cook, so why don't you just grab any of your stuff and bring it here?"

He was drying his hair with a towel and peered at her over the half wall separating the bedroom and living room. "Like move in?"

"Yeah, like move in."

He cocked his head and shrugged. "I like the sound of that. You think Rosie and Ansley would be cool with it?"

"Well, they kind of already thought you did," she replied, chuckling.

He'd been there so much except for the previous few weeks, Rosie had already asked if they were living together. Maybe a little too hopefully.

"Oh, well that settles it. Yeah. Tell you what, I'll run over to grab my stuff first, then we can go to the pier?"

"Take my car if you need it."

He looked at her and laughed. "I won't need it."

When he came back later, he wasn't kidding. He had a backpack and another duffle. That was it. Clothes, a toothbrush, another pair of shoes, and a couple of jackets. That was all he owned. And she thought she didn't have much stuff. She cleared a drawer for him, and he was moved in.

"Are you ready to go?" he asked, as he put the last of his stuff in the drawers. "Might want a sweater or something. It's chilly."

Sam walked over to the drawers, pulling one of his hoodies out and slipped it on. "Landlord rights."

He came up to her and kissed her. "What's mine is yours."

"Not much from the two people in the world who own the least," she kidded.

They cut through the side of town and out to the pier. It was a long walk, but Sam was enjoying being with Smitty without all the *will they, won't they* bullshit. She took his hand openly and watched him without fear of being caught.

She'd never actually been up on the pier. It was bigger than she'd imagined and stretched far out into the water. They used to jump off the end? Smitty said when he was really little they held carnivals on the pier, but as time went on they phased out all of that. Now, it was just a place for tourists to take pictures of each other. Luckily, on this day in December, it was cold and they were pretty much alone.

They made it to the end of the pier where there were benches facing the ocean. Sam turned around to look at the shore for perspective. It was so far away. She peered over the railing at the water. She couldn't see how deep it was, and Casey's face floating down away from her popped in her head. She quickly shook it away. Then the memory of Smitty leaning over Aidan in the backseat of her car whispering something, while tears rolled his cheek, came to mind. She glanced over at him. He was staring out across the ocean, his thoughts impossible to read.

"That night, with Aidan. When you were in the back seat with him. What did you say to him?"

Smitty peered at her from the side of his eyes and breathed out. "Truth time, huh? I told him I'd fucked everything up, but that Casey was the closest thing I had to a brother. I promised I'd make things right. I told him I didn't know how since I couldn't bring Casey back, but that I'd somehow fix things."

"How?"

"Sam, I don't know. I haven't gotten that far yet. But somehow I need to pay for my part in all of this."

"You lost Casey too. Isn't that enough?" she asked.

"I don't know. But I honestly don't think so," he answered quietly.

The conversation scared her, so she dropped it. There was something he wasn't saying, and she felt it would open a door she couldn't close if he said it. They were having a nice time and she didn't want it tainted. She also knew she needed to tell him about herself, in order for them to move forward. She took his hand, leading him to the bench.

"Okay, you were honest with me, and I told you that night on the stand that there were things you didn't know about me. I need you to know those things, so I don't end up fucking everything up like I do."

Smitty nodded and they sat on the bench. This would be easier for Sam if she didn't make eye contact.

"I have things I can't really explain or know what it's called. But I end up making really bad decisions because of it. It's been this way since I was a kid. I don't seem to attach to anyone or anything. It's as easy for me to walk away from something, as it is for me to start something new. I don't feel anything. Like I'm not there. Even if I like something at first, the moment it in any way makes me feel vulnerable I just get rid of it."

Smitty watched her, listening, taking it all in. He kept her hand in his, running his finger over the back of her hand in small circles. She told him about Miri and Ty, and how that ended. He didn't flinch. She told him how she drove all night but didn't remember driving. How that happened a lot. She'd just look up and not know where she was or how she got there. How she looked in the mirror and didn't recognize herself sometimes. How she mostly felt like she was watching herself on television from another room. How she'd never been in a committed relationship because as soon as the other person needed something from her, she ran. He was quiet and when she finished, he squeezed her hand.

"Sam, you didn't run from me. No matter how hard it got. It's okay to feel vulnerable. It's okay to be scared. When you're with the right people, you won't feel that way. Do you feel that way with me?"

She had but didn't anymore. She shook her head.

"As far as not feeling connected or feeling outside of yourself. You're feeling the way I wanted to feel, which is why I took drugs. Being inside my skin sucked, it was like having fifty radios playing in my head at the same time. You need to find a way to be in your skin just like I do. To find a place where you feel it's your own. It's going to take time, but I'm here with you. You hold me accountable; I'll hold you accountable. Deal?"

Sam felt years of tension from keeping her secrets ease a little. She'd finally told someone, and they didn't run away screaming. His experiences with addiction and loneliness helped him to understand where she was coming from. She let out a breath she hadn't realized she'd been holding and met his eyes.

"Deal."

Chapter Twenty-One

The holidays came up fast, and the restaurant was busier than it was during summer. Between holiday parties, people on vacation, and kids home from school, Sam was working seven days a week. The town increased the lifeguard hours from the middle of December through the week after New Year's to compensate for the increased foot traffic. Smitty and Sam were only seeing each other on her nightly break, and when they finally climbed into bed well after midnight. They agreed to forgo celebrating outside a string of lights they put in the window and getting each other one gift.

Christmas morning Sam climbed out of bed exhausted. The crowd on Christmas Eve had been rowdy, and they'd needed the police help to escort people out who wanted to continue to party into the early morning hours. She hadn't gotten home until four in the morning because the bar had been trashed and cleanup had taken hours. Fortunately, she and Smitty were both off since Ryan offered to take Christmas day for the overtime, and Natalie closed the restaurant for the day.

Smitty was already up and had coffee on. Sam stumbled over to the pot and poured a cup, rubbing her eyes which were still blurry from lack of sleep. Smitty was sitting on the loveseat, reading the paper with a cup of coffee in hand and smiled at her.

"You could've slept in. I was being quiet, so as not to disturb you." He glanced at her disheveled appearance. "Rough night?"

"You have no idea. It's like at the holidays people get extra drunk because they have to see family. Some guy took his shirt off and was standing on a chair yelling 'I am scrooge' at the top of his lungs, while he swung his shirt around like a lasso. It was fucking exhausting."

She sipped the hot coffee and waited to feel it go all the way down, hoping for an instant energy boost.

"Come here," Smitty said softly. "Let me see you."

She plopped down on the couch next to him and let him pull her in close. He smelled so nice, coffee mixed with his smell, like wood and the ocean. He rubbed her neck with one hand and held her tight with the other. She rested her head against his shoulder, feeling the tension in her neck loosen.

"Merry Christmas, or Happy Holidays, or whatever," he murmured in her ear.

"Whatever, as long as we're here and not at work," Sam mumbled. "Dinner at Rosie's and Ansley's, don't forget."

"I won't. But for now, I have you here all to myself."

She agreed with that sentiment. She'd had enough of people for a long time, even though she needed to work the next day. She got up and went to the bedroom, pulling a package out from under the bed. She walked back in and handed it to him.

"Merry Christmas."

He took the package and turned it over in his hands. He opened the paper to expose a set of professional chef knives with their own carrying case.

"Wow, Sam, these are beautiful."

"Well, I heard you cussing every time you had to chop stuff with my discount store knife."

He laughed heartily. "Yes, singular. Knife. I can't wait to use these. Too bad we have to go somewhere for dinner."

"I'm sure they'll let you bring them and help." She winked at him.

He jumped up and went to the kitchen, reaching up to the top of the cabinet above the fridge and took down a small box. Smart, she couldn't see up there. He came over grinning and handed it to her. It reminded her if he'd been alone on his birthday, he'd likely been alone on holidays too. For eight or nine years. She started to open the box, but he put his hand over hers to stop her.

"So, I got this for you, but I added something."

"Okay?"

She was confused by what he meant. She opened the box to see a silver beaded bracelet with a small spiral seashell dangling from it. She took the bracelet out and ran her finger over the shell.

"The shell. I found it when we went to the state park on my birthday. I put it in my pocket to remember when we were sitting on the beach. You were so pretty, the breeze blowing your hair off your face, and I was buzzing from kissing you. In case, you know, things didn't work out, I wanted to put the shell with the wood you gave me. But since here we are, I drilled a hole in it and attached it to the bracelet."

Sam was truly touched at his thoughtfulness. She handed it to him and put her wrist out for him to clasp it. He kissed her wrist once it was on. Sam blushed and touched his face.

"You know, you don't have to wait for dinner to use those knives," she hinted. "I could eat."

He laughed and gave her a playful shove.

"Alright, alright. Let me whip something up." He stood up and headed to their tiny kitchen.

Sam watched him dig through the fridge and noticed he'd put on a few pounds. He was still too thin, but he was clearly eating again. She got up and came around the side of the counter he was on. She put her arm around his waist. He smiled, turning his head to her. She reached up and kissed him long and slow.

"I'm glad you're here." She didn't mean just in their home.

He didn't miss her reference and nodded, tucking a stray hair behind her ear. "Me too. I would've hated to have missed all of this."

She left him to cook to get changed. She went to the bathroom to brush her hair and stared at herself in the mirror. She touched her face and it made sense, her finger touching her face reflecting in the mirror. She gave herself a little wave, feeling silly seeing herself waving back. Okay, so that was something, right?

She clicked on the radio as she came back into the kitchen. An upbeat Tejano song was playing. Smitty bopped his head along to the music. Sam resisted the urge to dance along to the music but decided to just let go and started dancing around the room. Smitty saw her and grinned. He came over, putting his hands on her hips, and they swayed to the music. The food on the stove started to sizzle, so he went to tend it, giving her a quick kiss on top of her head. Sam kept dancing, letting the music move her. It faded off and she laughed, sitting on the stool. Smitty was using his knives, cutting peppers and onions rapidly, as he threw in the hot pan. Sam didn't mind just sitting and watching, but she didn't want him doing everything.

"Do you want my help?" she offered.

"God, no," he said, never turning.

"Hey!" She rested her chin on her palms and pouted.

"Sam, what's cumin?"

She had no clue. Was it a vegetable? As she racked her brain to try to think what it was, biting her lip in concentration, he turned around to see what her response was and started cracking up.

"Sorry, that was too funny. Cumin. It's a spice. You looked like you might hurt yourself there, trying to figure it out." He was still laughing. "You really want to help?"

"No. Not now, I don't. Okay, I never did. Besides, my view from here is nice."

He winked at her and turned back to cooking. Once the food was done, he presented it to her like a waiter. "Breakfast burritos."

"What makes them different from regular burritos?" Sam asked, peering at the stuffed delight on the plate in front of her.

Smitty came around and sat beside her, sliding the salsa in her direction. "We're eating them for breakfast. Well, that, and I added potatoes."

Sam couldn't even finish half of hers; it was so big. Smitty ate all of his, so she offered the rest of hers to him. He gladly took it and ate that too. He was definitely eating again. After breakfast, they sat and talked, listening to music until early afternoon. Sam was starting to feel sleepy and decided if she was going to be able to stay up to go to Rosie's and Ansley's, she'd need to grab a nap.

"Hey, I'm beat and am going to lay down. I don't want to leave you alone though."

"Sam, no get some rest. Today has been perfect. Well, almost perfect."

She picked her head up from the couch and glanced at him. As soon as she met his eyes she knew. She grabbed his hand. "Alright, come on. But seriously, after that, I have to sleep."

He got up and practically dragged her to the bedroom, pulling off his clothes as they went. She laughed and happily climbed into bed with him.

When she woke up later, the sun was starting to get lower in the sky. Shit, what time was it? She got out of bed and looked at the clock. They were due over next door in forty minutes. Smitty was nowhere around. She found the most festive outfit she had, which wasn't much. A red peasant top, a black flowing knee-length skirt with little red roses embroidered on it, and black boots. She was just finishing getting dressed when Smitty came in. He was already dressed in a sage green, button-down shirt, and dark blue jeans. They stared at each other and both felt the spark. She shook her head, pointing at the clock. He laughed and nodded.

They made their way down to Rosie's and Ansley's house and went right in at Ansley's request. Rosie's dad was over as well and was sitting in an armchair in the corner, looking at a photography book. He glanced up with a friendly expression, his eyes widening with surprise when he saw Smitty.

"Smith?" He stood up and put his hand out.

"Mr Michaels! Hey, how are you?" Smitty took his hand and shook it.

Smitty turned to Sam. "This is Mr Michaels. He was my fifth-grade teacher. This is Sam, my girlfriend."

"And my Dad," Rosie chimed in, as she brought hors-d'oeuvres to the coffee table.

"Nice to meet you." Sam shook his hand.

"Smith, how are you doing? I try to keep tabs on my former students and well...well, how are you?" Rosie's dad flushed, obviously trying to not bring up Smitty's drug use.

"I'm okay, Mr Michaels. Better. I'm sure you've heard a lot of things about me, but I'm doing okay."

Mr Michaels nodded his head and eyed Smitty, not seeming completely convinced. He sat back down in the chair, crossing his legs. "Good to hear. You were a smart kid."

Ansley stepped into the room and gave a knowing look. "Did I hear you say girlfriend?"

Smitty's ears turned red and he laughed, as he was shoving a stuffed mushroom into his mouth.

"You know, you could've shaved off months if you'd just listened to me," Ansley joked while pointing her finger at them.

"It's all on me," Sam confessed. "I was delusional."

"Oh, I know. Anyone could see that boy was carrying a torch for you," Ansley chided.

"Carrying a torch? Ansley, who even says that anymore?" Rosie called out from the kitchen.

"I do," Ansley whispered, as she leaned down to give each of them a hug. "I knew it."

Ansley left to help Rosie, and Rosie's dad excused himself for some fresh air, leaving the two of them alone. Sam reached out and touched Smitty's ear, which was still hot to the touch.

"That true? Were you carrying a torch for me?" she teased.

"For fucking ever." He grabbed her and kissed her hard on the mouth, sending waves of desire through her.

They were called into dinner shortly after, and the table set was stunning. The amount of food could have fed twenty, not just the five of them. They ate until they were stuffed, and the food still seemed hardly touched. They were sipping on coffee after dinner when Rosie stood up and clinked her glass. All eyes turned to her.

"So, Ansley's art gallery opening was a big hit! A gallery owner from New York came through on vacation and has asked Ansley to do a show there, to leave some of her work permanently on display after. Not to mention, her art is flying off the walls at the gallery here. Because of this, we've decided to officially submit to be foster parents!"

The table erupted in cheers and congratulations.

"How soon could that happen?" Smitty asked.

"Well, since we're open to siblings, older children, and special needs, they told us it could be anywhere from a few weeks to a few months once the paperwork is finalized," Ansley explained.

Rosie's dad got up and hugged Rosie, his eyes filled with tears. They embraced tightly, Rosie pulling back to look at his face tenderly.

"Stop, Dad, you're going to make me cry," she said, wiping tears from her eyes.

He hugged Ansley too and placed his hand on the side of her cheek. Before long everyone was a little teary. Their home was made for children, and whoever got them as parents were going to be well-loved children.

As the evening wore down, Smitty and Sam took their leave. Rosie's dad stopped Smitty at the door and he shook his hand again, giving him a kind but firm look. Like Rosie, he wanted to know the kids he'd taken under his wing were not struggling. Smitty nodded in response. He was okay. Watching them, Sam realized just about the time Smitty was getting addicted was when Mr Michaels was his teacher.

The conversation from the evening had left her with unanswered questions she wanted to get off her mind. They got to the top of the stairs, and she paused to gaze up at the night sky. It was crisp and clear, the stars twinkling in the dark expanse. She took his hand, rubbing her fingers over his knuckles.

"Do you think you'll want children one day?" she asked, her words guarded.

Smitty didn't answer right away and when he did his voice was low. "I don't think so. My childhood wasn't great. I'm barely getting by as an adult. I don't think the idea of bringing another child into the world is such a good thing. Especially not for me and the obvious reasons. How about you?"

"No. I think I've always known it wasn't right for me. When other kids were playing with dolls, they were the mothers, and I was the aunt. My brother has kids and while I like seeing them, I don't feel any maternal instincts when I'm around them. I just want a life where I'm loved, love someone, and am still happy getting out of bed. I care about kids' welfare, but to be honest until they are like teenagers, I just feel like they are fragile and breakable. And loud."

Smitty chuckled. "What about dogs?"

Sam watched him in the moonlight and knew he alone was enough for her. She'd never even expected to find this. She opened the door and pulled him inside. She wrapped her arms around him, sliding her hand under his shirt.

"What about them?"

Chapter Twenty-Two

Winter at the beach after the holidays was dead. The beach and pier were empty most of the time. The town laid off the lifeguards until March, and the restaurant was only open Thursday through Sunday. Smitty took on some day labor work to fill the time and cover things. It gave them a lot more time together but also made the days seem longer. Smitty focused on learning more recipes, perfecting others to fill the time.

One evening after he'd made Korean Bibimbap for dinner, it piqued Sam's curiosity how someone who had been basically living on the streets was such an amazing chef.

"Who taught you how to cook?" she asked.

They'd moved out to the porch to stargaze. She sat at the little table with a cup of tea. Smitty was sitting on the floor of the porch with his back against the rails, his legs stretched out across the stair opening, smoking a cigarette. He took a drag and stubbed the cigarette out.

"Me."

Okay, now Sam had to know.

"What do you mean? When?"

"So, as I told you, my parents would go to conferences a lot. They'd leave me with frozen pizzas and money to get myself microwave meals. Basically, I was eating like you." He winked at her, wrinkling his nose.

"I hated it. That food is disgusting. Inedible. Sometimes when they were home, we'd go to restaurants in other towns but unlike other kids, I'd order the most unique item on the menu. If it had an ingredient I didn't know, I'd have to try it. It was never enough, I wanted more. I started using the money they left to buy my own ingredients. I checked cookbooks out of the library and tried every recipe I could find. Miriam, the library lady, would get in cookbooks from other libraries for me. I tested out recipes from other cultures and convinced my mother to let me buy different spices. They didn't care for what I made, being pretty meat and potatoes people. Sometimes my dad gave me a hard time about wanting to cook, but since it kept me out of his hair and out of trouble, he let it slide."

"Damn, that is utterly impressive." Sam meant it. She couldn't think of a time she'd actually even used a recipe. "Have you ever thought of being a chef? Like a real one, not a fry cook?"

He nodded, then shrugged. "No car. The places I'd want to cook at are towns over, and I didn't have a way to get there. And I'd never be a fry cook. That food is only one step above the canned shit you ate."

"What about now? You can drop me off and use the car. I don't need it. In a pinch, I could always walk to work."

He eyed her, thinking it over. "Maybe. I need to take care of some things first, figure some things out. But I'll look into it. In the meantime, I'll just have to cook for you."

"Please! It's like fine dining every night. I don't think I'd ever be able to eat canned ravioli ever again."

"Let's hope not. That's like playdough immersed in slimy red goo." He pinched his nose in disgust, imagining it.

Sam pictured Smitty as a teenager, pouring over cookbooks and buying fancy spices. It countered the image of him taking ketamine and getting fucked up. He was an enigma. She'd spent her life staying in the middle of the road, and he'd spent his life searching for paths off of it. She moved to sit next to him on the porch floor, stealing his warmth. He rested his hand on her thigh and gave her a light kiss on her head. He glanced down at her.

"So, tell me more about you as a kid."

She didn't have much to tell. "I was boring. Traditional family. Parents married, an older brother who was nice to me. I was okay in school. Participated in things enough to keep the school and my parents happy. Brad, my brother, was the real star of the family. His grades were perfect, he excelled at sports, got a scholarship to college. Married, two kids. Honestly, I loved it because he fulfilled everyone's hopes. It took the pressure off me."

"If you could chase your dream, what would it be?"

"Hard question. I was never a kid who had this, like, goal. You know how you said teachers would go around the room and ask kids what they wanted to be? I'd just make something up, so they'd move on. I had nothing. Some kids were so focused on an end goal. I was just getting through day by day. It's always been like that. Everything was just sort of gray all the time."

Smitty rubbed his thumb on her thigh, as he pondered what she'd said. "Maybe you just haven't found the thing that excites you yet."

"Maybe, or maybe I'm just one of those people meant to be a grocery bagger or bartender for life. Maybe not everyone has a thing."

"No, even grocery baggers have aspirations. You just have to find yours."

That sounded like work to Sam. Trying to find something. She'd tried that in college and ended up getting frustrated and quitting. She sighed and shook her head.

Smitty squeezed her leg lightly. "No rush, some people don't figure this out until later in life."

She nodded but somehow it still made her feel like a failure. Rosie was driven to work with children, Ansley had art, Smitty was an amazing cook. Everything she did was mediocre. She could excel at whatever she was shown, but it didn't excite her. Her brain was able to pick up almost anything and repeat it, but never once had she just wanted to learn something out of passion. She had no initiative.

Smitty sensed her frustration and put his arm around her. "Sorry to bring it up, Sam. Don't stress about it. You work hard, you take care of things. You're a beautiful, funny person. One day you'll come across something that will excite you and you'll know. Until then, I'll have to be the only thing that excites you."

She laughed and poked him in the ribs. "Full of yourself, aren't you?"

He drew away from her finger and kissed her gently. "It's true though, isn't it?"

"Yes," she murmured, her face flushing from his kiss.

The next day at work she leaned on the bar and peered around at her co-workers. Were they living their dream, or if not, did they have one on the back burner? Chris was in college for computer science. Jimmy cooked and was in a band. Natalie owned the place and gardened in her free time. Taylor was just focused on guys, pretty typical for her age. But was anyone actually doing what they wanted? She sighed and wiped down the counters.

At the end of life, did most people just do what they had to for the paycheck, and not what they wanted to? That was a depressing thought. She racked her brain to think of anything as a kid she pretended to do. Or anything, in particular, she was drawn to. Nope, she was a boring, flat kid. She didn't sing or play an instrument, she didn't want to be a teacher or a mother, she didn't love animals or plants. Nothing. She couldn't think of anything. It had always been just finishing one task and moving on to the next. Rinse, repeat.

Smitty came by later from his day labor job at a hotel, which was renovating rooms in the down season. The bar was so slow Sam was able to take an actual break, and they sat on the patio to eat. He'd packed leftovers for them to eat, much better than the food from the restaurant. Now that he was cooking for her, she couldn't even stomach the fried fare from work.

"So, how are things going at the hotel?" she asked, taking a bite of the gourmet sandwich he'd made from the leftovers.

"Painting. I fucking hate painting," he replied, showing his paint-splattered hands.

"I'm sorry. But it *is* kind of sexy." She made eyes at him.

"You're so weird," he replied, laughing.

"It's strange seeing the lifeguard stand and not seeing you in it."

"It's strange not being there. Don't take this wrong, but in the previous years I looked forward to the winter months, and the town closing it because it meant nothing interrupted getting fucked up for two months. January and February are usually a blur."

Did he sound wistful? Sam pushed down the knot it made in her stomach. She reached out and touched his hand, concerned. "Smitty-"

He met her eyes. "No, Sam, don't worry. I got this. Just remembering."

"Okay. Talk to me though if you feel like it."

"You know I will. I won't hide things from you." He squeezed her hand and stood up. "Alright, you better get back to work. I'll see you at home?"

His exit seemed abrupt to Sam. Like he couldn't wait to get out of there. These conversations were never going to be easy. She nodded and stood up quietly. There was no magic wand, and she didn't want to feel like a nag. However, they were friends first, she needed him to remember that.

"Smitty, you need to treat me like your friend. You need to tell me the hard stuff and if it's ugly, then it's ugly. I'm not your girlfriend first, I'm your friend first. Don't shut me out, okay?"

He stopped and stared hard at her. His eyes had that old edge to them. He shook his head and twisted his mouth into a smile, which wasn't a smile. He looked away before he answered.

"Fine. I want to use, okay? I absolutely hate working day labor. I think about using all day when I'm there because it's so fucking monotonous. It sucks. It's like this constant pull at me. Life is pretty much flat, except when we're kissing or fucking, and I can't do that all the time. As much as I'd love to. I'm on the edge right now. I can handle it, but it's fucking miserable. Sometimes I want to blow my brains out."

Sam stood frozen by his words. She'd asked for it. She wanted honesty, and it did not come more honest than that. She walked over to him, kissing him as hard as she could. He was holding himself tense as a board and relaxed a little. She pulled back and met his eyes, holding his chin in her fingers.

"Kiss me as much as you need to. Fuck me as much as you want. Smash things, scream, cry, yell. Whatever it takes to get through this. Just don't shut me out."

His eyes softened and he took her hand from his chin, kissing her softly. They stood resting on each other for a moment before he spoke, his voice sounding rough.

"Thanks, Samantha. I needed to hear that. Thanks for forcing that out of me. So, uh, get home as soon as you can, huh?"

She knew what he meant. She smiled slyly. "I will."

He grinned sheepishly and headed towards the parking lot. Sam watched him leave, seeing the police pull in. She peered at the clock inside. That was strange. They never started patrolling this early. They were moving slowly, looking around, and as Smitty hit the parking lot, they stopped and got out. She watched as they approached him and her stomach dropped. They were talking to him about something. She could tell it was serious. He glanced back at her for a second, and panic rose in her. His eyes were scared.

What had Aidan said to her that night in the bar? That eyes were on Smitty? But he hadn't sold or used in months. Her ears started ringing loudly, and everything was moving in slow motion. They talked to him for a while. Maybe it was nothing. Maybe they were talking to him about something else. She went inside and wiped down tables near the windows, so she could keep an eye on what was going on. She thought she saw one of the cops laugh about something and started to regain a little hope.

Smitty turned to motion to the restaurant, and Sam held her breath. The cops shook their heads at whatever he was saying. Smitty glanced back at the restaurant, and Sam thought for a moment their eyes met. He shook his head slightly, his shoulders slumped. He turned back to face the cops, their demeanor had turned much more serious. Sam burst into tears when she saw them loading him into the back of their car.

She heard someone screaming the word "no" and tried to figure out where it was coming from before she realized it was coming out of her own mouth.

Chapter Twenty-Three

Sam bolted out of the restaurant as fast as she could towards the parking lot, trying to get to them, her feet tripping in the sand. She fell to her knees right before getting to the pavement and looked up to see them driving away. Smitty saw her and met her eyes, as he put his hand on the window towards her. Natalie was following close behind Sam, from when she heard the scream in the restaurant and saw what was happening. She came to Sam and grabbed her, helping her up. Sam was crying so hard she could hardly see. But she saw Smitty's eyes, his beautiful golden eyes. All she saw was defeat.

"Come on, honey, you can't do anything at this moment. Let's go inside and figure this out." Natalie had her arm around Sam, guiding her towards the restaurant.

"Natalie, they can't take him! He stopped all of that shit!" Sam bawled.

"Shhh, let's just get inside and go to my office. People in this town don't need any more fodder than they already have."

They went inside, and the few customers in there were staring wide-eyed at Sam. Natalie glared at them and waved them off. They averted their eyes immediately, staring at their food and drinks in front of them. She led Sam to the office and shut the door behind them, handing Sam some tissues.

"Look, Sam, I know this is hard, but you can't change anything right now. Whether or not Smith straightened out, he did things. Illegal things. They're at least going to question him. I take it you've never dealt with that side of the law?"

Sam shook her head. Middle of the road, suburban Sam had never even thought about it. Things like this happened in movies, not to her. She blew her nose and stared up at Natalie with red eyes.

"What's going to happen?"

Natalie sighed and sat back in her chair, making it creak with the weight. She rubbed her chin thoughtfully. "To be honest, I'm not sure. Depends on what information they already have. They obviously know something. Maybe someone talked to them. What they know, who can tell? They could be just trying to find out things, and not know all that much. Does Smith have a lawyer?"

"No. He was pretty much living on the streets until he moved into my place. He doesn't have any money. He doesn't have anything."

"He has you. What about his parents? I remember them from a while back, they seemed well off enough?'

"They won't talk to him, haven't for years."

"Shit." Natalie shifted in her chair, leaning her elbow on the desk. "I guess now would *not* be the best time to try and reconnect, huh?"

It would've been funny if it wasn't so fucked up. Sam laid her head on her arms on the desk. She was all Smitty had, and she wasn't much.

"Fuck, Natalie. What the hell are we going to do?"

Natalie reached forward, placing her hand on Sam's arm. "What you're going to do is wait. Going down there and making a scene won't change anything. They'll likely give him a public defender. You don't have enough information at this point to do anything else. Wait for his call."

Sam sat up and nodded. Natalie was right. She was the last person to be any help to Smitty. She wiped her nose and brushed the hair out of her face. She'd never felt so small, so helpless. Natalie leaned forward, her eyes serious but kind.

"I've dealt with the law. I won't get into details, but things will play themselves out. He isn't innocent, you know that. But I can see the change in him. Anyone that knew Smith from before to now, can see he's fighting his demons. That may help. Ultimately, if they have evidence, then he and you will need to prepare for what is coming. If they don't, he may be fine."

Hearing that sent fear through Sam, and she choked back a sob. She didn't know how to prepare for the worst.

Natalie gave her a hard look. "Sam, when you walked through my door the first time, I knew you were a strong woman. You came in here with that knot on your head and a black eye, then conned your way into the job. Yeah, I knew. You may just be the best person to have his back right now. Why don't you head out and stay by your phone? I can close up."

    Sam stood up, feeling wobbly and disoriented. She tried to smile at Natalie, but her lips wouldn't move. She bobbed her head and went to the bathroom. The flickering lights made her feel like she was outside of her body, and she leaned against the wall. Not now. She splashed water on her face and blew her nose again. Her brain settled enough to leave. She held her head high while she walked past the bar and through the dining room, knowing all eyes were on her. Fuck them.

    She didn't drive straight home because she knew once she was there she was going to pace like a caged rat. She drove around the town, attempting to keep her mind busy. After a few rounds, she knew she couldn't put it off any longer and drove home, praying Rosie and Ansley wouldn't see her. Their home was quiet. only Rosie's car was in the drive. She reluctantly climbed the stairs, stopping on the porch to smoke a cigarette.

    Once inside, she checked her phone but there were no missed calls. Anxiety made her jittery and she couldn't sit still, checking her phone every ten minutes. Nothing. What was going on at the police station? Were they questioning him? Was he just sitting in a cell? It was evening, so it didn't seem likely they'd get him a lawyer until the morning. She bit all of her nails down to the quick and started on the skin around her thumbs until they bled.

    She showered and put on pajamas, knowing she wasn't sleeping that night. She smoked cigarette after cigarette on the porch and continually checked her phone. Nothing. She put on a pot of coffee and watched out the window, hoping he'd just come home. The street remained dark and empty. Wanting to feel close to him, she climbed into bed and held his pillow against her chest.

It smelled like him, which only made things worse. Still, she heard no word.

After three cups of coffee, her anxiety was through the roof. She felt like screaming but didn't want to scare Rosie and Ansley. She screamed into her pillow until she was hoarse. Why was he not calling? She put on the television for background noise, but everything just made her angry and she cut it off. She dozed off on the couch before dawn and woke up with a pounding headache.

Her phone still showed no missed calls, no messages. She thought about getting dressed and going down to the police station but thought about what Natalie said. It wouldn't help. She couldn't stay in the house, so she put on her sneakers and ran to the pier. It was early, and she was the only one in sight. She ran to the end and back a few times. She checked her phone. Nothing. She started to feel like she was going to lose her mind and ran back to the end of the pier. She screamed as hard as she could. It disappeared into the wind. She leaned on the rail, sobbing.

She'd come to this town with no ties, no people, nothing that bound her. Just a random town with random people. She'd never planned to stay so long and had set it so she could leave whenever. Now, she was attached in a way she'd never felt before. To a guy she'd only known for around eight months. She thought about Smitty, Casey, and Aidan, wondering how in such a short time she could care about so many people, who would just leave. All her life she'd been the one to move on. It was karmic punishment.

Depleted, she walked slowly back home. The world was waking up, and she didn't want to be around the eyes of the town. She rounded the corner to see him sitting on the steps. She blinked.

He was still there. She got to the bottom of the stairs and stared up. His head was down, and he didn't see her.

"Smitty?"

His head jerked up, his eyes red from lack of sleep, crying, or both. He jumped up and moved fast down the stairs to her, enfolding her in his arms. She melted into him with relief. But something was wrong. He was tense, shaking. She stepped back and peered up at him. Tears ran down his cheeks, and he shook his head at her.

"Smitty, what?" Her voice sounded so small, she didn't recognize it.

"Sam, it's bad. I really fucked up this time."

She began to feel faint and took his hand to lead him up the stairs. When they got inside, he collapsed on the barstool and put his head in his hands on the counter. He smelled like exhaustion and sweat. Sam rested her hand on his back, feeling the stress pouring out of him.

"What did they say? What's happening?"

He didn't answer at first. He wouldn't look up either. Sam started to get truly scared.

"Smitty, please tell me something."

"Sam. They know. They had an informant who gave my name. They stopped me yesterday to tell me as much and said they wanted to question me. I went with them to get it over with."

Sam sat on the stool next to him and took his hand firmly in hers. He squeezed hers in appreciation. But he was there, in their kitchen. He was home. That had to mean something. He took a deep, shuddering breath and continued.

"They assigned me a public defender, but told me if I'd accept the charges they could get me a plea deal."

"What does that mean?" Sam only knew law terms from television, which was usually highly inaccurate.

"It basically means if I confess and say I'm guilty, I can get less time."

Time? Like jail time? Sam started to panic, breathing heavily. Her hands felt cold. Smitty turned and held her tightly. She clung to him, not wanting to let go.

"Hey, hey, calm down. We can get through this," he whispered into her hair.

She thought her head would explode and jerked back away from him off the stool. Her eyes darted all around the room, as she tried to think of what it all meant. This couldn't be happening, there had to be a way around it.

"You said no, right? They can't prove it. It's just someone saying your name. They could be lying." She was bargaining.

"But they aren't," Smitty reasoned.

"So fucking what! Tell them no."

"Sam." He came over to her and reached out.

She pushed away. "Smitty, don't."

"Sam, I did this. I made these choices, it's time to pay for them," he said softly.

"So, you're willing to throw away everything we have for this?" She was crying now.

"Jesus, Samantha, you're the most important person in the world to me. I'd like to believe we aren't throwing everything away. I fucked up. I wish I could go back and make different choices. To save Casey. But I can't. There isn't a way out of this. There is only a way to have less of it."

Sam wasn't ready to relent. There had to be some way. They could pack up and leave. Just drive and disappear. She'd done it so many times before, she knew the ropes. They could do it again.

"Let's leave. I have money. We can just go," she pleaded.

Smitty came over again, taking her hand. She let him, in the hopes he agreed with her. He breathed out deeply and shook his head.

"I can't, Samantha. Please know I love you, and I don't want this. But I have to." Smitty met her eyes, and she could see the truth.

"Just tell them you didn't do it. Tell them they're wrong."

"It's too late, Sam. I already confessed," he said quietly.

A white-hot light shot through her head. The next thing Sam knew, she was tripping down the stairs and running. She didn't know where to but ran until her lungs felt like they'd explode. She needed to get away, to blur her mind. No matter how hard she ran, she couldn't break free this time. It wasn't something she was leaving behind.

This time, it was a part of her.

Chapter Twenty-Four

The lifeguard stand seemed like the empty shell of an abandoned building. Sam stood staring up at it and related. Of course, she'd end up here. It was where it all started, it should be where it all ended. It was locked up inside, so she climbed the ladder and sat on the porch with her feet hanging off. The ocean continued its steady beat against the earth, with no regard for the suffering of the inhabitants. Sam tried to process what had just happened.

Smitty had confessed, which meant he'd get jail time or really prison time. What did this mean for him? For them? How much time? She didn't know anything about any of this. She sighed and rested her chin against the bottom rail. If he confessed, why then was he able to come home? It was all so confusing and big. Massive, like the ocean.

"I thought you might come here." His voice was tired but gentle. "We have to talk, Sam."

"I know."

The run had worn her out and cooled her down for a bit.

Smitty climbed the ladder and sat next to her, both of them watching the waves crash against the shore. Out in the distance, a dolphin was surfacing and diving. Sam wanted that freedom. Bitterly, she considered Smitty probably did too. She glanced at him, and he looked back. How were they going to do this?

"How much time?"

Rip the bandaid off, right?

He blew out his breath, shaking his head. "Public defender says it depends on the plea deal. They're going forward with the fact that I haven't been selling for a few months, haven't used, and have some stability in my life."

"How can they know all of that? Are they taking your word on it?"

"Oh, hell no, they've been watching me for some time. And I took a drug test when they brought me in last night."

So, Aidan was right. They'd been keeping tabs on Smitty for months. Of course, they had. It was a short trail from Casey to Smitty. Sam wondered who the informant was. It could be anyone. Smitty was never careful. He was an addict who was slowly trying to kill himself.

"Why, Smitty? Why couldn't you just deny it?"

"Well, one, they had me dead to rights. If I denied it, went to court, and was found guilty, I could get locked up for a long time. Like years. Two, I did it. I know you don't get it, but this has been eating me alive. Casey was my friend and while I get I didn't kill him, this all started with me. With choices I made."

"Casey was dealing with his own issues. The ketamine wasn't the reason he died." Sam's dream flashed through her mind again, him looking at her and letting go of the rail.

"Don't you think I know that? I know Casey committed suicide," Smitty replied, his voice rough.

She was surprised and stared at him. "How-"

"Sam, he was my only real friend here. We talked. I saw him struggling with the world we live in, with how different he felt. He never talked directly about suicide, but he talked about feeling out of place. We spent seven years getting fucked up together. Things come out. Casey didn't know who he was, who he was supposed to be. He was depressed. Fuck, I guess we both were. But we couldn't help each other, or at least didn't."

He stopped and lit a cigarette. They handed it back and forth, smoking about half of it before either of them spoke. Sam had so many questions, but he needed to lead this.

"I think they knew that too. The police, I mean. His death isn't part of the charges. He had ketamine in his system, yeah, but he had to have climbed over the railing, so he didn't just fall off the pier. I'm being charged with selling, possession, and some other shit. But not Casey's death. But it doesn't mean I didn't have a hand in it. I could've not sold it to him. I could've been a better friend."

"Smitty, two drowning people can't save each other."

"I know that. But one drowning person can tell someone on the beach to stay away. And I didn't. I had him join me in the water. Except *he* drowned and I didn't."

Sam couldn't dispute this. Not everything was black and white. Smitty was a kid at the time, who'd made really bad decisions for himself and opened the door for others. But he wasn't malicious or trying to hurt anyone. They were teenagers. Casey would probably have found another source had it not been Smitty. Or was she just trying to reason this away?

"The night with Aidan. That was the lit match." Smitty picked at the wood on the railing as he went on. "I'd been trying to convince myself I wasn't at fault, that I wasn't a bad person and almost believed it until we saw Aidan. He was around the age Casey was when Casey started coming around and getting fucked up. Maybe a little younger, but not by much. When I saw him behind the gas station, high out of his mind, it all came crashing down. Then he told me he knew I'd sold Casey the ketamine, and I knew I couldn't run from this. I sat with him that night, all I could see was Casey as a teen. How everything from the point he started coming around, spiraled down until he died. I didn't want that to happen to Aidan too, and I knew I had to be accountable somehow."

"Aidan got out though."

"Hopefully, he left but it doesn't mean he got out."

"I talked to him, he's not Casey. He regrets that night and seems determined to move past it." Sam believed this.

Aidan was young, but wise, and saw what it did to Casey. He'd watched from the outside as it destroyed his brother's life.

Smitty nodded, not convinced. "I sure hope so."

It was warm for a winter day, and people were starting to walk the beach. Sam didn't want any more attention than they'd already had.

"Can we move inside? I feel like people are watching us."
They weren't, but Sam felt it anyway.

Smitty stood up, lit another cigarette, and grabbed a key
from the top of the doorframe. He opened the door, letting it air
out for a moment while he finished the cigarette. He put his hand
down to her and helped her up. Her legs were sore and stiff from
running, then sitting. They went inside, pushing the flotation
devices aside. It was musty but at least private. Sam sat on the floor
to let her legs stretch out. Smitty sat across from her, one of his legs
stretched out towards her, the other pulled up with his arm around
it. He stared at her until she felt self-conscious and she looked
down.

"You're so beautiful, Samantha. I'm sorry. I'm sorry you
met me, and I dragged you into all of this."

She glanced up and met his eyes. Pools of amber. She
didn't know what to say. She was glad she'd met him, but now this
was going to hurt more than anything. She nodded, drawing her
knees to her chest, her arms clutched around them. He moved over
and put his knees around hers, wrapping his arms around her like a
cocoon. She fought back tears. She needed to be strong to get
through this. She rested her head against his shoulder, as he rubbed
his hand up and down her back.

"How were you able to do it? To confess? I would've been
so scared," Sam whispered.

"I was fucking terrified. But it's like surfing, you just need
to focus on the way you need to go, even if it's daunting. You look
down the wave and when you need to go down it, you turn your
head and your body follows. I knew I needed to confess and own
this, so I turned my head and my body followed, so to speak."

"What if you hadn't?"

"Sam, despite the charges, had I not confessed I would've ended up killing myself."

His words were so honest and raw, Sam stared into his face. He would have. Either by using again or just ending it. She placed her hand on the side of his face, as tears slipped down her cheeks. He wiped them away with this thumb, cupping her face in his palm. He leaned in and kissed her gently, the salt of her tears on their lips. When he pulled back, tears were in his eyes.

"I never wanted to put you through this. Had I known you'd eventually come into my life...I don't know. I would've had something to live for. To be driven by. I was just trying to get through each day, and now I look forward to waking up with you every day." His words were pained and regretful.

Sam needed to ask the hardest question of all and built up the courage to ask it. "What happens next?"

Smitty met her eyes, this was going to be hard. "Part of the deal with confessing is I got twenty-four hours to get my affairs in order. I have to be back at the police station tomorrow morning to go before a judge for sentencing. I only have today and tonight."

Sam wanted to scream but bit it back.

"When will I see you again?" Her voice was shaky and fearful.

Smitty shook his head and grasped her hand tightly, more to steady himself. "They are saying even with the plea deal, I'm looking at probably at least six months in prison, maybe more."

Sam stared at him, her eyes big and wide. At least six months? She'd only known him a little longer than that. He brushed her hair out of her face and sighed.

"I know. I can't ask you to wait around for me, it's not fair. But I'm asking you to come home with me and spend the next however many hours we have left together. I just want to hold you and be in our place."

"Okay," Sam whispered.

They were silent on the way home, holding hands as if they were walking the plank. Sam's mind was numb. This was a nightmare she'd wake up from. Except it wasn't. She had less than twenty-four hours with the man she loved, then he was just gone. She was going to lose her mind. She couldn't bargain or deny anymore. He was doing this to save his own life.

The apartment was solemn when they got inside. They stood in the middle of the living space, not sure what to do next. What had been so familiar, was now foreign. Smitty turned to face her.

"Are you hungry?"

She shook her head. She was, but the idea of having to chew and swallow food was nauseating. He nodded and led her by the hand to the bedroom.

"We're both exhausted, let's just lay for a bit."

They climbed on top of the covers, holding each other closely. This was it. They both knew it and tried to absorb as much of each as they could. They ran their hands over each other's bodies and kissed over and over. It was like drinking water from a well in the desert. They couldn't get enough. Sam ran her fingers over his lips, attempting to make her fingers remember how they felt. Smitty traced her cheekbone with his thumb. They took off one another's clothes and made love slowly, trying to make it last. When they were done, she laid down on his bare chest and listened to his heartbeat. No matter how they tried to stop it, time flew by.

The sun started to dip in the sky and the familiar panic welled up in Sam. How could she stop time?

"Smitty, I can't do this. I can't watch you leave me." She sounded like a scared little girl.

"I'm not leaving you. I'm not, I promise. I *will* come back to you. Sam, I'm scared too."

Of course, he was, she reminded herself. He was the one going to prison. She had to be here without him, he was stepping into a world he didn't know. A world where survival wasn't guaranteed. She needed to stop being so selfish. She couldn't fathom what he was going through. Not only was he losing her, but he was losing everything. She rolled over, pressing her chest to his.

"I'm sorry. I'm scared for you. You're kind and sweet, you don't deserve this. I'm being selfish," she replied softly.

He pulled her to his mouth, holding her lips for a moment before letting go. "Be selfish, be angry. I *do* deserve this. I spent most of my life only thinking about myself and what I wanted, how I felt. This is my penance. My regret is that I dragged you down with me. You don't deserve this. I do. I don't deserve you."

Sam met his eyes and an urgency to not let him go filled her. She kissed him deeply and ran her hands down his body. It was dark out, time was slipping away. They took each other with such a sense of urgency, it was like they were trapped in a dance of love and rage. Pain and pleasure. As he released into her she clung to him, knowing she couldn't hold on. Sweaty and spent they fell back, breathing hard. Smitty turned on his side and pulled her close, kissing her breast.

"I don't deserve you, but you are mine," he murmured, his lips grazing her skin.

She ran her fingers through his hair, which was damp from exerting energy. She was his, and he was hers. Her penance for all the people she hurt was losing him. She started to cry. Smitty moved up, wrapping his body around hers. She turned in towards him and sobbed, her tears making his chest wet. He tucked her head under his chin and ran his fingers down her back.

"I'm sorry." He repeated it over and over softly, rubbing her back until she had no tears left to cry, and she fell asleep exhausted.

In the morning he was gone.

Chapter Twenty-Five

There was a note on the counter, next to the twisted knot of wood Sam had given Smitty for his birthday. She saw her name scrawled on the paper, and it was neatly folded in half. She couldn't face what was inside and put on a pot of coffee. She felt empty, broken, not ready to open the wounds. She drank a cup of coffee and slipped on her sneakers. Running at least required her energy, if not her mind. She went down the stairs, the cold air hitting her lungs. She ran through town, keeping her eyes forward and tried not to picture what was going on with Smitty. He was going before the judge for sentencing this morning, then what she didn't know. It was a done deal; it was the amount of time he'd receive, she didn't know about. She hoped he'd be allowed to call and let her know something.

She reached the end of the strand and turned around to run back, deciding to cut down to the beach on the way home. The beach was fairly empty, and seagulls took flight in front of her as she ran towards them. Her legs were burning, but her mind pushed her on. By the time she got to the access point to cut back towards home, her legs felt like they might give out. She slowed down and jogged at a lighter pace the rest of the way. She coughed when she got to the top of the stairs, cigarettes taking their toll.

After showering and dressing, trying to avoid staying in one place for too long, she checked her phone. There were no messages or calls but it was only pushing noon. Just as she set the phone back down it rang from an unknown number. She never answered unknown calls, but her gut told her to pick it up. She answered and the other line crackled.

"Sam! I'm glad you picked up." Smitty's voice sounded stressed. "I don't have much time, they limit calls."

"Hey." It was all she could get out.

"Hey, I'm sorry I didn't say goodbye. You were sleeping and I knew it would just fucking suck."

"It's okay. I miss you."

"Damn, I miss you too. Did you find my letter?"

"Yeah, but I couldn't read it yet. I wasn't ready." She sounded apologetic.

"No, read it when you're ready and hold onto my birthday gift okay? I want it safe for when I get out. Uh, so, I went in front of the judge and pleaded guilty to accept the plea deal. Shit, they are motioning me to wrap up. Sam, please listen to me, this is important."

"I'm listening," she replied, her words just above a whisper.

"I got eight months. I know we were hoping for less. I can shave off some for good behavior according to my lawyer, but he couldn't tell me how much. They're moving me to a correctional facility upstate tomorrow," he was talking fast, trying to get it all in before they cut him off.

"Smitty, this fucking sucks. Eight months? I've only known you that long."

"I know, Samantha. Damnit, my time is up. I have to go. I love you. I really, really love you." Voices were in the background, telling him to end the call.

"I love you too, Smitty."

"I'll send you information, like where I am and an address, as soon as I can. Sam, you're everything to me."

With that, the phone line went dead.

She sat at the stool, her mind reeling. Eight months, upstate. She wouldn't see him again for eight months. She didn't belong here, and now she was here without the only reason she had to stay. She opened his letter.

Samantha,

Something I never told you.

The morning you were in the parking lot, the morning we met, I saw you pull in. I was sleeping in the lifeguard stand and saw headlights. I looked out and saw your car parking. You got out for a minute and stared at the ocean. You were so beautiful, your hair blowing off your face. You seemed so lost, and I wanted to go to talk to you but thought that might freak you out. You got back in your car, so I stayed awake to keep an eye out to make sure no one messed with you. I let you sleep for a while, but then it was getting busy and hot, and I didn't want you to overheat. I knew Ryan was coming on duty and didn't want him to get to you before I could. I wanted to meet you.

Every day I wanted to talk to you. To get to know you better. You were so closed off, and I knew if I tried anything you'd run. I kept my distance, so when Casey came to me talking about you, I knew I might have missed my chance. He also had a thing for you. You two seemed to hit it off and I didn't want to step in. I didn't know how you felt about any of it because you never showed anything.

After Casey died wasn't the right time either. You needed a friend more than anything. Hell, I did too. When I opened up to you and you stood by me, you became my best friend. I didn't want a day to pass without talking to you, you made it easy. You listened so kindly. I fought off wanting more, seeing that you were afraid to let it go any further. But I wanted you so badly.

Then the night with Aidan. It brought up everything with Casey and the person I'd been. I was so ashamed. I couldn't sleep. I couldn't eat. I seriously thought about killing myself but held on to our friendship. Then I saw Aidan talking to you and thought all was lost. When you confronted me, I was going to get so fucked up I'd stop breathing. But I love you, and I had to tell you everything in the hopes you wouldn't leave me. That you'd see I never meant anyone harm. Not Casey, not Aidan and not you.

It was the hardest thing I've ever done up until leaving you this morning. But for me to put that part of me in the past, I have to pay for what I did. I knew that the night we took Aidan home and he lashed out at me. I know you know all of this, but I had to put it down on paper to get it out of me. As part of coming clean.

I don't expect you to forgive me, or stay with me. I want you to. But I know you run when things get tough and this is as tough as it gets. We already lost Casey, and now I put you in the position to not have me. I own that. I release you if you want to go. It will kill me, but I deserve what I get. I'll write to you when I can. I won't call because I don't want to put you on the spot, as much as I'll want to hear your voice.

I love you, my Sam. You changed my life for the better.

Love,

Smitty

She set the letter down and ran her fingers over his name. She didn't know what she'd do. Everything had happened so fast; she was still just dealing with the moment. She couldn't foretell the future. She loved him, but eight months was a long time. What would she do for eight months? She opened the letter and read it again.

Casey had a thing for her? That was news to her. With all of the pretty, young beach girls making eyes at him, she'd never thought of them as more than friends. While she was four years older than Smitty, she was seven years older than Casey and the thought hadn't crossed her mind. She'd found him attractive but had seen him more like a little brother. She was protective over him and enjoyed his company.

However, she truly loved Smitty. She'd cared about him fairly early on, but it wasn't until after Casey died, she'd even considered being more than friends. Now, she couldn't imagine life without him. She'd gone from being a loner to finding a part of her in him. Eight months could certainly change that, but she couldn't think about it. She called Natalie to let her know what was going on.

Natalie sighed, hoping for better news. "I'm sorry, Sam. That's a long bit. Look, take as much time off as you need. It's slow and I can handle it. Is Smith okay?"

"I really don't know. They rushed him off the phone. I only got that info."

"Yeah, they'll do that, fucking jail. I'm here for you if you need me. To talk, vent, whatever."

"Thanks, Natalie. I appreciate it. I'll call you when I'm ready to come back. It'll be just a few days. I can't be sitting around with nothing to do."

They hung up and Sam went to lay in bed. She put her hand on Smitty's side, almost expecting it to still be warm. It was cold to the touch. She pulled her hand back and stared at the ceiling, replaying events over and over but getting nowhere. No matter what, they were where they were. There was no going back. She got out of bed and went to the kitchen. She saw Ansley and Rosie outside and decided it was best to tell them herself before town gossip made its rounds. They waved when they saw her, then saw the look on her face.

"Sam, are you okay?" Ansley came over, her eyes filled with concern.

"No. Smitty's been arrested. He'd been selling ketamine, he stopped but it didn't matter," Sam explained. "He pleaded guilty; they gave him eight months."

A look passed between Rosie and Ansley. They knew about him selling and using. The whole town did. Rosie came around and hugged Sam tightly. "I'm so sorry. I know that must have come as a shock."

It had; Sam realized.

While the rest of the town had known, she'd had her head in the sand. She'd hoped by him deciding to stop, it would all go away. But that's not how things worked. People went to jail all of the time for things they regretted. Jails were full of good people who'd made bad decisions. Sure, there were people there who had no regrets and would repeat similar crimes over, but there was no separation based on this.

Ansley touched her shoulder. "We're here for you. I know that doesn't mean much right now, but if you need a shoulder to lean on, you have four here."

While she appreciated their gesture, it wasn't their shoulders she wanted to lean on. She'd rolled the dice and lost. She went back to her place and sat at the stools. No one was cooking dinner tonight. There'd be no laughter or intimacy. It was just her now, she needed to get used to the idea. She drank cold coffee and read his letter again.

What was he doing right now? He didn't have a letter from her to read. He'd been cut off while they were talking before she could tell him how much he meant to her. Tomorrow he was going to yet another facility where the people there were deemed guilty, whether or not they were.

She worried for his safety. She worried for his sanity. She worried for her own. Smitty had so much potential, which was now on hold if not destroyed. Prison could change him. He could come out bitter and disillusioned. He might not want to cook, surf, or do anything after serving time. The funny, sensitive guy that left her this morning, might be gone for good.

The thought turned her stomach.

The system wasn't meant for rehabilitation. It was meant to punish only, no matter the outcome. He might come out worse.

She could wait for eight months and not even know the person who came back. It was too much to think about, her brain was capped out. She laid in their bed with her hand on his pillow, trying to send him love until she fell asleep alone.

Chapter Twenty-Six

If anyone in the town had their doors open to Smitty, by the time the news traveled through about his arrest, they'd been firmly slammed shut. They'd been kinder to Casey's memory. After all, Casey was just a junkie to them, Smith was a seedy drug dealer. The lowest of low. They didn't even really gossip, just spit at the mention of his name. There were no kind memories, no admission of connection. It was as if he'd never existed outside of this fact.

Fortunately, word also spread that Sam was his girlfriend, so people shut up when she came by. She did get more than her fair share of stink eye, but as long as they didn't talk trash about Smitty, she didn't need to confront it. If they had, she would've pointed out that the drug problem still existed in the town, and their own kids were falling prey to it while they were busy talking shit.

A couple of weeks after Smitty left, a letter came in the mail for him. It was addressed to Smith Sinclair. Damn, his parents were pretentious. It sounded like he should've been wearing a little British school uniform. From birth, they were creating an image of their child he couldn't or didn't want to live up to. Smitty Sinclair at least sounded more down to earth. She opened it, knowing he wouldn't be able to. It was a termination letter from the town about his lifeguard position.

Due to recent circumstances coming to light, we have no choice but to terminate you effective immediately. Please turn in any uniform pieces and keys you have in your possession. You are further banned from setting foot on any lifeguard property indefinitely.

She ripped it up and threw it away. Obviously, due to recent circumstances, he wasn't around to turn that shit in. It was all so tiresome. Instead of looking inward and evaluating if the problem existed deeper in their community, it was easier for them to pretend it was one or two people. Just some bad seeds. So, the kids growing up here would never get help. Drugs would be prevalent, and there would always be someone else to blame. Not in their home, not their kid.

Sam had become more accustomed to being alone again. She hated it and ached to feel Smitty's arms around her, but she fell back into her normal routines. Eating like crap, too much coffee, too many cigarettes. She'd started running every day to expel pent up energy. But things around her were starting to go gray again. She didn't know how long she'd be able to hold out here. She began to hate the town. Around every corner was a memory of someone she missed, or a judging eye from people who thought they knew who Casey and Smitty were. People became petty and mean during the offseason, not having tourists to gripe about. They turned on each other like caged animals.

Fights broke out more often at the bar. People would speed up to cut Sam off when she was crossing the street while running. Residents didn't wave, or worse scowled and turned away from other people, muttering disparities. The only friendly people were the morning beach walkers and those picking up trash off the sand. They seemed to have a greater appreciation for the winter beach life.

Sam kept squirreling away money, living off as little as she could. She didn't want anything to stop her from leaving when the time came. She only bought what she needed to get by. She also had Smitty's clothes and while his pants were way too long for her, she wore his shirts, hoodies, and jackets regularly. His smell was starting to fade, but she tried not to focus on that. Just wearing them gave her comfort.

He didn't write or call. She didn't want to feel slighted, but she thought he'd need her more. Weeks passed with no word, and she felt shut out. Maybe it was too much for him, so it was easier to just let her go. Maybe he'd already changed. Her mind drifted more and more to leaving the town. Now, she had nothing left. After a month, she started to make a plan. She was in a lease with Rosie and Ansley until the end of May, and she'd honor that. That would give her time to save more money and figure out where she could go. It was already almost mid-February. The season would start in the next couple of weeks for spring break and bleed straight into summer.

Mid-February. It didn't dawn on her until she got to work and it was packed, but not with the normal drunks and old people.

Young couples, dressed too nice for the sticky tablecloths and fried fare, filled the space. What was going on? She glanced around, seeing flowers and way too much pink and red. Valentine's Day. It was fucking Valentine's Day. She'd never been a fan, but now she had to spend the evening watching couples stare into each other's eyes, and make promises they wouldn't keep.

She took her station behind the bar, trying not to glare at customers as they came up giggling, being a little too outward with their physical affection. She kept her head down and served drinks as fast as she could to get the customers the hell away from her. It wasn't that she cared about Valentine's Day, or missed Smitty anymore than usual. It was that she was alone in the true sense of the word. No friends, no family, no significant other. She felt like a hunchback with one eye standing behind the bar, serving all the self-proclaimed pretty people.

Fortunately, on Valentine's Day couples eat, have a few drinks, and head out to continue their celebrations between the sheets. By nine, the bar was empty for the most part. Jimmy and Taylor cut out, and since Chris had decided to go full-time to school, Sam was the dishwasher for any remaining dishes. After the last customer left, she locked up and went back to do the dishes. Natalie swung by before she left to grab the deposit, so she wouldn't have to in the morning. She poked her head back to where Sam was.

"Hey, I wasn't sure if you were still here. I have something for you. It may be something that can offer a little hope."

Sam was finishing the last of the dishes and dried her hands. She followed Natalie out to the bar. Natalie had photos spread out on the counter.

"These are from our reception here when Gus and I got married. We had a photographer walking around inside and on the beach, snapping pictures since we didn't have wedding photos. I was going through them to put into an album and came across these two. I thought you might want them."

She slid the photos over to Sam. Sam peered down and put her hand to her chest. One was of her and Smitty, sitting out on the patio. He was saying something, and she was looking up at him laughing. The next one was of them dancing on the lifeguard stand. His arm around her waist, her hand on the back of his neck. They were staring at each other in a way she didn't know they had. Like they were the only two people on earth.

Sam glanced at Natalie with tears in her eyes. "I can have these?"

"I want you to have these. Sam, I'm seeing how you're pulling back inside your shell. I know how much you're hurting, and while I don't have much to offer, I do have these. Maybe it's just a small reminder that there is something to hold on to. I've known Smith most of his life, and he never looked at anything or anyone the way he looked at you. I know it's hard to understand all of this right now, but I want you to have something to hold on to."

Sam hugged Natalie as hard as she could. She and Smitty never had pictures together, or even of each other. Now, she had something to look at to remind herself of him. Natalie laughed and scooped up the rest of the photos.

"I'm glad I caught you, I know today is tough. I was doing the album this evening while Gus and I were celebrating over wine and cheese. As soon as I saw them, I grabbed all of them and rushed right over, instead of waiting until later to grab the deposit.

I think Gus thought I'd lost my marbles. Anyway, let me get back to him, finish celebrating. See you tomorrow."

After Natalie left, Sam sat at the bar and gazed at the photos. Smitty was so beautiful, so alive in them. The way he was staring at her in the picture of them dancing, sent shivers down her spine. His eyes were locked on her face, soft and intent. His mouth turned up in a slight smile. His arm holding her close. She sighed and slipped them in her bag with napkins around them to keep them from getting smudged.

When she got home, she put the picture of them sitting on the patio on the fridge and put the other one on the plant stand on his side of the bed. She needed to get a frame for it. She whispered a message to him into the air, hoping somehow he'd get it, even if just as a feeling or thought of her.

"Smitty, I miss you so much. It's Valentine's Day. I'm guessing that doesn't mean much where you are. It doesn't mean anything here either without you. I'm worried about you. I don't know what's happening there, or what's going through your mind. I wish you'd write. I just need to know that you're okay. I'm thinking about leaving this town. There's nothing left for me here, except reminders of you and our life before all of this. I'm not sure what I'm holding on to. I love you. Damn it, please write."

She breathed out and stared at the ceiling. In her mind, she pictured him laying back, staring at the ceiling and thinking of her. All she had to work with was television shows about prison, so she put him in that scenario. She had no clue what it actually looked like where he was. She pictured a small cell with a pair of bunks, a sink, and a toilet. She didn't know if he was in a cell with anyone else or alone. All she could imagine was him laying in his bunk.

A few weeks later, Rosie knocked on her door with mail for her. The weather was starting to turn warmer, so Sam had all of the windows open and the radio playing. Rosie handed her the mail and invited her to dinner, more of a demand than a request. Sam hadn't gone over since the holidays and accepted, much to Rosie's delight. Sam was grateful for the people who were still around, making sure she was okay. She needed to live her life somehow.

There was a postcard from Aidan of the Seattle Space Needle. She flipped it over and it made her smile.

Hey Sam!

We made it to Washington. Took a trip to Seattle. Wow! Did you know there is a whole world out here?

I'd love to hear from you.

Aidan O.

She chuckled at him adding his last initial like she had tons of other Aidans sending her mail. She stuck the postcard on the fridge next to the picture of her and Smitty. It made her feel good inside. Hopefully, Aidan was doing well and happier where he was. She flipped through the rest of the mail, which was mostly junk, when a small envelope fell out.

She recognized the handwriting immediately, and her hands began to tremble. It had been two months since Smitty had been arrested, and the first time she'd gotten anything from him. She opened the envelope carefully, drawing the letter out. She took a deep breath and opened it.

Sam,

Sorry it has taken me so long to write. It took me a while to get used to life here. It's all so unfamiliar. Everything is pretty much scheduled by lights. Time to get up, lights cut on, time to go to bed, lights cut off. We're told how and when to do everything. They have activities we can do, but it's a little bit like an insane asylum. I've been reading a lot to try and pass the time. The book selection isn't great, but it's better than nothing

They got me into the kitchen when they heard I could cook. I spend a lot of my day cooking. Cooking being used loosely at best. It's worse than the food you used to eat. Mostly reheating frozen food. But it keeps me busy and helps the days pass.

I've had a lot of time, too much time, to think while here. I've realized how unfair it is for me to expect you to sit around, waiting for me to get out. I love you so much, but I recognize you're giving up way too much for me. I don't deserve it. I just want you to be happy and find your place. I'm not worth sitting around waiting for. You should go live your life, and if our paths cross again maybe we'll get it right next time. I'm sorry, Sam. You deserved better.

Love,

Smitty

The letter made her feel worse than not hearing from him at all. At least before, she could picture him pining for her. He was telling her to leave. She'd already been contemplating it, but this was a slap in the face. He signed it 'love', which pained her even more. It was confusing and hurtful. She folded the letter and stuck it in the kitchen drawer with his other letter, the wood knot, and the birthday candle she'd found when cleaning out her bag. She wasn't sure if she'd write back. She had his address, but the conversation seemed pretty final.

She was grateful for Rosie's invitation, as she needed something to distract her brain. She headed down and walked right in back to the kitchen. Ansley was washing vegetables in the sink and smiled at Sam.

"Hey, glad you came!"

Sam plopped down on the stool. She wanted someone to talk to. "I got a letter from Smitty today. He says I should stop sitting around and waiting for him, that I should just leave."

Ansley turned around and stared at Sam, her mouth in a straight line. "Oh, he does, does he? And what do *you* think?"

"I don't know. I'd already started planning my eventual escape anyway, but him saying that fucking hurts."

"Sam, why are you here? I mean, do you think you came to this town just for him? Or do you think you came for another reason?"

Sam thought about it. So far, nothing else stood out. She met Casey, and he died. She met Aidan, and he moved. She met Smitty, and he was telling her to leave. Everything else about the town was mundane. The beach was pretty, but there were beaches all over the place. She could work a crappy bartending gig anywhere. She was glad she'd met Ansley and Rosie, but no matter where she went, they'd always be her friends. She shrugged at Ansley.

"Sam, I believe we're brought to places not just for the people we meet, but how it can make us grow. Maybe there is something here you haven't discovered yet. You have time. See if you can find it."

Sam had never thought of it that way. She'd always seen things as so random. Rosie came in and gave her a quick hug. She sat down next to Sam.

"I heard part of that from the other room. I want you to think about something. Ansley and I didn't have to come here. There were so many other accepting places where we didn't have to justify our lives together. People here only accepted it because I grew up here, and I think they're scared of Ansley."

Ansley gave a little bow. "Exactly. People here still aren't thrilled seeing us hold hands, or kissing in public, but we aren't here for them. We're here for our own reasons. You aren't here for Smitty, even though he may be part of it. You're here because something wanted you to come."

Sam nodded and thought that over. She'd no idea what she'd be here for but would think about it. It was only the second week of March. She had two and a half months to figure out if she was going to leave once the lease was up.

"So, are you going to write him back?" Rosie asked tentatively.

"I don't know. He doesn't seem to want me to." Sam bit her lip. Saying the words cut like a knife.

"Sam, you don't truly know what he wants, you know? You're going through things but around familiarity. He is going through things, far away from home, alone, with no control over his life. Take his words with a grain of salt. He's trying to survive. He's put himself in a bubble, maybe so he hurts less. Just think about it. You may be his only lifeline."

Rosie's words were truthful and gave Sam a different perspective. She smiled and nodded at Rosie. The pain in her heart eased just a bit. Rosie was always good for some encouragement.

"Let's eat." Ansley shoved platters into each of their hands and opened the back door to the porch.

They ate dinner around the back table, the promise of spring in the air. For the first time since Smitty was arrested, Sam felt hopeful. She helped them clean up and headed home. Once inside, she took a deep breath and relaxed her shoulders. In order for her to move forward, she needed to find what was inside her that was holding her back.

By the time morning rolled around, she knew what it was and headed for the beach.

Chapter Twenty-Seven

The weather was warm, and the beach was already buzzing with locals by the time Sam got there on her run. She had one focus and scoured the beach until her eyes landed on what she was searching for. On the far side of the pier, a group of teens surfing were coming out of the water for a break. She ran towards them and slowed to a walk to catch her breath before speaking. As she approached, one of the kids standing guzzling a sports drink eyed her, seeming confused. He held his drink in midair and furrowed his brows. He had light brown hair and blue eyes with freckles across his nose. They all seemed so confident, she almost lost her nerve. But shook it off and walked right up to him.

"Hey, sorry to bother you. I saw you surfing. Any chance you could teach me the basics? I can pay you." Her voice wavered a bit, but she put her chin up and met him in the eye.

He glanced from her to her friends, who were watching with a mixture of amusement and shock. He turned back to her and shrugged. "Sure, you have a board?"

Shit, she didn't and it hadn't occurred to her to bring one. She shook her head stupidly.

"You're going to need one. Hey, Mike, can this lady borrow your board for a bit, so I can show her some stuff?" he yelled back to a long-haired guy, eating a sandwich.

The guy, Mike, glanced at her and laughed. He motioned to his surfboard, which was laying behind him. Sam walked over and took the board, muttering an embarrassed thank you. She slipped off her shoes and brought the board back over to the first kid.

"To get started, have you ever even been on a board or anything?"

"No."

He sighed. "Well, this will be fun. I'm TJ by the way."

"Sam."

"Okay, Sam, the first thing you need to do is attach the leash to your back foot. This will depend on if you ride regular or goofy, but you may not know what that is until you get up and try it. So for now, attach it to your dominant foot."

"What's that for?" Sam hadn't seen Smitty or Casey using one when they were surfboarding, nor were any of these kids using one.

"So, unless you want to constantly be chasing your board long distances, or popping other surfers in the face, this will keep control of your board when you fall off. And you *will* fall off. All beginner surfers should use one, most intermediate too. Until your surfboard becomes part of you, and you grab it without thinking, you need to use a leash. Some people will always need to use it."

He grabbed a leash out of a bag, showing her how to attach it to the board and her foot. They headed towards the water with their boards. Fear rose in her stomach, and she pushed it down. She needed to do this. He peered back to make sure she was still with him and nodded.

"Let's just start by riding some white-water waves, the whitewash, get used to the board and footing."

They went out waist-deep. He waited for a set of waves and jumped on his board, making it look flawless.

"You can lay first, and then get up if that's easier. You need to hold your board by the rails and keep the nose straight towards the waves at your side. You don't want it getting caught by a wave and smacking you in the face. I've seen some seriously broken noses by people who didn't know what they were doing. Okay, a set of waves is coming. You want to try?"

She waited for the waves, grabbed her board by the rails and got on, first laying down, then getting up on her feet. She was immediately knocked off into the water and was glad for the leash because she had no idea where the board went until it tugged on her leg. She got up and prepped for the next set of waves.

"No worries, Sam!" TJ yelled towards her. "Remember, a lot of this is feeling it. You have to find your footing."

He grabbed the rails of his board and jumped up, darting along the face of the wave. She followed and did a little better this time, getting up for a second before the waves knocked her off again. She kept at it for about thirty minutes, and each time felt like she was staying up longer and traveling further. She jumped off as the wave ran out.

TJ made his way over to her. "You're catching on! Next time don't jump off. Shift your weight to the tail of the board to slow down and sit, one leg on each side, to finish the ride. If you're ready, we can try paddling out. I need to head to the beach for a bit to meet with my friends. Mike needs to leave, but I can give him his board later. Keep practicing and I'll be back in a bit. Unless you're too tired?"

She was but wanted to get this down. "No, I'm good."

By the time he came back, she'd gotten the hang of riding the whitewash enough to feel like she could practice on her own. He gave her thumbs up watching her.

"You ready to paddle out?"

They waded out until she was up to her chest, jumping over the waves as they came to them. Once a wave had passed, TJ got on his board, laying with his chest down. She imitated him.

"So, we need to paddle out through the white-water waves, through the break. You need to get speed up, so you can punch through. We're trying to get out of the surf zone and hit the lineup. In other words, we're trying to get to the bigger waves. You want to paddle like you're making an *S*. Really dig in. Watch me." He waited until a set of waves passed and began paddling out, his arms making a snake formation.

She followed his lead, moving her arms in the same formation. Her arms quickly became tired, but she pushed on.

"Paddle hard!" he yelled back at her. "To get over the waves you need to press up like this."

He pushed his arms up to lift his chest off the board. He seamlessly rose over the wave. Sam tried to repeat what he'd done, but she must have done it wrong because the wave caught the board, flipping her over. This time she swallowed water and got disoriented on what direction was up. Again, the leash tugged at her leg and she surfaced, pulling the board back towards her. She coughed and blew water out of her nose.

TJ paddled up to her. "You alright? You took on some water on that one."

Sam nodded and got back up on the board. TJ rode the board on his stomach, back towards the shore to about where they'd started. She followed and they started from the beginning. It took a few more times, but Sam got the press down and learned how to get over waves with the board. She was exhausted. TJ could tell and circled in next to her.

"You did great for the first day."

"That was fucking amazing," Sam said, grinning.

"And you haven't even gotten up on a wave yet." TJ laughed. "Let's call it quits for today."

"Can you keep teaching me? After today, I mean?" Sam asked hopefully. "I don't know the going rate, though."

He thought about it. "Me either. Why don't we say fifteen an hour? And you need a board. I think Mike will want his back."

"That sounds great! You don't know how much this helps me. I'll get a board before our next lesson. Can you meet the day after tomorrow at about the same time? I think I'll need a day to recover after today."

TJ nodded and they rode back towards shore, letting the waves carry them in. As soon as she put her feet back on the sand, they wobbled and she stumbled. TJ grabbed her, laughing knowingly.

"Yeah, you'll build up strength and get used to the switch."

She unhooked the leash, handing him the board.

"Should I look for anything in particular for a board?"

"About the same as Mike's. He's only a little taller than you and weighs a little more. You should talk to Ansley down at the surf shop, she can help you get the right one."

"Oh, I know Ansley! She's my neighbor."

"Cool. Yeah, she's the expert. Hell of a surfer too, she used to compete when she was younger. Still surfs, I see her out here sometimes in the morning finishing up when I'm starting."

All things Sam had no clue about. She could picture Ansley surfing, though. Long, tan legs braced as she owned the waves, her curly blond hair flowing behind her. Sam would have to ask her about it.

"Thanks, TJ! See you next time."

"No problem. You may be sore tomorrow."

She already was. She walked home, each step reminding her of muscles she didn't know she even had. It took twice as long to get home and climbing the stairs was shaky. She got in and popped a couple of aspirin. She laid on the bed to rest, picking up the picture of Smitty and her dancing. She thought back to when she saw Casey and him surfing effortlessly, laughing together. It was so beautiful. Not like her swallowing half the ocean today. She groaned and rolled onto her side. Running was one thing, surfing was completely different. She'd have to practice to get stronger. For now, though, she was just going to lay there and not move.

The next day wasn't any better, and she was glad she'd said to take a day in between lessons. There was no way she was getting on the board. She was moving like a ninety-year-old who'd just had hip surgery. She took more aspirin and got dressed in the easiest clothes to get on. Her legs and arms were on fire. She grabbed her car keys and slowly crept down the stairs. She needed to get a surfboard.

Ansley's car was parked on the side of the surf shop, leaving space for Sam to park right outside of the doors. She made her way in and peered around. There were boards of all sizes, shapes and colors. She wouldn't even know where to start. Ansley came out from the backroom, her eyes widened with surprise.

"Hey, Sam! What're you doing here?"

"Well, I came to buy a surfboard. I have no idea what I'm doing, though." Sam laughed sheepishly.

Ansley came around the counter and moved over to some boards on the wall. She sized Sam up, pulling a couple off.

"So, I take it you're just beginning? No sense in spending too much while you're learning. These are fun boards; they cover a wider range of waves. Both of these should be about right for your weight and height. How long have you been surfing?"

"Since yesterday."

"Oh! Okay then. You may want a nose plug too."

"Yeah, I learned that the hard way. If either board is good, I'll take the yellow one with blue flowers."

Ansley took the board up to the register and snagged a pair of nose plugs. She rang everything up, then grinned at Sam. "How are you getting it home?"

"Uh, in my car?"

They both looked out at Sam's small car parked out front. Ansley shook her head.

"Probably not. We have surfboard roof racks. I can help you install it." She grabbed a roof rack and put it on the counter, adding it to the total.

"To get started isn't cheap, but you don't buy stuff all the time. If you like surfing and want to progress, I'd recommend having a board made for you. But this will do for now. Threw the nose plugs in for free and gave you a discount. Total is three-hundred, ninety-nine dollars, and forty-six cents."

That was the most money Sam had ever spent on any one thing, not including necessities like rent. She looked at the board and knew she was okay with it, handing Ansley her card. They took everything out and Ansley installed the roof rack, showing Sam how to take it off and put it on if needed. They secured the board to the rack. It made Sam's car look like an image on a postcard. She'd have to get a picture and send it to Aidan.

"So, the kid, TJ, who is teaching me, said you used to compete?" Sam asked, slipping the nose plugs in her bag.

"Indeed, I did. In college. Until I got injured and had to quit surfing for a while. Now it's just for me. TJ is a good kid and a decent surfer; he'll be able to show you the ropes. "

"How did you get injured?" Sam didn't know if it was appropriate to ask, but she was curious.

"I got too cocky and misjudged my distance, smashing headlong into a pier piling. Cracked my skull," Ansley replied dryly.

"Damn. That's scary." Sam stared at the board with new respect and fear.

"Yeah, it took me about a year to recover, and my balance or memory still isn't one hundred percent. Ended my competition days. I surf for enjoyment only now. It's okay, though, surfing is the most amazing feeling, like flying but over water. Just don't let your guard down. One second of being distracted can end with you being seriously hurt."

Sam got in the car, considering Ansley's words. While even little kids were out learning to surf, and a lot of people did it like second nature, the ocean was powerful and there was always risk. Serious risk of injury or death.

The real question Sam had to ask herself was, why did knowing that excite her so much?

Chapter Twenty-Eight

TJ was there as promised the next day. Sam was more prepared this time with her board and nose plug. He grinned and checked out her board, turning it over to admire its newness. Sam felt a weird sense of satisfaction knowing it was her board. She couldn't put her finger on why, but she beamed with pride. TJ nodded his approval and grabbed his board.

"You want to practice what you learned the other day, or pick up where we left off?"

"Pick up where we left off. I still need to build strength, and I might fizzle out if we practice first. I can practice after."

Sam wanted to make sure she got up today.

TJ led the way into the water and Sam followed closely behind. They were in an area with no one else, making her feel more confident. When people watched, she felt like she made mistakes she wouldn't otherwise. They moved out to chest-deep water and got on their boards, paddling hard to get out to the bigger waves. Once they got out, TJ sat up on his board. Sam did the same.

"Once you're out here and want to catch a wave, you need to be ready. If you miss your chance, let it pass and wait for the next one."

"How will I know when I'm ready to go up?" Sam could already start to feel the rhythm of the waves move past her.

"When you start to feel the wave rise, that's when you pop up. You want to paddle out and as soon as you feel it, do it."

The waves had moved them towards shore while they talked, so they laid back on their boards and paddled towards the waves. Sam felt the wave start to rise but moved too slow and ended up being knocked off by the turbulent top of the wave. She got back on the board and paddled again, feeling the rise and popped up. It wasn't graceful, and she lasted only a second before falling off. She was glad for the nose plug. She wasn't giving up. She paddled, again and again, trying repeatedly to get up, each time feeling a little more in sync with the waves.

TJ watched and gave pointers while he successfully caught wave after wave. She watched his form and his footing, attempting to copy those. When it happened she wasn't expecting it. She felt the wave rise and got up, setting her footing, then she remembered what Smitty had said about looking where she wanted to go and her body would follow. She turned her head, her hips shifted, and she caught the wave, riding it briefly before her own surprise caused her to scream in delight as she fell into the water.

When she surfaced, she couldn't stop grinning. TJ was grinning too, giving her a thumbs up. After that, each time she could feel it more and more. Exhausted, she paddled over to TJ.

"It is cool if we go to the shore and eat something? I'm running out of steam."

"Of course. You're doing great!"

They paddled towards the shore, letting the waves ease the work. Once they hit the beach Sam flopped onto the sand, every ounce of her body tingling. TJ sat down next to her and grabbed chips out of a bag. Sam pulled out a sandwich and they ate in silence. TJ turned to her; his face twisted in thought.

"Hey, you're Smith's girlfriend, right?"

A pit formed in her stomach. How should she answer that, and why was he asking? "Yeah, I suppose."

"You know, he taught me how to surf. I was like six, maybe seven or so, I think he was in high school. A bunch of us would pester him when he was surfing. Finally, he started showing us things whenever he was around. It was really cool."

The image made Sam smile. No one spoke well of Smitty anymore, and she wasn't prepared to hear it. It made her feel pride and heartache at the same time.

"That's really neat. Thank you for telling me." She pushed her foot around in the sand, looking away.

TJ was watching the waves and glanced over at her. "I heard he got locked up. Selling and shit. That really sucks. I only know him from back then, but he was always cool to us kids. He gave us the time of day. I know he's a good guy."

Sam met his eyes and nodded slightly. Smitty was a good guy. TJ finished his chips, slipping the empty bag back into his pack. He grabbed his board and stood over Sam.

"You ready?"

"I am. TJ, it means a lot to hear that about Smith. People here are so quick to judge and blame him for everything." She squinted up at him.

"People here have no fucking clue what is actually going on. Most of the kids are using K. I stay away from that shit because I see how stupid it makes them. Drugs were here before Smith and will be here long after. The type may change, but kids here will always be using something. It's how they cope. Anyway, come on, let's get back in."

He ran towards the water. She snagged her board to join him, happy to move away from the conversation. For the next hour, they practiced everything he'd taught her. He always pointed out little tips that would make it easier, make it more fun. She didn't think she'd ever laughed so hard in her life. It was exhilarating. Part of her liked the connection of Smitty teaching TJ, and TJ teaching her. It was that line that connected them all again. Finally, their time was up, and they headed back to the beach. She grabbed thirty dollars out of her bag and handed it to him. He smiled, sticking it in his bag.

"You still want me to teach you?" he asked, slipping on his shoes.

"Definitely. I'll practice on off days but if we can meet a couple of times a week that would be great."

"Yeah, okay. I was on spring break this week and back to school next week. So, like weekends? I'd say afternoons, but there are a lot more people around and it's harder to get a clear spot."

She was back to work the next day and needed a couple of days to recuperate. Weekends worked. "Can you meet Saturday and

Sunday mornings? I work at the restaurant those days but don't go in until three. How about nine in the morning?"

TJ nodded, grabbing his things. Sam picked up her bag and board, liking how it felt. They walked together to the parking lot. She loaded the board in the rack. He was on foot, carrying his.

"Do you need a ride?"

"Nah, I like the walk after surfing. Gives me time to think and improve." He paused, glancing at the lifeguard stand. "Don't let anybody tell you anything bad about Smith. This town, they like to talk shit. It's their hobby because they don't have anything else to do, you know? Don't stress it."

He headed off, his board under his arm with his backpack slung over his shoulder. It made her think of Aidan. She snapped a picture of her car with the board on top to send to Aidan. On the drive home, she saw all the cute little cottages with their kids' toys and windchimes differently. It was a town of dark secrets, and kids getting lost in the blackness. For every little kid playing in the front yard, how many of them would end up addicted, end up alone, end up dead?

Casey's beads swung from the rearview mirror, and she held them in her hand. Smitty had regretted not getting a set when Casey had offered to buy him some. When she got home, she took them down and brought them inside. She wasn't ready yet, but she knew what she needed to do. She put them in the drawer with Smitty's letters, wood knot, and candle. The time would come.

After a long hot shower to ease her aches, she threw on a t-shirt and skirt, walking barefoot around the apartment. Even her body felt different after surfing. Like she felt it more. Like it existed more in the space. It dawned on her, she hadn't had an episode of not knowing where she was for a while. Not since she and Smitty had gotten together, perhaps before. She honestly couldn't remember. She put on the radio, and when a song came on she liked, she danced around the living room unabashedly. It was an odd feeling to be so in her body. She rubbed her arms, appreciating their smoothness.

She made her way to the kitchen and touched Smitty's knives. She was tired of eating shitty food and missed his gourmet meals. She could never make what he did, but she could try something. Before she knew it, she was heading for the grocery store. Instead of grabbing whatever was canned or easy, she grabbed fruits and vegetables. She still had all his spices, oils, and seasonings. She could figure out something. She saw some edamame pods that Smitty had bought before, grabbed those and a bag of rice. She'd try to make the stir fry he'd made. How hard could it be?

She walked home with bags in hand, feeling pretty proud of herself. In her life, she'd never made anything from scratch. Everything was processed, pre-made, simple. Once she was in the kitchen, she didn't know where to start and tried to remember watching him cook. Rice. He'd put on rice first. She read the bag and followed the instructions. After she got that going, she tried to cut the vegetables like she'd seen him doing, nicking herself in the process. The knives were wicked sharp, so the blood pooled up quickly. She grabbed a paper towel, wrapping it tightly around the injured finger, which was starting to throb.

The veggies got cut one-handed and were ugly. Sam laughed at her attempt, as she threw them in the frying pan. She added oil and seasoning. Edamame. She'd forgotten that. She threw all the pods in, and the pan started to sizzle. She kept stirring everything until she thought it was done. She tasted the rice, which wasn't perfect but not terrible. She turned everything off and served herself a plate. She took a small bite. It wasn't Smitty's delicate fragrant food, but it was edible. Like surfing, she'd need practice. Still, she ate two plates and saved one for lunch before work the next day.

With the kitchen cleaned and everything put away, she stepped out to smoke a cigarette. Rosie was out prepping the garden beds for planting and waved.

"Hey, Sam! What are you up to?"

"I cooked dinner," Sam said proudly.

Rosie laughed and stared at her weirdly. Sam realized most people had no idea an adult woman would've never cooked a meal before. She chuckled, rubbing her face with her hand.

"I mean, for the first time. I've never cooked a meal before. I've heated up stuff but never bought, chopped, and cooked from scratch."

Rosie's face was priceless. It was twisted up, her head cocked and brows furrowed. She shook her head, trying to process what Sam had just said. She blew out her breath, nodded her head, and giggled.

"You're crazy, Sam. I don't get you, but I love you all the same."

Rosie went back to her gardening. Sam finished her cigarette and stepped back inside. Her house smelled good, like a restaurant. Like when Smitty was around. It dawned on her that she didn't have to wait for someone else to do something for her. She could learn anything. She was learning how to surf; she could teach herself how to cook. An empowered feeling came over her, coming to this realization.

Her whole life she'd been waiting around. Waiting for her parents to do things for her, to tell her what she needed to be doing. School had told her how and when to do her work. Landlords told her when to pay. Bosses told her what her job was. She was always waiting for the next command. She wasn't invested. The only time she was doing what she wanted was when she ran away from problems. That was the only power she'd felt over her life. Now, she wasn't running. Now, she could have power by choosing to do what she wanted, how and when she wanted.

This revelation was like a weight off of her shoulders. She went to the drawer, pulling out Casey's beads. He'd been trapped by believing he was stuck here. Smitty was trapped by believing he didn't matter. She'd been trapped by believing nothing she did was of consequence. None of them was actually trapped, except by themselves. Casey was free to go and leave this town. Smitty mattered simply because he existed. Sam changed every circumstance she was in, for better or worse.

She sat on the stool, her mind reeling. It was like a flood gate had opened. She grabbed a piece of paper and started writing.

Smitty,

I received your letter but didn't know how to respond to it. Or if I should. I'll be honest, it hurt me. That you could even think I was just sitting here waiting for you out of obligation. After all we went through together. You still have a lot of growing up to do. I love you. You are my friend, you were my lover. I don't know what the future holds and will make decisions based on what I feel, what I want. You aren't setting me free because you don't own me. I'm my own person.

I'm sending you Casey's beads because you need them more than I do. He was there for you in your darkest days and is there with you now. I've been here for you by my own choice, from my own heart. I thought what we had was stronger than all of this, but now I don't know. I feel like you shut me out and that hurts. I care about what happens to you. I know you're going through a lot, but you aren't alone. By believing you are, you have made us both be.

By the way, I used your knives.

Love,

Sam

It was harsh and short, she knew. She couldn't not write to him, but he needed to hear it honestly. She didn't have an envelope to mail it with the beads, so she put them back in the drawer. She stared at the photo of them on the fridge and removed it, sticking it in the drawer with the letter.

Over the next few weeks, she worked, took surf lessons, and learned to cook. The Sam who'd shown up in the town eleven months prior had evolved. This Sam found a passion in surfing she never knew she could. When she was cutting through the waves, she felt alive. She went every morning and sometimes joined Ansley at dawn. She saw and felt herself as a whole person. Instead of avoiding situations, she faced them head-on.

By the end of April, she went to the post office with the letter, beads, and picture packaged up in a box to mail out. It felt freeing. She had a month left to decide what to do. This time, the decision wasn't going to be rash, based in fear and detachment.

This time, Sam was in control and knew what she wanted.

Chapter Twenty-Nine

May came in with a bang, with Ansley and Rosie getting a call about three siblings needing immediate foster care. A three-year-old, five-year-old, and six-year-old, the five-year-old with developmental disabilities. The oldest was a boy, the two younger were girls. They accepted on the spot, the children needing urgent placement, as they were being housed in temporary care. It gave them only a couple of days to get the house ready. The children would be enrolled in Rosie's preschool until the following fall when the two older ones would start at the charter school.

Ansley cleared the extra bedrooms of any of her art supplies, moving them to the garage. Children's furniture was shuttled in, the larger of the bedrooms readied for the two girls and the smaller for the boy. Play equipment filled Spork's backyard. He sniffed and peed on everything, leaving Rosie to keep hosing it off until he felt he'd marked it as his own. Child-proofing made their once flowing home into a series of gates and latches to figure out. Overnight, it went from the home of two unencumbered adults to the home of a family with children.

By the time the children arrived a couple of days later, the home was a child wonderland. They were brought by a social worker and greeted by their new parents at the gate. Sam watched from her place above, not wanting to interrupt their special moment. She also didn't want to get attached to the children, as she'd decided she was leaving around the end of the month. It was going to be hard enough, without having to say goodbye to a whole new set of people.

The youngest girl cried and didn't know who to cling to, her black curly hair tied up in a couple of twisted pigtails on her head. Rosie swept in, kneeling before her, talking softly. Sam couldn't hear her, but her words were having a soothing effect on the child, who put her arms around Rosie's neck. The other two were curious and were peering around the garden. They almost looked like twins, being so close in age. The middle child wore thick glasses, which accentuated her large brown eyes. The older boy eyed Ansley from the social worker's side, obviously wanting to talk to her. Ansley gave him a quick wink and he smiled, showing a missing tooth.

The social worker was handing them paperwork, and they moved inside to finalize the process. Sam was happy for them, but part of her felt like it was another sign, telling her it was time to go. They needed time to get to know their family and get situated. Things were starting to fall into place, and this time she was taking time to do it right. Grabbing her bag, she drove to the restaurant for her shift. She wanted to get there early to talk to Natalie and give her notice. She hoped it wouldn't put them in a bind, but she needed to stop making decisions for other people's benefit.

Natalie was sweeping when Sam walked in. Sam took a deep breath and touched her on the shoulder. Natalie turned and smiled, her eyes immediately reading the room.

"Hey, Sam! You're here early. What's up?"

"Hey, can we talk?"

Natalie eyed her and nodded, knowing what was coming. They walked to the office and sat down. Sam knew she just needed to start before it became bigger than her voice.

"So, Natalie, I appreciate all you've done for me and for letting me work here. You've been such a good boss, and a friend," she paused, thinking of the next words.

Natalie leaned forward and patted her hand. "Sam, I know. I've been seeing it for a bit now. You've grown so much since you first came here, what, almost a year ago? I don't expect you to stay forever. I hate to see you go, but I understand. How long have I got you for?"

"I'm leaving around the end of the month." Sam choked up saying the words. "It's just that I came here randomly and never really planned to stay. Then everything with Casey. And Smitty going away."

At this point, a tear did slip down her cheek. She never thought she'd be able to care so much about people in such a short time. This was much harder than leaving Miri. She wiped the tear away, put her chin up, and smiled, meeting Natalie's eyes.

"It's just time. I didn't want to leave you hanging, and I wanted to give you as much time as possible to replace me."

Natalie sat back smiling. "Don't you worry about that. Gus can take your place; he's getting too old to barback and we'll find some young kid to replace him. We'll miss you, but no one should stay in a place longer than they can grow. When it's time, it's time."

"Thanks, Natalie. I feel like I'm stuck in a memory, instead of moving forward. There's a whole world out there, and I need to see what's next for me."

"I'm proud of you. You've really changed. By the way, I've seen you surfing in the mornings sometimes when I come for the deposit. You're a natural."

Sam blushed at this compliment. It had only been a little over a month since she started surfing, and now she couldn't imagine her life without it. Nothing in her life had given her such a feeling of freedom and power. It was a drive in her she couldn't explain. Wherever she went, it would have to be near the ocean.

"I can't believe everyone doesn't do it," Sam mused.

"Not everyone knows how to dig that deep. You're stronger than you give yourself credit for. I'm sorry about Smith. It takes some people a while longer to know what's up. Forgive him, and yourself. You both got knocked down pretty hard."

They had. Each of them coming into everything with their own demons. Then losing Casey, finding each other, and being ripped away from each other, just as they were gaining their stride. There was no one to blame. Sam was hurt but not angry. Sometimes things just didn't fall into place as they wanted. At this point, she needed to step forward and see what was out there for her. Like losing Casey, it was something she'd learn to deal with and put in a safe place in her heart. The memories were fond, and she hoped maybe at one point she and Smitty would be able to be friends again. Not feel trapped by circumstances.

The next morning, Sam woke to the sound of children laughing and playing. Spork was barking nonstop. She stepped out on the porch and saw the two older children playing in the backyard, Ansley running around with them. The littlest one was still clinging tight to Rosie. Ansley saw Sam at the top of the stairs and waved.

"Sam, come meet the kids."

Sam reluctantly went down the stairs and into the backyard. She needed to talk to Ansley and Rosie about leaving anyway. The boy ran up to her and handed her a flower he'd picked.

"Thank you! I'm Samantha." She took the slightly wilted and sticky flower. "What's your name?"

"Marcus."

He ran off, disappearing into a large plastic boat in the yard, followed closely by a very excited Spork. Rosie came up, carrying the littlest one who refused to look at Sam. Her tiny arm was so tight around Rosie's neck, it looked like she was going to cut off her circulation.

"And this little angel is Tori. Victoria. Her sister over there on the swing is Lanie. Short for Delanie. Girls, this is our friend Sam."

The children were uninterested in this information and kept playing. Except for Tori who'd become an extension of Rosie, firmly planted on her hip. Rosie called the kids to come inside for breakfast, leaving Ansley and Rosie in the backyard alone. The yard fell blissfully silent.

Ansley came over to Sam, breathing hard from chasing the kids around the yard. She was glowing. "Aren't they great? I'm already exhausted."

Sam laughed. "They are. What's their story? I mean, how did they end up in foster care?"

"It's really sad actually. Their father died in a car accident a few years ago, leaving their mother to raise them alone. Tori was just a baby at the time. A couple of months ago, the mom was diagnosed with terminal breast cancer and is now at the point she is in hospice. We've been given permission to call her every day and let her know how the children are doing. Until-"

Her voice trailed off. Until.

"Oh." Sam didn't know what to say.

Those poor kids, losing everyone they loved and knew at such a young age. They probably didn't even comprehend what was going on with their mother. She thought of Rosie losing her mother young, and how life seemed to connect in cycles. Rosie understood better than anyone and would be a good source of support for them.

"We've already put in to adopt them and their mother has agreed. She just wants to make sure they stay together and are loved in a stable home before she passes."

"So, no other family?"

Ansley shook her head, giving a small shrug. "I really don't know. They don't tell us more than that. The mom is too weak to talk much when we call, she mostly just listens to the kids. We want the kids to have the ability to keep those connections as they grow. Hopefully, someone will reach out."

Crying came from inside, and Ansley bolted for the door to see what happened. Sam followed behind but nothing serious was going on. Lanie was frustrated because she'd knocked over her glass of juice. Ansley quickly jumped in to clean up the spill while Rosie refilled the glass, helping Lanie wrap her fingers tightly around it. Sam shifted uncomfortably, waiting for the right moment to tell them her news. Once all of the kids were happily eating, she took it.

"Hey, I need to tell you something. I know this is kind of out of the blue, but I'm moving at the end of the month."

Rosie's eyes widened, causing her eyebrows to raise comically. Ansley was quiet. Sam felt horrible for springing it on them, feeling the need to over-explain.

"It's just that I need to figure out what's out there for me. Smitty obviously has moved on, and I don't think working at the restaurant until I'm old and gray is in the cards for me. I want more. I want to feel like I do when I'm surfing. I want to be passionate about things." She stumbled through her words, trying to make sense.

Ansley laughed softly and came over to put her arms around Sam for a second. "We weren't judging you, just a little shocked. We've liked having you as a neighbor and kind of always imagined you up there. Like an Auntie. You'd mentioned thinking of leaving a while ago, but we weren't expecting it so soon. Where are you moving to?"

"I'm not sure yet. Still trying to work that out. I've been saving money for years, especially while working here. I have almost nine thousand saved, so I figure that gives me time to figure things out, try a few things."

"It's time for Sam to choose her own adventure," Rosie said gently, chuckling.

Exactly.

If she found this town on a fluke, imagine what was out there for her to explore and discover? The kids were getting restless, so Rosie's and Ansley's attention shifted to them. Sam figured it was best to leave, allowing them to focus on their children. She motioned towards the door.

"Hey, I'm heading up for coffee and to go surfing. I'll let you know more once the date gets closer, but it'll be near the end of the month." She headed towards the door, as the volume of kids' voices got louder.

"Oh, hey, Sam?" Rosie yelled over the din. "There's mail for you on the table by the door. It came yesterday while you were at work."

Sam scooped up the mail and walked out. Almost immediately the handwriting caught her eye. What appeared to be a very thick letter from Smitty. A sense of fear came over her. She'd no idea what he had to say and wasn't sure she was ready to face it.

She set it on the counter while she made coffee. She wondered if she should just not open it, just leave things as they were. She considered this over coffee, then decided she wasn't in her right mind to make the choice. She grabbed her board and headed for the beach. She wanted to get into the waves, to not think about anything for a while. It was still early, so she found a clear spot to surf, pushing herself as hard as her body and mind would let her.

By the time she was too exhausted to push any further, a few hours had passed. She was hungry and headed home, knowing what was waiting for her. She slid the key in the lock and pushed the door open, her eyes immediately drawn to the spot.

The letter was still sitting on the counter unopened, taunting her. She stared at it and decided no matter what he had to say, she needed to live her life for herself. Not reading it wasn't changing that. To move forward, she had to be aware of all sides, whether or not she agreed with them. She ripped it open, taking out what appeared to be seven or eight pages in Smitty's scrawled handwriting. Her heart did a flip, and she couldn't deny she still had feelings for him.

She laid the pages flat on the counter, took a deep breath to settle her nerves, and began reading.

Chapter Thirty

Samantha,

I got your letter. It was an eye-opener, and I felt ashamed after reading it. You're right, I'm not here to tell you what you should do. That was shitty of me and for that, I'm truly sorry. I was only thinking of where I was coming from. Being here, it's hard to think about the outside world and what other people are going through. It's honestly better if I don't. When I first got here, I'd think back on our life together, our home, you, and it would hurt so much. It made each day creep by, and I thought I'd lose my mind. Sometimes, I'd dream about holding you, then wake up in this fucking place without you and have to fight back panic attacks. So, I pushed it all down and away, so I could get through my time here. But it doesn't mean I didn't want you.

Thank you for Casey's prayer beads. That meant the world to me, and I know it must've been hard sending those to me since Aidan wanted you to have them. Luckily, they let me keep them, as they saw them as a protected religious item and figured I couldn't hang myself with them. Funny, but not funny. I wear them every day, they are my connection to the outside world. The picture you sent hangs above my bunk. I know things have changed, but it makes me smile when I see it. You laughing is the most beautiful thing I've ever seen. Before you sent those, I had nothing of my own. Most of the guys here have their areas plastered with pictures of family, religious items, letters, drawings from their kids, things like that. Up until you sent those, I just had my bunk and a blank wall.

Inmates here come and go. I'm on my second bunkmate, Joe. He's pretty quiet, in for assault. He beat someone so bad, they almost died. You'd never know it though. He's soft-spoken and reads a lot. You'd think he was like a high school history teacher. Who knows, maybe he was. We stay out of each other's way, for the most part. I'm not trying to connect to anyone here. I want to get out and put it behind me. I have the top bunk, so I use it as a place I can escape from here to be alone to think. You'd think in here, being alone would be bad but until the lights cut off at night, and for a bit after, it's always fucking noisy. People are constantly yelling. Makes me crazy.

Fights break out a lot here. Everyone feels trapped, obviously, so people fight over the dumbest shit. Most are minor, just scrapping, but I've seen people taken out on stretchers. Some guys are in for years, and it takes its toll. The long-timers learn the system and adjust it as their life. It's usually those here for shorter periods who explode and go off, but the long-timers have no problem setting them straight. They rule the place. I've had a few fights but nothing serious. Some bruises and scrapes, one cut I needed stitches for, which left a scar on my side.

I didn't start them, but you can't take a beating, you have to fight back. Otherwise, you get marked as easy prey. Have to make it out alive.

　　Everything here is micromanaged. There is no privacy. I guess that goes without saying, but until you live it, it's hard to understand how demeaning it can be. It has truly opened my eyes. I'll never so much as cross the street wrong if it means I'd have to come back here. Some guys are on a revolving door in and out of here. I don't get it. I mean, I'm not in their shoes, but in mine I'd rather die than come back again. I just want to walk as far as I want, get into the ocean, cook real food, feel the sun on my face. I could go on. I want to do everything.

　　The positive side is it has helped me deal with my addiction. Not only would it be hard (but not impossible) to come by here, but just freedom is going to be all the high I'll need. I'm not stupid and know I'll have triggers on the outside, but I feel like I'm more prepared to deal with them. I'll get help on the outside as well. Sitting here, I can look at my previous life and see how I took for granted the aspects of it that I had. Including you. You stood by me, and I was so wrapped up in my own shit I didn't appreciate you the way I should have. I'm really sorry.

　　I wrote to my parents when I first came here and told them everything. They didn't respond. I suppose I didn't expect them to, but it still hurt. I guess a drug addict, inmate son isn't something they are willing to deal with. I feel like I never measured up to what they wanted. But I needed to get it all out there and let them know anyway, to allow myself to resolve my relationship with them and move on. I guess at this point I have no one, and I'm not feeling sorry for myself, just accepting the fate I laid out through my choices. Made my bed, now I have to lay in it, right?

I do see a correctional counselor once a week named Brian. He's a nice guy, but not sure it's helping. I think he's burnt out from working within the system. We talk about what got me put in here and plans for the outside. He lets me know my options, gives me things to read. Sounds like when I get released I'll get a parole officer, and have the option to go to a halfway house in a nearby city to get back on my feet. Seems like my best option, since I have nothing to go back to there. I'm sure the town wants nothing to do with me and to be honest, I don't want anything to do with them either.

On that note. I'm not sure if you're planning to stay or leave. Either way, can you put my things in a box and leave them with Ansley and Rosie? As soon as I can, I'll arrange to either come and get them or have them shipped to me. It's not a lot I know, but the knives you gave me mean a lot to me, and I only have the set of clothes I was wearing when I was booked. When I'm released, they'll give me that set and my wallet, but that's all I'll have. Well, that, Casey's beads, and the picture you sent. I never had much, but it's strange to only have what you can carry on your body as your only possessions.

I'm so sorry I fucked this all up, Sam. I kick myself every day for all of this. I didn't handle any of it right, I know that. I'll spend my life regretting what I did to you, Casey, and Aidan. The three of you mean everything to me. Casey tried to reach me so many times, and I laughed him off. I'm so fucking ashamed of that. Casey was one in a million, and I was so busy wanting to get fucked up I missed all of the signs. You know how much that hurts? Aidan now has to carry that burden because he was too young to be able to help Casey, and I just didn't. I hope one day Aidan can forgive me.

Where do I start with you? This one is going to hurt, and I hope I can get it down in writing like it is in my head. First, you're hands down the best thing that ever happened to me. Please know that. I'd like to think had I not been arrested, we'd be living our peaceful little life in that tiny-ass apartment above the garage. It was perfect. Now living in a cell, that apartment seems spacious. I can't believe I ever even had that for a moment. I don't know if I'd have completely kicked my addiction, though, on my own, and I'm glad I didn't put you through that. I'm a complete, selfish dick when I'm fucked up, and I'm glad you never really saw that side of me.

I love you, Sam. Nothing will ever change that. You're the first and only person I'd ever felt that way about. I'd fight off sharks for you. But see, in this scenario I'm the shark, right? I'm the one who hurt you and I can't fight myself off. But what I can do is not ask anything of you. Like you said, I don't own you and don't have the right to ask you to be around for me. I won't. However, I'll go to my grave loving you and hating myself for destroying the beautiful thing we had. You deserved so much better than me.

Not that I think you would, but don't write back to this address. I got word I'm being released early, June third, on good behavior. Honestly, I just think the system is so saturated they need the space and in their mind, I'm less of a threat to society than some of the other guys in here. I'll move to the halfway house and try to figure out what the hell I'm going to do with the rest of my life. It's weird to be this old, having to start over again. No money, no job, no family. And as a felon. Man, I sure know how to fuck everything up, don't I?

If you can, let Ansley and Rosie know I'll send for my things as soon as I can. Let me end with this. Sam, you are a gift. You changed my life, and you'll be in everything I do for the rest of my life. If I could go back and do things over I would, just to keep you. To hold you in my arms again, to hear your laugh, and cook dinner for you.

I know there are no do overs, though, and can only tell you how sorry I am. I hope at some point that will be enough, and you can find it in your heart to forgive me.

Love,

Smitty

Sam closed the letter and stared out the window. In a couple of weeks, it was coming up on a year from when she first met Smitty in the parking lot. A year ago, she'd never met him, Casey, Aidan, or anyone else in this town. A year ago, she was planning her thirty-first birthday with Miriam, a simple take-out dinner at home, a movie, and drinks. This year, she was arranging a move, learned to surf, taught herself to cook, and was planning an afternoon at the pier by herself for her birthday. This year, she'd had her heart broken for the first time ever. She didn't recognize herself from the woman she'd been a year ago, who didn't recognize herself in the mirror. She felt more connected to herself and her body than she ever had and was making decisions out of desire, instead of fear or necessity.

She didn't blame Smitty for being in his own head at the time. He'd been through a lot, not all of his own making, and had never been taught how to deal with things or find a peaceful place within himself either. He'd been running like she had, he was just using different tools to get there. In a way, it'd been amazing they'd been able to be there for each other at all, considering their individual circumstances. She folded the letter and stuck it in the drawer. As she closed the drawer, it felt like closing a chapter in a book. She had a few weeks to wrap everything up here and head out.

On her birthday a few days later, she turned her phone off, packed her backpack with food and water, and walked to the pier. Her parents and Brad would likely call, and she didn't want to have to put out the energy it took to talk to them. Not yet, anyway. She wanted today to be about herself and reflection. The pier was busy, but the bench at the end was surprisingly empty. She set down her backpack, claiming the space, and pulled water out, heated from her walk. She sat on the bench and gazed out over the ocean, feeling its draw.

The day she first arrived in the town, and since then, she'd thought it was something about the town that had seemed so familiar, so much like home. At this moment, she realized it wasn't the town, it was the sea. It had been calling to Sam her whole life, its waves a metronome in her blood. It had centered her and helped her find passion. Surfing had brought her together, body and soul, giving her a reason to live. For that, she was grateful for the fallout with Miri, who she never heard from again. She hadn't really expected Miri to respond. Some choices couldn't be changed, some injuries never healed. Miri was done with her and rightfully so. Sam accepted not everything was tied up with a neat bow. But it drove her to this town, to the ocean, and eventually to herself. Everything in her life had been a catalyst to get her to this moment, to find what was missing inside of her.

She ate the food she packed and spent the next couple of hours meditating with the ocean. When she was ready, she packed up and headed to the end of the pier. She breathed in the salt air, feeling light spray against her cheeks. She felt Casey there and thanked him for recognizing in her what she hadn't seen in herself. A light breeze kicked up, blowing her hair off her face. She liked to think that was Casey hearing her, letting her know he was okay. She imagined putting her arms around him and promised to take him with her. She could feel his energy moving around her. No matter what, in life or death, he was a part of her now.

She strolled home, taking the time to go down extra streets, to take everything in and imprint it in her mind. The beach-themed cottages with small yards, painted pretty pastel colors. Once she left, she didn't think she'd ever come back, she'd already done what she'd come to do. When she got home, she went to the bedroom and picked up the bracelet Smitty had given her, turning it over in her hands and put it on. It had been too painful to look at, much less wear, since he'd been gone. Regardless, he was part of who she'd become, and she wanted the reminder. She loved him, and his friendship had helped her define who she was now. There are no mistakes, she repeated in her mind. He'd always be part of her like Casey was.

Her phone was blinking with messages. She listened, knowing she couldn't put it off. As expected, her parents called, told her they loved her and hoped to see her soon. Now more than ever, she appreciated their commitment in her life, reminding her she mattered and was loved. The next message was from Brad, the kids yelling happy birthday in the background, which made her laugh. The last one she wasn't expecting, and the sound of his voice sent shivers through her body.

"Hey, Sam, it's Smitty. I know I'd said I wouldn't call, but I wanted to wish you a happy birthday. I didn't forget. You've been on my mind, well, all of the time, but especially today. I hope you find a way to celebrate which makes you feel as special as you are. I wish I was there to make you dinner, to hold you. I love you. Happy birthday, Samantha."

She replayed it a couple of times, warmed by the timbre of his voice. She rubbed her finger over the seashell on the bracelet she was wearing and smiled. Then she grabbed her surfboard, loading it up to go for an evening surf. By the time she was done surfing and driving back home, she knew where she was going and was ready to start packing.

Chapter Thirty-One

The next couple of weeks flew by. Before Sam knew it, the end of the month was looming. She started tying up loose ends to close doors on her life there. She returned her library books and said goodbye to old Miriam, who only remembered her on certain days. She donated anything she didn't think she'd need to the thrift shop and began packing everything she wouldn't need in the last week or so. She packed Smitty's box of things and set it down, begrudgingly putting his clothes she'd borrowed in it. She pushed it next to the door and wrote his name on it.

The following Saturday, she met with TJ for her last surf lesson from him. It was way more bittersweet than she thought it would be. She was already at the beach when he came up eating a doughnut, looking like he'd just climbed out of bed. He waved the doughnut at her and smiled.

"You ready, Sam?"

He was already heading for the water, so rather than stopping him, she followed his lead. They hit the water and caught every wave they could, laughing and falling in the process. He didn't have much to point out to her anymore. After a couple of hours of surfing, they came back to the beach and sat on the sand. She looked at him, seeing his sun-bleached hair and freckled nose. For a minute she could see Smitty at the same age, already deep in addiction and her heart ached for him. Smitty had been just a kid.

"So, TJ, this will be our last day. I'm moving away in a little over a week."

He glanced over at her and nodded. "You don't need me anymore anyway. You caught on in like two months, in what some people can never get. Where are you going?"

"I'm not for sure, but maybe a little further north, I think. Definitely near the ocean. As long as there are good waves, I think I'll be good."

She dug in her bag and pulled out a hundred-dollar bill, plus the thirty for the lesson. "Here, for all you've done. Think of it as a tip."

TJ took the money and stared at it for a second, then shoved it in his bag. Teenagers weren't all that shy about taking money. He grinned at her. "Thanks, Sam! I could use it right now too. Eyeing a new board."

"You should keep teaching, TJ. Kids around here need someone to show them the ropes. You know, to be there for them."

"Maybe I will. I'm sorry to see you go. But honestly, I'm out of here as soon as I graduate. My friend Aidan moved out to Washington state, and it sounds so much better than here.

Anywhere has to be better than here. Like you said, as long as it's near the ocean."

She should've figured he knew Aidan; they were around the same age and probably in the same class. Aidan just might be the line out of this place for some of these kids. TJ got up and threw his bag over his shoulder, extending his hand out to shake hers. She grasped it and smiled up at him.

"Thanks, TJ. Hey, I'm thinking over an idea for the kids here with surfing and would like you to be involved. I don't have much to go on yet, but I'll ask Ansley to reach out to you if I can get it formed."

"Sounds good, I'm open. Nice to know you, Sam. Good luck!"

He picked up his board and headed down the beach. Sam gathered her things and went to her car. She threw her bag in and loaded her board, rubbing her hand down it, now scuffed and broken in. This had been her ticket to freedom. No matter where life took her after this, surfing would be a part of it. She headed for the surf shop to purchase another board before she was somewhere where she didn't have such expert advice.

Ansley rang her up and helped load the board. This one was lime green with a dark blue line running down the middle. It looked pretty next to Sam's other one. It would be the last thing she purchased in this town. She drove slowly through the town, gazing at the people and the businesses. It would always be driven by the same focus, by the money of tourists and not the needs of the people. It had been this way for decades and nothing was changing it. The residents served the tourists, simple as that. She loved being near the beach but knew she needed to go somewhere that wasn't solely focused on tourism and offered a life to the locals. Somewhere people stood a chance to thrive.

Her last few shifts at the restaurant were almost too busy for her even to get nostalgic. Like last year when she moved there, it was always swamped with tourists. Gus was behind the bar helping, getting everything down before she left. A young guy, Greg or Grant, she didn't hear when she was told and was choosing not to ask, had stepped in as barback. Taylor was directing a couple of new waitresses who Sam also avoided, so she could just disappear when the time came. Jimmy was still cooking in the back and gave her a quick hug on their last shift together. He told her to stay cool and ducked out. Sam wished all goodbyes were that easy.

On her last night, as they were wrapping up, Natalie came over and slipped her five hundred dollars plus her tips, hugging her. "A little extra to help you get where you're going. I'll mail your last check once you know where you're going to be. You need to stay in touch. Just send me a postcard now and then. Once you have an address, send it my way."

"I will, Natalie. Thank you. For everything. I'll miss you."

Sam hugged Natalie, biting back tears. Natalie winked at her and went to help Gus close down the bar. Sam stopped at the door, glancing around one last time. The table where she first sat with a knot on her head, and no clue what she was doing in this town. Casey's chair, where he joked with her while she worked, that Aidan later sat in to tell her he was leaving. The table where the people were talking shit and Sam finally snapped. The patio where she and Smitty sat, laughing and talking. Her eyes drifted over the lifeguard stand, empty since the last shift of lifeguards had gone home for the day. She walked over and climbed up, sitting down where she usually did. She placed her hand where Smitty would sit next to her, feeling the cool wood. After a bit, she got up.

The door was locked, so she peered in the small window. The floor where they'd fallen asleep the night he'd confessed to her about using and selling drugs. The corner where he'd cried with her about everything before he went to prison. Her heart ached and she took a deep breath, letting it out with a shudder. She turned and gazed down to the spot where she'd first seen Casey, laughing and falling back on the sand. She could see it all so clearly in her mind. A movie that played over and over.

They'd all been so alive and present at the time. Circling each other, living their lives until one by one they fell off, leaving Sam standing there alone. The faces she now saw were mostly unfamiliar. People would come and go. In a year from now, it would be a new set of faces and eventually, they'd be replaced too. Sam climbed down and stood looking up at the lifeguard stand. She rested her hand on the ladder one last time and walked to her car. She sat staring out at the ocean, a sense of heaviness weighing on her. It was time to go. She put the car in gear, driving out of the parking lot for the last time.

At home, everything was packed by the door. She began hauling everything down to the car, so she wouldn't have to do it in the morning. She needed to get an early start. It was still not a lot, but a bit more than she'd come with. She had Ansley's art piece and snagged one of Rosie's off the wall. Added to it were a tent, sleeping bags, and a propane stove. She wanted to be prepared and give herself time to find the right place. It all fit neatly in her car. She'd wait to load the surfboards until the morning. She went back up to the empty apartment and sat in silence. She could see Smitty cooking and jamming to music in the kitchen. The porch where they'd sit and smoke, staring at the stars. The bed where they made love, holding each other in good and bad times. She knew it was time to go, but why was it so hard? She laid down to try and sleep for a couple of hours before she needed to get up and drive.

Morning came and Sam was groggy but ready for the next chapter of her life. She did one last check under the bed, in drawers, and in the closet. She had everything. She just needed to load the surfboards and stop at the gas station for gas and coffee. She carried the boards down, leaning them against the car.

"Not trying to sneak away on us are you now?" a voice teased from behind her. Ansley and Rosie were at the fence, little Tori beside them, holding Rosie's hand.

"No, I just wanted to get loaded up first, so it wasn't awkward," Sam lied. She was totally trying to get out before they saw her to avoid a painful goodbye.

Ansley came around and loaded the boards while Sam fished around her bag for her keys. She pulled off the house key and handed it to Rosie. Rosie's eyes glistened with captured tears.

"You know you always have a place with us. Ansley is taking over the apartment for her art studio, but we're leaving the bedroom up there intact. You better come see us. Seriously, Sam, you are family."

"Thanks, Rosie. You've been so wonderful to me. I couldn't have asked for better landlords. Neighbors? Family, really. I'll send you my address as soon as I have one if you can hold onto my mail."

Sam reached across the fence and hugged Rosie's neck. Behind Rosie, two little heads appeared in the window, waving at her grinning. She waved back; grateful she didn't have to say goodbye to them as well. They disappeared as quickly as they appeared. Sam turned to Ansley, who was leaning against the car eyeing her.

"Boards are on there securely. But if you feel any type of shifting once you hit the highway, stop and fix it. You don't want those flying off at high speed. Best case scenario, they just shatter into bits on the highway. Worst case scenario, you take someone out. But you should be fine."

Sam reached in her bag and drew out three hundred dollars, handing them to Ansley. "I want to start a fund in Casey's name that pays for surfboards and lessons for the kids here, who otherwise wouldn't be able to afford them. Even if they can, I want to make sure they have guidance from the community and a support system. Like a mentorship program. I know this isn't much, and I'll send more as soon as I start working again. I'd love it if you could oversee it here. I mentioned it to TJ, well not exactly, but I let him know you might be reaching out for his help. I mean, if you're interested."

Ansley's eyes lit up and she grinned. "Hell yeah, I'm interested! That's a great idea. I bet I could get the surf shop owners to offer boards at cost for this. I'm sure we could drum up more donations too."

"I'd like it if the high school kids could be involved in teaching and other things. That's where I'd like TJ to get involved. If he could oversee the lessons side with you, I think it would be good for him and a focus for other teenagers. I'm not sure how it all works but wanted to get it rolling. Once I'm settled, I can call and we can talk more about setting it up as a nonprofit. Maybe call it Casey's Trust?"

Ansley nodded thoughtfully and agreed. They hugged each other and Sam choked up.

"I love you both. I'll stay in touch, I promise," she said roughly.

"You had better," Rosie replied. "We're holding your mail hostage."

With that, Sam climbed into her car and rolled the windows down. She started the car and Rosie picked up Tori, who gave Sam a little wave. Sam waved back and pulled out. As she drove down the street, she peered in her rearview mirror watching them standing waving at her car, and she let the tears fall she'd been holding back.

She stopped into the gas station to fill up and grab some coffee for the drive. As she came out and heard the door chime, it made her smile. She'd come full circle and it was time to go. She put her chin up, feeling excitement stir inside for her next adventure. She took the long route through town, past the library, grocery store, and little shops by the beach. Then she hit the edge of town, looking back. It was time. She turned the car out of town and drove until she hit the highway. She accelerated and merged in, letting the line connecting her to the town snap.

She drove for a couple of hours, taking in the scenery. Finally, she pulled off to eat something and stretch. She stopped at a roadside park and found a picnic table to eat at. She'd prepped enough food for the trip to save money, and to make sure she made good time. The boards were still secure on the roof, thanks to Ansley. She grabbed a blueberry muffin and orange juice out of her cooler and sat cross-legged on top of the picnic table to eat.

There was plenty of money in her account, which would buy her time to figure out what she wanted to do and get a place to live. She just needed to get there and start building her life. She still didn't know what she wanted to do with her future. Surfing had ignited a passion in her she didn't know existed, and she knew she couldn't keep working mindless jobs. Something would come to her. She just had to be patient and let it.

Checking the time, she saw she needed to get back on the road to stay on track. She threw her trash away and headed for her car. As she got close, the sun glinted off the boards on top, making her stop in her tracks. She peered at them, the way they curved just right. She ran her hand down the boards, thinking about how the right board with the right person made the experience feel like an extension of one's body while they were riding the waves. She didn't know why the idea hadn't occurred to her sooner, and the giddiness of a child on Christmas morning ran through her body.

She started grinning and couldn't stop, even as she pulled out and back onto the highway. It had been staring her in the face for the last couple of months. She let out a deep breath and her shoulders relaxed, as the pieces of her life started falling into place. She just had one piece left to figure out. About an hour later, she pulled off the highway and headed down a county road. She checked the time, it was almost nine in the morning. She'd made good time and hoped everything else she needed to do that day would go as smoothly.

Anxiety bubbled up in her stomach and she pushed it back down. There was more than one path, she reminded herself. If this didn't work out, she'd still be okay. She'd adjust to set her sails elsewhere if needed.

She drove into the parking lot, staring at the large expanse of buildings she was hoping would connect her with the next step.

Chapter Thirty-Two

The sun reflected off the razor wire wrapped around the tops of the tall fences of the correctional facility, hurting Sam's eyes. She put her hand over her eyes to block the sun and see if anyone was coming out. The guards in the towers seemed to be watching her, making her feel like she'd done something wrong. She reminded herself she hadn't, and she had every right to be there. She got out to stretch and lit a cigarette. She had no idea how this would go, or if she should even be there, but she followed her gut and came anyway. She wanted to at least try.

She'd called a few days earlier to find out when Smitty was being released and made sure she was there on time. He didn't know she was coming. He was planning to board the shuttle, which was idling outside the gate to take him to the halfway house. If he didn't want her there, she was only a few hours off track and would just head on. She chewed the side of her thumb and smoked her cigarette, eyeing the walkway leading out to the gate. It was empty.

After some time had passed, she began to question herself. Had she gotten the date wrong? It was June third. He'd told her that, and when she called the guy she spoke to had confirmed it. Had he already been released? She pushed down the panic threatening to come out. It was okay, the time was right, the date was right. She just had to wait. About thirty minutes later, an interior door opened and a group walked out. Two guards and three inmates. Sam spotted Smitty immediately since he was taller than the rest of them. His hair was cut short, all the bleached ends gone, and he'd lost his beach tan. He was too thin and appeared older than he had the last time she'd seen him. She watched as they made their way through the series of fences. He was joking with one of the guards.

He didn't see her and paused at the last gate to look at the paper he was holding in his hand. As they started to load onto the shuttle, the brightness of the surfboards on Sam's car caught his eye, and he glanced over. She was leaning against the car, not sure what to do. He looked from the boards to her, his eyes a mixture of surprise and confusion. He said something to the guard and walked towards her, stopping about ten feet away. Her voice caught in her throat.

"Hey." It was all she could get out.

"Hey," he replied. "What's with the surfboards?"

"I learned to surf."

"Did you then?" Smitty laughed softly but didn't come any closer.

She started to feel like maybe she shouldn't have come and stood awkwardly, staring at him. Time seemed to stand still. She put her hand out to him with the pack of cigarettes and lighter in it. "Smoke?"

He slowly came over and took them, his fingers brushing hers. He turned, heading to a trash can on the side of the parking lot and threw them in. Sam's mouth hung open with surprise. He came back over, this time a little closer to her.

"Hasn't anyone ever told you those things can kill you?" he asked, his voice just above a whisper.

"A lot of things can kill you," she answered, remembering her first break at the restaurant.

She moved towards him and paused when she got to him. It was like a wall was dividing them, not letting them get any closer. They stood watching each other when he put his hand out to her. She took it and he drew her towards him. She wrapped her arms around him and he did the same. They clung to each other for a while, letting the stress fall away. They held on, not wanting to break the trance, not saying anything.

Finally, Sam pulled back and really looked at him. His light freckles were more prominent not being hidden by a tan, giving him a boyish charm. His eyes seemed tired and older, the depths of golden brown somehow deeper. Smitty gave her a small, nervous, goofy grin. She ran her fingers across his lips, which were soft from being out of the sun.

"I didn't expect to see you," he said, never taking his eyes off hers. "I didn't think you'd come for me."

"I wasn't sure if I was coming. But I had to try."

"You had to try? Sam, I should be the one trying. I'm the one who fucked this all up."

"Well, either way, here I am."

With that, he leaned down and kissed her. Her hand gravitated to the back of his neck, pulling him in closer. A light sigh escaped him, and he held her tighter. The heat of his body made her feel weak, so she stepped back to keep her footing. He ran his hand down her cheek.

"Damn, I've missed you."

"I've missed you too, Smith. Can we go? I feel like we're being watched," she said, eyeing the towers.

"Oh, we're being watched."

They moved towards the car, still unsure of each other and what would happen next. Smitty ran his hand along the boards. He turned to her; his eyes inquisitive.

"That's awesome you learned to surf, but why two boards?"

"One's for you."

He stared hard at her, biting his lip. "Sam, are you saying you still want me in your life? I mean, I get it if you're here to just give me a ride. But do you want me to be with you?"

"I always have, that never changed. That's why I'm here. I figured I'd come, and if you didn't want to go with me I'd just leave. With two boards."

He tipped his head back and laughed genuinely at this, making him seem more like the Smitty she knew. "Not go with you? Sam, I wanted this every day I was in that hell hole. I can't go back to that town, though. I just can't. I don't belong there, and I'm sure no one wants me back."

"We aren't. Neither of us belongs there." Sam motioned to the stuff in the car.

Smitty glanced in and understood. "So, where are we going?"

"Let's get in and we can talk. I want to get out of here as soon as possible."

"You have no idea," Smitty commiserated.

They climbed in the car and Sam started it up, guiding it out of the parking lot. Smitty turned, glancing back and shook his head as the correctional facility disappeared. He sighed and flipped off the sign as they pulled out onto the main road. Sam reached back and handed him a little box. He opened it, taking out his knot of wood and birthday candle. He turned them over in his hand, smiling.

"Thanks, Sam, you kept them. Do you have my knives too?"

"I do. They're in the back with your clothes. I threw away the lifeguard shorts and shirts, though, after they terminated you."

"Fair enough. So, you said you used my knives?" he asked, cocking his head.

"Yes! I taught myself to cook. Well, sort of. Not anywhere close to what you do but no more canned or microwave meals for this girl."

"Of course, you did." He laughed and sat back in the seat. "What now?"

"I wasn't a hundred percent sure what you were allowed to do now," Sam confessed.

"I don't have to see my parole officer for three months. I have to let them know if I move. They have Rosie's and Ansley's address for now. If I move out of the area, they'll assign me one where I'm at. I can't cross state lines yet, though."

"Okay, that gives us some time. I was thinking about the Outer Banks? We can check a couple of places out. Places with good restaurants and near the ocean with good waves. I have a few places in mind I researched."

Smitty shifted uncomfortably in his seat. "Sam, I don't have anything. No money. I'm a felon, no one is going to want to touch me. I'm starting at zero. Well, below zero really with this on my record. I've nothing to offer."

Sam reached in her purse, pulled out her bank book, and tossed it in his lap. He opened it and raised his brows at the total.

"You have all of this?" he asked incredulously.

She nodded, smiling at him. "I came prepared."

He rolled his window down and leaned out towards the opening, breathing in the fresh air. His shirt had pulled up slightly in the back, exposing his waist. Sam reached out and ran her fingers across his skin, causing a jolt of electricity in her body. He sat back and grabbed her fingers, putting them to his mouth for a quick kiss.

"Eyes on the road," he teased.

"Sorry," she mumbled and focused back on her driving.

His fingers touched her neck lightly. Then he squeezed her thigh and left his hand there, causing warm ripples up her leg. "Don't be sorry. For the last almost five months, I've imagined your fingers on my skin and didn't think I'd ever feel them again. I'm not convinced this isn't a dream, and I won't wake up in my bunk with months of time left to do. If it is, it's a good dream."

They pulled off for gas after about an hour, and Sam ran to use the bathroom. Smitty filled the tank while she went into the gas station. She grabbed a couple of bottles of water and almost grabbed cigarettes, deciding better of it. As she was checking out, she watched Smitty at the pump. He finished pumping and stretched, his long arms almost touching the overhang above. He walked to the back of the car and leaned against it, watching the cars on the road drive by.

Sam hadn't considered how new everything would be to him again. How his mind would have to reprocess once familiar things. That even being able to walk freely in and out of doors would be an amazing gift. They had time, there was no rush. She walked out and handed him a water bottle. He opened it, taking a big swig. He wiped his mouth and grinned at her.

"Thanks. Hey, can I get to my clothes in the back? I'm really not digging wearing the shirt I was arrested in, you know?"

She opened the back and dragged his box forward. He dug through and found his knives, hugging them to his chest with a comical grin. He set them down and grabbed a t-shirt to put on. He glanced at the gas station, deciding if he should go in to change, then decided to just change in the parking lot. He pulled off his shirt and threw it in the box. Sam tried not to stare, but the scar was bigger than she'd imagined, running from below his rib to his waistline. It was still purplish-red, in the early stages of forming scar tissue. Someone had wanted to hurt him. He pulled the new shirt over his head and caught her eye.

"Hey, it's nothing, superficial."

"It doesn't look like it."

He had Casey's beads around his neck and adjusted them to sit on the outside of the t-shirt. He shrugged lightly. "Well, I guess I was meant to live."

She didn't know if he was trying to be funny or not, but it shot through her brain. He could have died. They wouldn't be standing here in a gas station parking lot. She would've never seen him again. Like Casey. She went over to him and hugged him as tight as she could. He put his chin on her head and rubbed her back like he always had.

"It's okay, Sam, that chapter is over. Some people didn't like me in prison. I tried to keep my head down and just get through. But people expect you to align in certain ways. I wouldn't. I've spent my whole life doing shit I shouldn't, and whether or not this was the right pedestal to stand on, I refused to get involved with certain groups while I was there. To make an example of me, I got jumped and cut with something on the way to the cafeteria. Some sort of smuggled or handmade knife. It missed my organs, thankfully, but probably not intentionally. I saw it coming at the last second and sidestepped the impact. Guards were on them in seconds. I needed stitches and recovery, but I promise I'm okay."

Sam stared at her feet. While he was in there fighting for his life, she was learning to surf. Then being mad at him for trying to survive and pushing her away, so he had the best chance to. Embarrassment washed over her. He lifted her chin and peered into her eyes, reading her mind.

"You had every right to be mad at me. You didn't know what was going on in there, and truth be told I *had* shut you out. I just want us to move forward and put this behind us. Please, Sam?"

She nodded and touched his face. "Okay."

They got back in the car and headed out. Smitty gestured to the stuff in the back. "I saw you had a tent and sleeping bags?"

"Yeah, I thought we could camp out until we figured out where we'd live. I checked into it, we can camp on some of the state park beaches and have contained fires there. We'll need to get a permit from the fire station when we pass through town. I have a propane stove too."

"Turning into quite the boy scout, Sam."

"I suppose. But I expect you to cook for me when we get where we're going."

"You know it."

It was getting past lunchtime. Sam asked Smitty to grab sandwiches out of the cooler, so they could push on. He grabbed a couple of sandwiches and apples. As they were eating, he noticed the bracelet he'd given her on her wrist and reached out to touch it. The seashell dangled, swinging lightly back and forth. She glanced over to meet his eyes and saw a deep sincerity in them. His voice was soft when he spoke.

"I'm really glad you exist, Samantha."

Sam felt his words, as much as she heard them. All her years of feeling like she didn't belong and not being able to connect to anyone or anything, including herself, were gone. For the first time in her life, she truly could say she was glad she existed as well.

Chapter Thirty-Three

They drove into the beach lot in the afternoon, tired from driving and needing to stretch. They'd snagged their bonfire permit and a couple of bundles of wood to get started. Sam cut the car off, staring out at the ocean for a moment. The waves were much bigger here, rougher, and would crest over their heads at times, creating barrel waves. The waves she'd learned to surf on had been to the top of her shoulders and up to Smitty's chest on a regular day, bigger with impending storms. It wasn't the huge waves she'd seen in pictures from California, but a good next step.

She expected to feel afraid but excitement bubbled up inside of her. Smitty's need to thrill-seek made so much more sense now, and she couldn't wait to share this with him. He was gazing out at the water, his face relaxed and a smile turning up the corners of his mouth, like in the picture she had of them dancing on the lifeguard stand. He met her eyes, raised his eyebrows, and gestured his head towards the water.

"You want to?" he asked but not really asking.

"You don't have to ask me twice!" Sam agreed breathlessly.

She grabbed her swimsuit and ducked behind the dunes to change. When she came back Smitty was in just board shorts, checking out his new surfboard. Ansley had helped, picking it based on his height and weight. Sam had picked the color. He flipped it around and nodded.

"Damn, that's nice. I owe you one."

"One?" Sam teased.

"Well, everything, but we can add this to the list." He winked at her, grabbing his board and headed for the surf.

As they came up to the water, it seemed to get bigger and bigger. They waded in and began paddling. Sam was proud that she was able to keep up. Smitty had lost some muscle mass in prison, and she'd gained some. In a way, they'd traded places, him losing the sun-touched parts of him, and her gaining them. Her dirty-blond hair had bleached out to a lighter blond while his was a much darker brown. That would change fast, considering they were going to be camping on the beach until they could decide where to go and find a place to live. And surfing at every chance they could get.

The larger, rougher waves knocked them down over and over until they could figure out its secrets. Within an hour, Smitty was riding like he'd always been there and Sam, while not as experienced, held her own. Neither wanted to stop until the sun started to dip in the sky. They needed to set up camp and gather firewood before it got too dark. They reluctantly came in and set their boards down where they'd decided to camp. Smitty grabbed the tent, setting it up while Sam collected firewood from a wood line near the dunes.

She was coming back with an armful of kindling and wood when she stopped to watch him work. He'd spread the tent out and was deftly inserting the poles, causing the tent to rise into shape. He hammered in the stakes all the way around and stood back to check his work. He seemed at peace doing the task, so in his element. She came up and dropped the load next to where they were building the fire.

"Have I ever told you how beautiful you are?" she asked quietly.

Smitty turned and grinned bashfully at her, his ear tips turning slightly red. He put two fingers to the corner of his brow and gave her a little wave, his appreciation of the compliment apparent. He went back to working on the tent, making sure it wouldn't blow away in the wind.

Sam carried the stove and cooler from the car, her stomach grumbling a reminder. Smitty grabbed a bag of groceries and sleeping bags. They focused on getting the fire going, digging a pit and filling it in with kindling and logs. Smitty got the tent ready for sleeping later and dragged over a fallen driftwood tree to sit on. Sam laid out a blanket by the fire.

Within thirty minutes, they had a fire going and the camp set up. Smitty was digging through the cooler and bag of groceries, deciding what to cook for dinner. Sam went to gather more wood and sat down after a couple of loads. Smitty was like a kid opening presents, pulling out vegetables, spices, and a cutting board with glee.

"You even have spices!" He was exhilarated.

"In all fairness, most of those are yours from before you left. I don't know how fresh they are. I only replaced the ones I used."

"Sam, I haven't had food with anything more than salt and pepper for nearly five months. This is fucking awesome."

He quickly got to work, chopping and sorting. Sam set up the propane stove, which had little fold-out legs to keep it off the ground. Smitty took over, throwing things in the frying pan, seasoning and tasting as he went. The air filled with delicious scents, and Sam's stomach growled so loudly Smitty heard it and laughed.

"I'm working as fast as I can."

Sam grinned and threw a seashell at him. He didn't look up, his focus solely on cooking. Within a short while, he had a steaming bowl of Indian vegetable curry in her hands. She breathed in deeply and closed her eyes, the aroma delighting her senses. If it smelled amazing, it tasted even better.

"Damn, I've missed you," she said between bites.

"I hope not just for my cooking."

"Well..."

"Hey!" He nudged her foot with his.

They finished off the food and rinsed the dishes, packing them back into the car to keep a tidy camp in case of rain. The sun had started to set, making a mosaic of the sky, casting oranges, pinks, and reds in layers all the way to the horizon. Casey's sunset. Smitty sat facing the ocean with his elbows resting on his pulled-up knees. Sam came over to sit behind him, slipping her legs around his and rested her head on his back. He put his left arm over her leg and leaned into her. He spoke softly, almost as if he wasn't speaking to her.

"You know, this morning when I woke up, I thought I'd be riding a shuttle to a strange city and sleeping in another strange bed. I'd accepted it and was going to make the best of things. Then when I came out and saw you leaning against the car, I thought my mind was playing tricks on me. Like you were a mirage. I was afraid to come closer and have you disappear. Then you offered me a cigarette, and I thought to myself that mirages don't smoke."

He started laughing at this, his whole body shaking from it. Sam smacked him on the leg. He grabbed her hand and held it as he went on.

"Sorry for throwing them away. But I want you around for the rest of my life. If I can quit drugs and cigarettes, I'm begging you to quit those. I need you here with me."

"I'm not mad. You're right, if you can quit much harder stuff, I can quit those. I might be a bitch now and then, but I can quit."

"Now and then?" he teased and moved quickly, knocking her gently back into the sand.

He was now facing her, grinning as he leaned over her. Sam wanted to just hold the moment and placed her hand on his chest, meeting his eyes. Everything that had happened from the day they met to now passed between them, and he laid down next to her on the sand, his head propped by his elbow. Their eyes stayed locked. Sam knew it was her turn to say something.

"I really did miss you. In everything that happened to me over the last five months, I came home wanting to talk to you about it. The first time I got up and rode a wave, I wanted to tell you so badly. When I was hurting, it was you I wanted to comfort me. I made do, I went to work and stayed busy, but at the end of the day, I needed my best friend to share things with. It was like you were part of my life and then just gone. Like Casey. I was mourning for you."

Smitty's eyes darkened, a sadness came over his face. He put his arm over her and shook his head. "I'm sorry I put you through that. I thought I was protecting you. But I guess you were dealing with your own sentence of sorts. I can only promise I won't intentionally do anything to tear us apart again. I'm not perfect, but I promise you that."

"I don't like to think of it that way, that I was serving a sentence, knowing what you went through. But we both were suffering, you know? It fucking hurt." Her voice cracked at the end.

"I know," he whispered.

He laid down on his back next to her, and they gazed at the stars. She laced her fingers into his, resting her head against his shoulder. The expansive sky and huge waves made her feel so small, so invisible. This was oddly comforting. She glanced at Smitty from the side of her eyes and watched him. His eyes were focused on the sky, giving him the aura of an innocent child seeing the magic of stars for the first time. Maybe after all of this, he could find the child he lost to addiction and make it okay for him. Release him to the past.

For what seemed like a peaceful eternity they laid and watched the sky, holding each other's hands. Sam dozed off and when she awoke Smitty was still awake, his eyes on the sky. She rolled over and put her arm on his chest. He placed his hand on her arm, giving her a tired but happy smile.

"You okay?" she asked, moving in closer for warmth.

"Yeah, just thinking. Appreciating."

The fire was starting to die down and Sam shivered. She placed her head on his chest, and he wrapped his arm around her, making her warmer. She could hear his heart beating through his ribcage, the rush matching the sound of the waves hitting the beach. She yawned and watched the waves in the moonlight.

"Hey, I'm not keeping you up, am I?" Smitty asked softly.

"No. Maybe. I just want to be here with you, for you." She was tired but didn't want the moment to end.

"Yeah. I think I'm afraid to go to sleep." He laughed sheepishly. "I'm afraid I'll wake up and this will all be a dream. Then it would be a nightmare."

Sam lifted her head and met his eyes. "I can think of something we can do to stay awake."

He didn't respond but didn't stop her when she got up and took his hand, leading him to the tent. He'd laid one sleeping bag down as a mat and the other to cover them, so they slipped under the cover. They took off their clothes and wound their arms around each other, quickly warming the tent.

They took time exploring each other's bodies slowly, savoring each moment. Sam traced the scar on his side and put her hand over it as if to heal it. He kissed her shoulder and rubbed her back lightly. Their eyes met and for a second it was like it was both of their first times. They laughed nervously. Sam slid her arm around his waist and pressed herself to him. They kissed deeply and as if they'd never been apart, they connected and let all inhibitions fall away. When she let him inside of her, causing her body to respond to his, she knew the only thing that mattered was they were together. She cried out as he shuddered and released, her body understanding what her mind had tried to deny. Nothing could keep them apart.

Afterwards, they held each other, basking in their reunion. Smitty's chest started to rise and fall with the comfort of sleep, and Sam took a moment to watch him. His face was relaxed, content. He seemed like a guy without a care in the world. She laid back down next to him and felt his breath on her shoulder, warm and steady. Sleep overtook her, and she fell into a deep slumber.

Sam was jolted awake in the morning by Smitty sitting upright, his face confused and his eyes darting around trying to figure out where he was. His breath was ragged and he ran his hands roughly through his hair.

To not startle him, she gently put her hand on his arm, "Hey, it's okay. I'm here."

His eyes landed on her and stared blankly, trying to process if he was actually seeing her. She reached up and put her arms around him, pulling him down next to her. He relaxed and kept his eyes on her.

"You're really here," he whispered, sliding his arms around her.

"I'm really here. You are free."

He sighed in relief and waved one of his arms in the air. "I'm free!"

Sam kissed him on the neck and sat up, searching for her swimsuit. "You want to hit the waves?"

A huge grin broke out over his slightly sunburned face. He sat up and reached for his shorts, slipping them on at lightning speed.

"Fuck yeah."

Epilogue

It had been a little over a year and a half since they arrived at the Outer Banks and found a place to live. A small one-bedroom cottage near the outskirts of town. Bigger than their apartment above the garage, but just by a little and almost twice as much in rent. Sam had made a huge dent in her savings for them to get set up and have time to find jobs. As Smitty had feared, being a felon made the higher-end restaurants turn their nose up at him. He ended up taking a line cook job at a high-foot-traffic but low-quality restaurant that didn't care who they hired, as long as they showed up for work.

Within months, Smitty was head chef there, updated their menu, and increased higher-paying clientele. After a year, every restaurant was knocking on his door, but he wanted complete control of the menu and kitchen. He turned them down, finding satisfaction in knowing they'd shunned him before. Now, he didn't want or need them. When a new high-end fusion cuisine restaurant opened looking for a head chef, he went in and wowed them with his skills. He was hired on the spot, doubling his salary and with full control.

Sam knew what she wanted when they arrived in town and just had to find it. There were a lot of surf shops in town, but she didn't want one who catered to people surfing on a whim or during vacation, buying premade boards. She wanted to learn the art of handcrafting a surfboard. She searched until she found a small surf shop on a side street, owned by an older couple who were avid surfers and built their own surfboards. She went in and bargained running their shop for them for lower pay if they'd teach her their craft. They shipped boards all over the world and were more than happy for the help. She caught on quickly, allowing them to make more boards in a shorter period of time.

Before long they became like second parents, inviting Smitty and Sam to events and family gatherings. Sam handcrafted matching boards for herself and Smitty, and she gifted them to him on their one-year anniversary in the town. They used them every day they could, surfing together before work.

Smitty was still sleeping after a long night, catering a high-end event for some of the town's elite. His name had spread, and the demand for his services was at an all-time high. Sam had let him sleep as long as she could, but checked the time and could see it was getting close to him having to head back to work. He seemed so peaceful, she hated to wake him at all. He was working hard, making a name for himself and a good life for them while she honed her surfboard building skills.

She brushed his now shoulder-length, bleached out hair off his brow and kissed him on the forehead. His eyes fluttered and he groaned. He rolled over, trying to go back to sleep. Sam looked at his back, muscular and tan. He held a good weight now working in the restaurant. She leaned in and put her arm around him.

"Hey, what time do you need to go to work? It's one."

"Soon," he answered without opening his eyes.

"How soon?" she asked, sliding her fingers under his waistband.

He grabbed her hand and opened his eyes. "Not that soon."

He pulled her over him, making her squeal. They took each other's clothes off and dove back under the covers. When they were spent, he kissed her and got up to take a shower. He stopped at the bathroom door and winked at her.

"That's a sure way to get me up.'

"Mmm. I have my ways."

He laughed, disappearing into the bathroom. Sam heard the mail being dropped off and went to check it. There was a packet in Rosie's handwriting. She poured out the contents on the table. There were pictures of the kids, who already looked so much older. A note from Rosie about happenings with the kids and charter school, which was adding third grade the coming year. There was also a gallery opening invite for Ansley's work in Raleigh for the next month. Sam stuck it on the fridge in case they could make it.

There was a news article from the Crestview paper, highlighting Casey's Trust, how they'd given out their fiftieth surfboard. It covered how the mentorship program was seeing a decrease in drug use among kids in the community, but also an increase of high schoolers who assisted with mentorship going to college. A scholarship program was currently in the works.

It was small numbers, but as the article pointed out, they'd only been going in the other direction prior to Casey's Trust hitting its one year mark. Funding had poured in once people saw the benefits, and they were able to secure nonprofit status. The best part was the picture of Ansley, TJ, a few other mentors, and a group of smiling kids, ranging in ages from six to fifteen, holding the surfboards they'd been gifted. Next to it was a picture of Casey at the beach smiling, standing with his surfboard, long hair wet from the surf. No longer the town junkie, now someone who made a difference through his life's memory. Sam stuck it on the fridge next to Ansley's gallery invite. They'd already agreed to open a chapter in the Outer Banks. Jim and Marie, the owners of the surf shop she worked at, jumped at the chance to head up the funding drives.

The other piece of mail which came was a letter addressed to Sam with the returned address from A. Osher. Aidan! She ripped it open, glad to hear from him after all this time. She'd written to him when they had an address and had settled into a routine, but never heard back from him.

Hey Sam!

Sorry it's been a long time since I've written. I've been pushing school, so I could qualify for scholarships. I appreciate you writing to let me know you moved and what's going on.

First, let me tell you how much it meant to me and my family for you to start Casey's Trust. We've been following as it's grown, helping so many kids. I've written to Ansley as well to thank her. You made my mom cry with gratitude.

And TJ! That was awesome to see. We were buddies when I was there, and he's planning to come out here after graduation. We're looking at a couple of the same schools.

I'm pursuing film-making and found a few schools that have good majors in it. My grades came up when we got here, so I have a couple of scholarships in the works. My school counselor said there should be no problem getting accepted at any of those schools with my grades and other stuff. He told me to write an essay talking about my experience and what happened with Casey. How it changed me. Weird, but I guess they want to know something about me. What sets me apart.

I'm glad to hear Smitty got out of prison and is doing well. Please let him know I'm not angry at him anymore. I'd say I forgive him but there is nothing to forgive. I did a lot of growing up here. Getting out of that town and looking back, I can see he was just as buried as Casey. Casey thought the world of him, like another brother. I don't know if Smitty knew that, but Casey told me that so many times. He really loved him.

Please let Smitty know that. Let him know he probably saved my life that night I was fucked up. I wasn't going to stop unless something stopped me. He stopped me. I was hard on him and said things I truly regret. Tell him I appreciate him and I'd really like to talk to him sometime.

My brother's brother is my brother.

I'll stay in better touch. I promise. You all are family to me. I'd love to hear from you. Send more pictures! I have the picture of your car with the surfboard on top you sent a long time ago, on my

bulletin board above my desk. It reminds me of the good parts of
home. Of you, Casey, and Smitty. My family.
    Maybe put you guys in it this time, huh?

                   Peace,
                     Aidan

    Smitty came in just as Sam finished reading the letter. He saw the article on the fridge and read it, as he gulped down a cup of coffee. He smiled and nodded, turning around to Sam to say something about it. He stopped when he saw her putting her hand out to him with the letter from Aidan in it. He cocked his head, furrowing his brows and took the letter. He started to read it and moved to sit on the couch once he realized who it was from. He finished reading it, then read it again. He folded the letter, holding it in his hands, his head down while he thought. When he looked back up, his eyes had tears in them. The last piece to healing was Aidan forgiving him, and he was given more than that. He was given a brother.

    Sam sat down next to Smitty on the couch, and he put his arm around her, kissing her on the top of her head. She wrapped her arms around him and put her face close to his neck, smelling him and feeling home. They sat reveling in the letter from Aidan and what it all meant. Sam had found Smitty and herself in all of this. Smitty had found something he didn't even know he was missing. He'd found a true family and been gifted a second chance.

Acknowledgements

Thank you to John Pape for being a sounding board on this novel. Your insight, honest words, and continued support helped more than you know! Kind of seemed like Louise was hanging around on our conversations.

Thank you to Clay Anderson for being a cheerleader with this process. You always gave me the boost I needed when I was feeling frustrated or self-doubting.

Thank you to Kekoa Davidson for your surfing insights. You know your stuff and I hope I did it justice. Maybe one day I can make it out there and we can go surfing!

Thank you to Brooke Cantrall for being willing to take photos once I realized the image I wanted was in your town. You went above and beyond! You have a definite eye.

Thank you to my family for tolerating my long hours while I wrote, edited, and stressed over this book.

Thank you to fellow authors Ben Meeks, Lillah Lawson, and Mab Morris for letting me ask questions and helping me try to find my way after fifteen years back into the writing world.

Thank *you* for reading!

If you or anyone you know is struggling:

American Foundation for Suicide Prevention: afsp.org

Anxiety and Depression Association of America: adaa.org

National Suicide Prevention Lifeline: 1-800-273-TALK (8255)
En español: 1-888-628-9454

Crisis Text Line: Text "HELLO" to 741741

National Alliance on Mental Illness: nami.org

To Write Love on Her Arms (suicide/addiction help): twloha.com

7 Cups of Tea Foundation (emotional online support): 7cups.com

Never Alone Initiative (tools and resources): neveralone.love

You are not alone.

Made in the USA
Coppell, TX
27 September 2021